Alex Christofi was born in Dorset and read English at the University of Oxford. As well as working as an editor, he writes occasional essays and reviews. His first novel *Glass*, also published by Serpent's Tail, was longlisted for the Desmond Elliott Prize and won the Betty Trask Prize.

PRAISE FOR *GLASS*

'Charming and funny . . . there's enough here to show you the author has plenty more to offer and that, like his hero, he definitely has his heart in the right place' *Daily Mail*

'Christofi's writing really does gleam with wit, inventiveness and an offbeat charm' Kate Saunders, *The Times*

'[An] impressive, tightly paced coming-of-age story . . . a multi-layered story that follows one man's refracted path through life's prism' *Financial Times*

'Entertaining and affecting' *Herald*

'A moving, funny coming-of-age tale' *Independent*

'A thoughtful, comic look at an ordinary life lived well' *Guardian*

'A rare novel . . . rollicking' *Dazed & Confused*

'A tale about growing up, one that's as funny as it is touching. A talent to keep an eye on' *Shortlist*

'A confident and frequently adroit first novel . . . enjoyably mercurial and quixotic' *Morning Star*

'Charming, quirky, unexpected . . . Christofi is a writer to watch. Witty and incredibly inventive' *Saga*

'A promising debut from an intriguing new voice' *We Love This Book*

'With a first novel this good, great things are surely in store for Alex Christofi' *BookHugger*

'A confident, swaggering entrance into the literary world . . . Skilfully swinging from brilliantly funny to dark morbidity, Christofi displays considerable mastery of his craft . . . An accomplished opening effort from a writer well worth keeping an eye on' *Hot Press*

'Günter Glass, with his flaws and his limitations, and his belief in the better part of human nature, is a great pleasure to spend time with. I was moved and amused and ultimately comforted by Günter's sky-reaching spirit and his quest for deeper meaning in a world of transparencies' Stephen Kelman, author of *Pigeon English*

'*Glass* is a brilliant novel with a first-person narrative voice that's so natural and understated, I found myself re-reading passages in order to relive emotional experiences that were happening as a result of the gentle, but Nabokovian precision of Alex Christofi's prose' Simon Van Booy, author of *The Illusion of Separateness*

'*Glass* was such a pleasure to read, funny, beautiful and perceptive. I found Günter a gentle, endearing hero, a unique little fish in an extremely moving bildungsroman. It struck a deep note about the fleeting nature of existence' Sara Crowe, author of *Campari for Breakfast*

LET US BE TRUE

ALEX CHRISTOFI

First published in Great Britain in 2017 by Serpent's Tail,
an imprint of Profile Books Ltd
3 Holford Yard
Bevin Way
London
WC1X 9HD
www.serpentstail.com

1 3 5 7 9 10 8 6 4 2

Designed and typeset by Crow Books
Printed and bound by Clays Ltd, St Ives plc

A CIP record for this book can
be obtained from the British Library

ISBN: 978 1 78125740 1
eISBN: 978 1 78283302 4

Penguin Random House is committed to a sustainable future for
our business, our readers and our planet. This book is made from
Forest Stewardship Council® certified paper.

MIX
Paper from
responsible sources
FSC
www.fsc.org   FSC® C018179

*Whoever believes in freedom of the will has never loved
and never hated.*

Marie von Ebner-Eschenbach

Paris, 1992

It would be easy to believe, Ralf thought, looking down at the river, that time was in the moment, falling and evading the hands like a down feather. But time was a process of fulfilment: time gathered. One left each moment behind and it rested there. How often had he walked past this spot without knowing he would be standing here today, with all these gathered moments, leaning over the stone wall to watch the river boats?

Part One

Part One

I

RALF, Paris and Deauville, March–April 1958

)

Ralf first met Elsa when she began punching him in the head. It didn't much hurt, since he had been drinking for a couple of hours already, but she had a surprisingly sharp aim. It would certainly have been preferable to begin with names.

It had happened in Jacques' bar, of all places, where Ralf had settled in for the night. Jacques was a barman of the ancient stock: gruff, suspicious of newcomers, his fingernails so dirty one could barely make out the lunula, his dishcloth employed to ensure an even distribution of grease across his glasses. But to be recognised and accepted in a place like Jacques' bar was a beautiful thing. One's glass got bigger and refilled itself; on warm evenings, one might doze in the corner for hours without being disturbed.

Ralf had sat at his usual table. Back in his student days, he used to drink in the Two Mandarins, celebrity-spotting, when he still thought he might complete his doctorate. The university had made the mistake of handing Ralf a lucrative sideline in the translation of scientific papers from the German (the most interesting research still being done by Germans, even after everything). But Ralf had discovered there was easier money still in tutoring language students at Berlitz, and he had set up a new life, albeit a temporary one, in the Marais. The buildings were condemned, which made them cheap, and it was the perfect place to get by while he formed a plan. He had his little maid's attic, bread and wine. Of course, the temporary became the permanent if you didn't mind waiting, and Ralf was beginning to see life as an accrual of the probable in the face of the possible.

About an hour before the attack, another of the regulars, Fouad, had woken up, smoothed down his moustache, wrapped his sleeve around his hand and screwed the ceiling bulb back into its fixture. Ralf suspected he did not have an apartment at the moment, difficult as it was to find a landlord willing to take an Algerian. In the few hours between finishing one job and starting the next, he would walk the streets, stopping at Jacques' to doze for an hour or two before the bar closed and he found himself back out among the rubbish and the trees. He always carried a copy of the day's paper with him, which lent him a certain urbanity, but which likely doubled as bedding.

Ralf made no attempt to conceal himself when Fouad's eyes met his own. Fouad waved him over. Once they had broken into a good bottle of wine, they set about solving the various political crises dogging the Fourth Republic, starting with the limpness of the coalition government and moving quickly on, as Fouad often did, to the war in Algeria, which he insisted on calling the 'war of independence'. Ralf fell back on his usual position, arguing that it was important to stand together, but political aims were poorly served by violence, implying as it did a lack of confidence in one's arguments. Fouad argued that the object was not to force the government's opinion, but to force them to listen. At the end of the bottle, they still hadn't found a solution that was acceptable to all parties, so Ralf went to the bar for another.

Jacques made him wait while he went to the cellar to replace a barrel, lifting the trapdoor beneath his feet and disappearing through the hole. A handbag sat on the counter. There was only one woman in the bar, so Ralf picked up the bag and went over to her.

'You left your bag at the counter,' he said.

She looked at him with affable bewilderment.

'Not mine. Here's mine.' She hefted her own on the seat next to her.

Ralf went back to the bar and opened the bag. Jacques was cursing as he rolled the new barrel up each step. Ralf found a lipstick; a bag of other assorted make-up; a diary, which he put to one side (it didn't have a name, but it did give times and places); a single deadlock key; a compact mirror. Sticking plasters; aspirin. A purse had sunk to the bottom. If he could get a name, or better still, an address . . .

Something hit him quite hard on the side of the head. He stumbled as he was punched a second time. The top of his ear stung. Someone was tugging at the purse, which he clutched tighter by instinct. A woman was screaming for him to let go.

'Thief! Give it to me!'

Ralf let go just as Jacques shoved the barrel up the last step.

'Call the police!' the woman shouted. 'This man was trying to steal my bag.'

'What? Ralf?' said the barman. 'He won't even let me round up his change.'

She looked across at him. He had one arm half raised to defend himself. She seemed to be deciding whether or not to keep hitting him.

'I was just trying—' he began. She burst out laughing. 'I was looking for your name,' he finished limply.

'Elsa,' she said, holding out her hand. Behind her, Fouad was putting on his coat. He grinned at Ralf, tucked his newspaper under his arm, and slipped out.

'Can I . . . offer you a drink?' Ralf asked.

She smiled.

'I just punched you in the head.'

'Yes, and now I need a drink.'

'All right. But I'll pay,' she said.

'No, don't worry.'

'I insist. It's your reward for finding my bag.' She stood next to him at the bar, smiling to herself. She had not apologised, as such. Jacques' expression implied he didn't care who paid, as long as they did it quickly.

They went back to Ralf's table and she took off her gloves, throwing one leg over the other.

'I hope you're not staying to keep me company?' Ralf asked. 'You seemed to have been on your way somewhere?'

'Only home, and I don't want to go back there.' She rested a cheek on the palm of her hand, one finger stroking the down above her ear. 'Why, have I interrupted your plans?'

'No, I'm not up to much at all tonight. Unless you count smoking.'

'Smoking isn't an activity. It's an ellipsis between activities.'

Ralf entertained the possibility she was being forward. He was terrible at flirting, because he hated taking risks.

'Well, then, I'm free all evening,' he said cautiously.

'Good. Then you must take me for dinner.' She drained her wine, stood and walked over to the phone booth. He drank as much of his own as he could manage, having only just sat down, grabbed her bag for the second time that evening, and threw a bleary smile at Jacques.

'Let him starve, then. I can't be there every moment of the—'

She saw Ralf, cupped her hand over the receiver and turned her back to him, as if the phone were a child and he a grenade. Her green overcoat hung from her shoulders as on a clothing rail, taut only where it was cinched in at the waist, making an illusion of her body. Ralf somehow hadn't noticed, while they were talking, how small she was, almost malnourished – she had seemed imposing at first.

He looked outside. Jo Goldenberg's had full covers. He stood waiting, holding her bag by a corner, in case holding it too naturally implied ownership. The smell of leeks and boiled meat wafted down from one of the apartments above. A couple of metres away a thin, grey cat watched him as it licked at a gutter. Holding the door open, he heard the metal of the phone cradle ring out dully as the phone was slammed.

'Let's get out of the Marais,' said Elsa desperately. 'Find somewhere fun. It's so stifling in these narrow little streets.' She was already off towards the river.

She led him off to the Left Bank and, from there, to the Tour d'Argent, a restaurant that had been doing very well without Ralf's patronage for several hundred years.

'May I take your coat, madame?' asked the waiter on their way in.

'No, you may not,' she replied.

'We have a cloakroom, if you feel it would be convenient?'

'I shall bear that in mind.'

She strode off in the direction of a window table, leaving Ralf and the waiter to hurry after her, Ralf shrugging helplessly at the waiter as if to confirm that she was not under his control.

The table was set with silverware and thick Egyptian cotton, three lit candles casting a warm, buttery light over Elsa's face and chest as she sat across from him.

'Our speciality is the pressed duck,' informed the waiter.

'What's special about it?' asked Elsa.

'The duck is eight weeks old, fattened for the last fifteen days and then strangled to retain the blood. It is a great delicacy.'

The waiter upended their gleaming wine glasses, and presented Ralf with a four-hundred-page wine menu. Ralf wondered how he'd come to be sitting here. He felt a surge in his stomach, as if he were falling backwards off a wall and was about to crack his skull against the earth. The colours here were nothing like the faded interiors of the Paris he knew.

'Pick something that goes with duck,' she said.

'I don't know what goes with duck.'

Elsa held up an arm, not taking her eyes off him, and waved her hand about. The sommelier arrived.

'Has sir decided what he will be drinking tonight?'

'We would like something that makes duck taste nice,' Ralf said, hoping she might acknowledge the challenge.

'What year were you born?' she asked.

'What?'

'What year?'

'1927.'

'God, are you that old?'

Elsa passed the heavy menu to the waiter.

'A nice red from 1927. And squash us a duck.'

The waiter obediently took up the book and went gliding off in the direction of the cellar. Ralf suppressed a smile. Elsa seemed to have sensed Ralf's discomfort, and was puncturing the waiter's superciliousness for his amusement.

From here, Ralf could see the people on the road below, the river, the Île Saint-Louis and Notre-Dame. How could he hope to reciprocate in a place like this, when even the view seemed to hold more interest than he could? He didn't even have the money to pay for the food, let alone the wine. She must know that, if not by where she found him, then by his clothes. But he had set his course – he might as well enjoy it. Browsing the other diners, he spotted one man with slick dark hair, large round ears and a preposterous moustache.

'Is that Dalí?' he muttered.

'Which one?' She swivelled her whole person, putting a hand on the back of her chair for leverage.

'Salvador Dalí.'

'I mean which one is he?'

'The one with the bloody Dalí moustache.'

'Oh. Yes, it is.'

'Aren't you interested?'

'Not really. Melt a clock, do a couple of statues, put them in a desert and call it something idiotic like "The Perception of Loss". He's hardly Da Vinci, is he?' She unfolded her napkin. 'And anyway, I thought he lived in Spain.'

The sommelier returned to present a dusty wine bottle.

'I'm sure it's fine, thank you,' Ralf said.

The sommelier removed the cork, a conductor giving the first flourish of his baton, and poured a splash into Ralf's glass. Ralf glanced up at him, and at Elsa, who looked ready to burst out laughing. He opted for a quick half-mouthful.

'Yes. Thank you.'

The sommelier started to pour, holding the bottle as an extension of his forearm, taking care not to touch the glass.

'Oh, just leave the bottle,' Elsa said. 'We haven't got all night.'

He knew he should be appalled but he thrilled at her rudeness. She seemed to acknowledge quite naturally that Ralf would betray himself to be with her. And it was true: he wanted to take her part. He felt a silent allegiance developing, a softening of the boundary he had put up around *me* and *mine,* the admittance of *us* and *ours*.

The waiter came pushing a trolley, his white apron covering his legs. He lifted a cloche to reveal two plates, on which sat two perfect duck breasts, pouring on a thick, dark, almost purple sauce. Then he spooned two soft little potatoes onto each plate and bid them a good appetite. It was done. The sauce was poured, the wine unstopped. He estimated the meal would cost him eight thousand francs. Perhaps they would be trusting enough to accept a cheque?

'Eat it while it's hot,' commanded Elsa. He looked over at Dalí, who had one eyebrow raised at his dining partner and was dabbing at his mouth with a napkin, then out at the Seine, which ran off towards the rest of the city and the Tower. Overhead, the clouds bruised and cracked. There was a brief flash of lightning, the thunder inaudible behind the glass. He was in the world's oldest restaurant, eating duck with a stranger who had just punched him in the head. The multiplier effect of probabilities necessary to bring all this about made his presence here as good as impossible. Certainly these things happened in the world, but never to him. These last few years, he had not lived every day anew but had worked towards perfecting the same day, over and over, interested only in subtle variations. Now, here, tonight, this beautiful woman had broken the cycle, without ceremony, quietly leading him away to a new day, with no intimation of what might come next.

He lifted his silver fork and pulled away the tender flesh. It was soft, almost melting into nothing as it landed on his tongue, and yet the flavour was rich, earthy and sweet. Like plums and gravy. He rolled his wine, watching it cling to the glass. It had sat for his whole lifetime untouched in a shadowless rack under the soil, trapped with a tiny bubble of the air that had existed before his father had died and they had fled Hamburg, before England, the war, the toil of learning to speak French not just correctly, but gracefully.

He took a sip. The flavour shuddered down the sides of his tongue, so tart it was almost sour, fighting against the heavy splendour of the duck.

'Are you crying?' asked Elsa suspiciously. She lowered her glass, from which she had been about to drink.

'Of course not,' he said, blinking. 'My wine caught in my throat.' She did not look convinced and held his eyes in hers as she drank her wine.

When he had finished his food, he excused himself and stood at the bathroom sink, caught between two mirrors. There were a great many of him, here in this *mise en abyme*, stretching endlessly out before and behind. He was here, real and alive, perfect copies of him strewn across the past and future, their movements tied to his own in the present. For all time, he would be here, and here. He smoothed his hair back, and in the abyss, every Ralf did the same, half facing him, half facing away.

By the time he sat down, the plates had been cleared.

'I've never seen you in Jacques' bar before,' he said.

'I've never been there before,' replied Elsa.

'What made you come in tonight?'

'I honestly don't know. I suppose I was lonely.' She smiled at him sadly and, unexpectedly moved, Ralf was on the verge of telling her how glad he was to have met her when the waiter returned to ask whether they would like dessert.

Ralf steeled himself as Elsa took a menu. He might borrow some money from M. Dague, his landlord, who had a pedantic brand of chivalry where money was concerned. Or he could take the waiter aside and explain the situation to him, offer to wash dishes. His tutees were quite flexible. It would take three or four weeks at most.

'Are you having dessert?' she asked.

'I'm quite full,' he replied. 'You?'

'No, not tonight.' She stood and put her coat on, picking up his hat. 'Come on, let's go for a walk.'

He could have laughed. They were charging it to her account. Why else would she have suggested it?

'Get your coat on. Quickly,' she barked. They'd barely set down their cutlery and she was already across the room and heading down towards the lobby. He followed her, muttering his thanks to the maître d', down the stairs and past the doorman. Elsa didn't stop for him – she had started down the road.

'Excuse me, sir,' called the doorman. He heard squabbling behind him and quickened his pace. 'Excuse me!' called the doorman again, insistent this time, walking. Elsa took off her shoes and started to run. Ralf broke into a run too, and the doorman gave chase.

Elsa disappeared, cackling, round a corner.

'You'll never catch us, you fucker!' she shouted.

The doorman was fast, for a big man, and Ralf's stomach lurched horribly as the sickly sweet aftertaste of the duck rose in his throat. He turned the corner but Elsa was gone, and for a long time there was nothing but the clacking of his heels against the cobbles, until he realised he had fled everything. There was no doorman, no restaurant, no Elsa – nothing except the fallen rain, running off into the gutter, the darkened chequerboard of art deco windows facing onto Saint-Séverin and a heart that wouldn't slow. He would get two and a half billion beats out of it if he was lucky, and he could hear it counting down. He felt sick and shaken. Alive, and at last.

Three days passed and Ralf had begun to resign himself to the fact that he had no chance of finding this Elsa. He didn't have a number or an address for her, nor even her surname. He turned over ways of finding her in his head all the same. But time dragged on, and on Friday he found himself outside Jacques' bar earlier than usual, the first of the regulars to arrive.

'Any sign of Fouad?' Ralf asked.

'No, he's off marching today,' replied Jacques.

'Pro-communist, or pro-Algeria?'

'How should I know? You're the one who spends every night arguing with him. Oh – I'm to give you this,' said Jacques, handing over a crumpled and greasy piece of folded paper. 'Drink?'

'I'll have a beer, thank you.' Ralf looked down at the note. Jacques sniffed and swallowed phlegm. The note said:

If you ever want to see your hat again, meet me at 5.30 pm by the restaurant on the Tour Eiffel.

Ralf turned the note over. The other side was blank except for Jacques' dirty fingerprints. Ralf looked at the clock.

'Did she give you this today?' he asked.

'It was a boy came in this morning while I was putting the chairs down. He was only in his shorts and cap, must have been freezing his little orphans off.'

'Can I cancel the beer?'

Jacques lifted the glass, scraping off the excess foam with his finger.

'I've poured it now.'

'Can't you drink it?'

'I'll drink it and you pay for it, how's that?'

'I'll pay you later, you bloody skinflint,' said Ralf as he wound his scarf tight around his neck. If he cycled quickly, he could make it there with time to spare.

He had a clear run to Saint-Jacques, perhaps the only church ever to have been built by butchers and destroyed by republicans. For reasons unknown, they had left the tower intact, so here alone it stood. He continued down the rue de Rivoli, passing buses at their stops. Grey and beige Vespas buzzed through gaps. The wind froze his knuckles and caught at the back of his throat.

Who was this Elsa, who was playing a game without telling him the rules, who had run off, leaving him behind as evidence? Her behaviour didn't make sense. He had to know more. At times he had wondered whether she was humouring him – he had almost felt he was boring her – and yet she had gone so far out of her way in his company. They were both, doubtless, banned from the Tour d'Argent. The stunt could not be replicated. It was as if she gave no thought to consequence. Ralf turned off to cycle through the Tuileries, named after tilers and planted for royalty. A passer-by was trying to stop her handbag from slipping down her arm as her child ran over to the fountain with a model boat.

'Dismount!' called a policeman, holding his hand out towards Ralf.

'Sorry, I can't, I'm late,' shouted Ralf over his shoulder as he swerved past.

The policeman made as if to give chase, but thought better of it as Ralf sped down the long, straight gravel of the gardens, negotiating his way through traffic at the Place de la Concorde and on towards the Pont Alexandre III.

If she had never contacted him again, that would have been the end of it. But she had kept the hat, leaving the night unresolved. She must want to see him. He had been thinking about that evening, going back over what she had said in the search for new meanings, wondering whether he had invented her glances. He had barely had a chance to find out anything about her. They had not kissed, nor declared any sentiments. Nothing was spoken aloud. What if she were simply to give the hat to him and go? But that was ridiculous. Why arrange to meet if one could have delivered the hat instead of the note?

Up ahead was the tower. Once condemned as useless, monstrous, giddy and ridiculous. It reminded him of that Hollywood vision of the war which had made Paris a place of brief sojourn between the realities of fascism and resistance. By the time Ralf had arrived in the city for his studies in late 1946, the alumni of the Resistance seemed to have swelled in number. A pâtissier who wouldn't serve Jews before the war claimed to have been supporting a family of ten in his kitchen cupboards, and so on. If they had really been so numerous, they would have run out of Jews to hide and might have invaded Germany with walking sticks and umbrellas.

As the Quai d'Orsay became the Quai Branly, he wondered why she had chosen this place at all. This was Baedecker Paris, a postcard backdrop. It seemed too overt and gauche a gesture for one who had taken such pleasure in flouting convention.

Still, here it was, a mass of struts, a crow's nest on the good ship Paris. Elsa would be up there by now, looking out across the city. The natural taper of the structure made it seem to recede beyond all measure into the sky. He leant his bicycle against a railing. A couple were smoking on a bench, not talking. A father was pulling his child out of a flower bed by the arm. He found the behaviour of children baffling. They seemed to have no associative memory. They were hell bent on collecting new sense experience: taste, touch, smell. They hadn't seen enough of life to presume. Beyond this, the imperfect control of their bodies and the comedy of their scale made them fascinating to watch.

Ralf could not remember having seen a child for years, but now he saw them everywhere. It wouldn't be the only thing to have passed him by in his twenties. But it wasn't the sudden appearance of children that shocked him, so much as the realisation that their parents were younger than him. They had five-year-olds, ten-, fifteen-year-olds, even. At some point, his path had diverged from that of others his age. Academia had split him off from the pack, and he had branched off from that too, so that he was now a living fossil, cut off and unlikely to converge. He knew rationally that the world hadn't run out of women for him to meet, but it sometimes felt like it.

He crossed the gardens to the long elevator queue. She would be gone before he reached the front. The attendant intercepted him as he approached.

'Sir, don't take the stairs.'

'Why shouldn't I?'

The attendant looked up.

'Even the lift takes eight minutes.'

'Well, I don't propose to queue for an hour and then wait a further eight minutes.'

The attendant shrugged. Ralf began to climb. Would he recognise her? He remembered her red lipstick, her coat pulled tight at the waist, the delicate frame of her collarbone. The perfect symmetry of her face somehow made it harder to recall. She was beautiful, he was sure of that. A heart-shaped face, almost pointed at the chin. But it was the idea of her.

Catching his breath at the top, he walked twice clockwise and once anti-clockwise around the platform. There was no lone woman; there was no one alone. He looked up at the ugly new broadcasting aerial above him. He should have searched the queue. Perhaps she was still at the bottom.

But why should he be nervous? He was a grown man. He was not a weeping young romantic and there was no reason to trust a perfect stranger. It was only a hat. He had no business going on wild goose chases around the city, climbing towers. Still, he was here now. He looked out at the city. The sun backlit the dark clouds in chiaroscuro and for a moment broke through, catching each drop of rain so that the sunlight fell not just on surfaces but everywhere at once, manifested endlessly through the air. He ran his hand through his hair, feeling the strange absence of his hat.

Ralf imagined the bells ringing across the city at the liberation, the bell of Notre-Dame ringing for the first time in four years, and wished he could have been here. Grenades and home-made incendiaries thrown out of anonymous windows, the enemy routed, the victory parade, General de Gaulle's arrival, the lighting of the eternal flame, the last enemy snipers, Allied troops gunning in the windows, kicking doors and retaking buildings, more parades, endless parades, Shermans parked in the road, the joyous uplifted faces of young women, Philip Morris cigarettes, pastis in the bars, owners ripping up the tabs. The joy of being alive and the certainty that you would remain alive, that one could utter the forbidden word, *future, futur.*

He'd known he was going to enlist before the war had started when his mother took in two children from the *Kindertransport.* They were brother and sister, and Ralf had been fond of them immediately. As they came off the train, they looked sick with nerves, just as Ralf had felt five years earlier, when he and his mother had made their own hasty departure for London, relying on a name and an address. They were clutching a sweet little booklet, *While You Are in England: Helpful Information and Guidance for Every Refugee.* Ralf had memorised his favourite section: 'Do not make yourself conspicuous by talking loudly, nor by your manner or dress. The Englishman greatly dislikes ostentation. The Englishman attaches very great importance to modesty, under-statement in speech rather than over-statement, and quietness of dress and manner. He values good manners far more than he values the evidence of wealth. (You will find that he says "Thank you" for the slightest service – even for a penny bus ticket *for which he has paid.*)' Later, he would find the two little strangers nestled into him like cubs during a night raid, encouraging them along with little snatches of English ('Talk in halting English rather than fluent German – and *do not talk in a loud voice*').

Throughout his childhood and adolescence, everything had been a matter of adaptation. He was soon used to the sirens, and would file onto the underground platform politely, letting go of the children's hands to hang his coat on a poster nail like the adults. He would lie down with his mother and the children in the jigsaw puzzle of bodies, and stare up at the lampshades waiting to see whether the lights would be turned off.

When he heard that Hamburg had been levelled by the

Allies, thousands of planes dropping thousands of tonnes of bombs, day and night for a week, it was as if the last barrier to participation had been breached. Buried deep beneath blankets of time, like seeds under snow, had been the town of his birth, a world of vague waters, birds nesting under eaves, the bellow of foghorns. Ralf had found himself unable to celebrate what was by all accounts an august victory, his sheets kicked and bundled around his shins in the night while he dreamed of a cyclone that melted asphalt, set fire to canals, sucked oxygen from cellars, the draught pulling people bodily into the firestorm, like dry leaves.

It took him months to reconcile himself to the news. Even then, he couldn't fully grasp that Hamburg no longer existed. Thinking of it was like exploring a gum that had lost a tooth. But when spring came, after his seventeenth birthday, Ralf signed up to the Royal Armoured Corps as Ralph Woodward. He had heard that joining a tank regiment was preferable to joining the infantry, since one didn't spend all day walking and all night digging foxholes. It was only after he had signed up that someone mentioned the terrible losses they had suffered in North Africa. Almost no one in a tank had survived longer than three months: they were a sitting target when the sun went down behind them.

He'd gone into training at Farnborough as a radio operator, because of his German. People were already muttering that the worm had turned, and quietly they began to prepare for a massive assault on Normandy. Ralf felt a great ferocity at the thought of conquering the conquerors. He wanted to ride a tank over German soil. He didn't particularly want to kill a German, he reflected as he applied thick black glue to waterproof the underside of the tank, but he rather thought he might kill a Nazi.

As the day of the assault approached, all leave was cancelled. Mobilisation was postponed a day because of bad weather, and they were kept in holding camps in a forest. They played cards, ate dinner, and waited. Just after midnight, they got the call, and the entire Second Army mobilised. The noise was so loud Ralf half expected the Nazis to hear them coming. They rode through the night, throwing their loose change glittering into the streets, women waving them off from top-floor windows. At Gosport, they slept on the pavements, the heavy Rolls-Royce engines ticking and cooling, until dawn.

Their sergeant gave them a breakfast of tinned peaches and cream, neither of which Ralf had seen since the start of the war. Holding the tin, he felt keenly that this was his last meal – that he would die in just a few hours, and it would happen too quickly for him to think anything of it. One moment he would be straining into his radio, the next a confusion of twisted metal, black bone and hissing flesh, piled up on foreign sand to be pecked at by seagulls and lapped at by the waves. He drank the last sweet juice from the tin, sad and appreciative to have been a creature that could taste at all.

Theirs had been the first vehicle on the landing ship, parked right up against the far ramp. It was dark and the sea was choppy. The chains securing the vehicles rattled. Ralf's head swam with petrol fumes. When his crew went up top, they could see ships everywhere, barrage balloons littering the skies like a ghost fleet. The coast appeared, then Gold Beach itself, and they were back in their tanks, Ralf tuned to receive orders.

They debarked through four feet of water, Spitfires buzzing low overhead. Knocked-out tanks were already strewn across the beach. Up on the cliffs, one of the houses was flying a French flag. The order was to push up the path – to keep taking ground come what may. It seemed to Ralf they had arrived too late to be of use here, almost as if they had run out of enemies to fight.

They put their first soldier down by running him over. Some moments passed before they could check their surroundings properly. The enemy soldier was clearly still alive, albeit pancaked into the mud, so Ralf radioed for the infantry to come and dig him out if they could.

Throughout that day and the next, they pushed through narrow hedgerows in single file. They all knew the foremost tank would be the first to be hit, so they played a slow game of Russian roulette, each tank taking its turn to lead for five minutes, desperately hoping not to encounter a dugout or a camouflaged 88, which they would never survive. At the end of their five minutes, they would drop to the back of the line, laughing with relief that they would live another twenty minutes.

The world grew colder. They swung east, stopping at night to make tea and read old newspapers by the light of burning towns. When they heard that Paris had been taken, it seemed almost as if the war was already over, though there was so much ground still to take. The Allies had dropped thirty thousand men from above, a cloud of paratroopers drifting through the air, wooden gliders spiralling down like injured moths. Under the sheer weight of numbers, Ralf began to hope he would survive to see the end of war.

By winter, they were pushing farther into the Netherlands, towards Germany. It was deathly cold, and Ralf was sick of being shot at. He was sick of the shriek of Nebelwerfer. He was sick of maintaining the tracks and of people hiding in foxholes. Ordinary worlds were being tortured into the new narrative. Farms became fortifications; his radio broadcast screams. He was sick even of the relentless cheerfulness of his crew, of their nearness, of their jokes about Germans, of their bodies, sweating in white undershirts. He was sick of fighting for days over a little bridge that he had never heard of. More than anything, he had begun to dread arriving in Germany.

Matters came to a head one night when they had settled down

with their dog biscuits, tinned butter and Spam. Ralf got out of the tank. It was his turn to brew tea. The snow had fallen some time back, and its surface cracked like a frozen lake under his boots, not soft or airy but large and crystalline, snow after Eden. Ralf's feet were beginning to smell dreadful. The skin around the ball of his sole had begun to turn to a kind of white mulch, and itched terribly. He wanted dry socks.

He lit the stove, stared into its little twilight, thought about flame-throwers. He'd seen a pillbox lit up with soldiers in it. Door handles were less than useless in a situation like that. Their gunner had made a tasteless remark about missing his Sunday roast as they had watched. Ralf tried to focus on what was in front of him. The tank. The fog. The rustling of animals in a nearby orchard. The hiss of the gas.

Far off, Ralf could hear an indistinct crashing and a low rumble. It sounded like thunder, though Ralf had an unproven idea that lightning didn't strike in mist. He put the water on. It sounded like cracking foliage. He began to feel the rumble through the earth.

'Get up!' Ralf shouted. 'There's something coming.'

The first thing Ralf saw through the mist was the dark, floating O of an anti-tank gun, gliding in ten feet above the ground, resolving into the hulking form of a Tiger tank no more than twenty-five feet away. Their Churchill was directly in the line of its 88, a monstrous gun like a telegraph pole. Ralf had never seen one so close before – it was designed to knock out tanks from a mile off. The gunner's sleepy head appeared out of the hatch.

'Drive!' shouted Ralf, running round to take cover.

The tank choked into life as the turret began to turn slowly clockwise, and Ralf knew he had to run. The Churchill could hit 40 mph when it needed to, and there was no way it could outgun the Tiger. He made it halfway to the orchard before he was flung to the ground. He turned his head, small and exposed without its helmet. The gunner was draped half out of the turret, uncaring, aflame. Ralf lost consciousness.

The next he knew, Ralf was lying in bedsheets behind the lines, watching others arrive on stretchers from Antwerp. When he had recovered sufficiently, his commanding officer brought him in for a horribly brief meeting, in which he was told that none of his crew had survived, and was given a note to take to logistics about being reposted.

Ralf was assigned to T-Force, with the brief to take control of Radio Hamburg, from which the turncoat and general Allied irritant William Joyce, aka Lord Haw-Haw, broadcast his English-language propaganda. On 30 April, outside the city, Ralf tuned in to Joyce's last broadcast. He was drunk, and spoke as if the problem was the Allied failure to properly apprehend what Hitler had been trying to achieve. *They are not imperious, they do not want to take what doesn't belong to them. All they want is to live their own simple lives, undisturbed by outside influences.*

By that time, Hamburg was defended by policemen and the Hitler Youth. Despite the odds, and indeed despite the suicide of the Führer himself, they put up quite a fight. Still, on 3 May, there Ralf stood, in front of Lord Haw-Haw's equipment, staring at the pre-recorded tape from which his last message had been broadcast. He rewound the last few seconds. *Germany will live. Because the people of Germany have in them the secret of life, endurance, will and purpose. And therefore I say to you, in these last words – you may not hear from me again for a few months – I say* Ich liebe Deutschland, Heil Hitler, *and farewell.* Ralf spooled the recording onto a can and found a case to take it as evidence.

He followed the wires along, testing out the connections. He switched on the equipment, waiting for the valves to warm up.

The gentle hiss faded in. He cleared his throat and watched the gauge's needle twitch. 'This is Radio Hamburg, a station of the Allied Military Government.' Ralf licked his lips. His sergeant watched him nervously, clearly uncomfortable about letting anyone broadcast a message in a language he didn't understand. The sergeant held the paper bearing the official message, which Ralf read out as clearly and properly as he could, sounding out syllables that made his heart beat manically, as if he were outing himself as the enemy. And then they switched off the equipment, and Ralf was allowed to go down to the office of records, where he asked after anyone bearing the name Wolfensohn. A search was made, and it transpired that his grandmother had died in '43, in the firebombing. Two years earlier, his grandfather had been taken away by train. Nothing was left of his childhood home, nor his grandparents'.

In 1946, Joyce was hanged and Ralf was demobbed. He was to take a train home via Paris. In the newspaper, he read that the British government had agreed to take a thousand minors from the camps, but they could only find 732 survivors. And perhaps it was selfish – certainly, his mother didn't yet seem to have forgiven him – but when the time came to board his train for England, he remained on the platform. England and Germany seemed, however unfairly, part of a grey continuum of sadness and arbitrary cruelty, whereas Paris was a city of possibility, glimpsed from a train window, standing near whole among the ruins of Europe.

It was getting dark. Ralf stood on the viewing platform for an hour or more, watching the lights come on. One or two at first, then more, and more frequently, until the city's filaments were bursting alight too quickly to count. This City of Tungsten. In time he would forget that he had ever seen this. He would take the lift back down, crammed in with all the couples. He scanned a last time over the deep blue sky and the city. Over there, the

Marais. And there, atop Montmartre, once *Mons Martis*, the basilica of Sacré-Coeur, where the crows nested.

Ralf wondered how he could have fooled himself so easily into thinking that a single chance meeting was the start of a long and significant narrative. It shamed him to think that he had cycled around Paris for a week thinking about her. He had imagined looking back at this time from the vantage of years. He had been nostalgic for the present, thinking it the soft stuff of memories. Sitting with a child on his lap, its little head under Ralf's chin, as they looked at photographs. *This is the restaurant where we first had dinner. We used to go back every year. And this is where we used to live.* He had underlined two sentences in a book he had been reading: 'Why does that tune haunt me? Indeed, why is there this music?' Every new thing he encountered had felt quite saturated with meaning, as if it were all draining down towards the same great subterranean river, and he could hear it rushing under every step.

He put out his cigarette and started for the telephone ringing at the bottom of the stairs. He would buy new pencils and a typewriter ribbon. He would begin to take his academic work seriously. He would find reward in it if he put the time in. He took the stairs two at a time and caught the phone mid-ring, the bell resounding as he spoke his first words of the day.

'Marais 2271?'

'Good morning. I have a call from London. Will you take it?'

'Yes, please put it through.'

'You can stay on the line, it shouldn't take a moment.'

He heard the quality of the static change from 'ç' to 's'.

'Mother?'

'Oh, Ralf. You're alive.'

'Well, yes.'

'You said you would call me on Tuesday and I didn't hear a thing. All day, I sat on the chair by the telephone, darned every sock in the house—'

'I'm sorry. It's been a busy week.'

'In what way, busy?'

'Tutorials.'

'All week?' his mother asked dubiously.

'And other things. I'm working on a new research idea. It's required a lot of time.'

'What is it?'

'It's hard to explain.'

'What's it called?'

'Does it matter? You won't understand it.'

He listened to the hiss.

'No. I'm sure you're right.'

The hiss, heavier than silence. She had always claimed the telephone was an amenity for the benefit of the lodger, but it was painfully clear that she had hoped they might speak more.

'Is it a young woman?' she asked hopefully. 'Is that why you haven't called?'

'No.'

The hiss, leaking into the gulf between them and expanding. They were already a sea apart, and threatened to fall altogether out of one another's orbit.

'Why don't you come home to me?'

He heard her chair creak. It would be the same wooden chair that the previous lodger had left behind four years earlier when he defaulted on two months' back-rent and disappeared. Furniture stayed in that house for as long as it took to disintegrate, and his mother was not above using her only manual tool, a hammer, to nail joints back together. He had not torn a single pair of trousers since he had left.

'This is my home, too.'

'You know the pharmacist? His daughter Rebecca is twenty this year – and so beautiful.'

He had stopped listening. He loved her very much but she dwelled on his shortcomings. She wanted him to gather a family about him, and yet she wanted him back in her second bedroom.

She had never really forgiven him for his failure to return to London after the war, or for losing touch with the two children they had taken care of. Every time she had asked Ralf when he was coming home, he'd told her he needed to finish his degree, or his research, or his teaching contract, his excuses getting gradually less credible, the intervals between her asking getting longer, until he had gently suggested that she take a lodger. Listening to her crying down the phone, he had hoped that this was a kindness – that, by giving her certainty, she might stop asking. Then, the last time he had visited England three years earlier, they had left so many silences, it had been as if they had set a third place at the table. They were unavoidable, the silences, measured out like Erik Satie's first *Gymnopédie*, the sustain of the third beat, the negative space of the expected note, the hobbled waltz. He couldn't bear it.

After melancholy assurances, he excused himself, crushing his keys softly in his hand so as not to betray the sound to his mother. He replaced the phone in its cradle and went to get his coat.

In the shop, M. Dague was sweeping up hair. Once upon a time, he had swept up hair of many colours, but now almost all the hair was grey. Ralf never asked how business was going, but there were six barbers' seats, and he worked alone. The apartment was cheap enough, but Ralf felt obliged to have his hair cut here, and M. Dague only knew one cut. He looked up brightly as Ralf emerged from the stairway.

'Let me show you something,' he said, fumbling through a

newspaper as Ralf came over. He turned to a page where a hair-dresser with a turtleneck stood smiling behind an exquisitely coiffed American celebrity. 'Now isn't that a spectacle?' Ralf nodded. 'He's opened a place on the rue du Faubourg Saint-Honoré,' M. Dague continued. 'Half the world living in boxes in Sarcelles, the other half pandering to these starlets. I could do it if I wanted to. I'm very good with women's hair.'

'I don't think I've ever seen a woman in here,' said Ralf absently, examining the actress's heart-shaped face, willing her to resemble Elsa.

'Nicolle comes in to give me my lunch,' M. Dague replied defensively. 'Look, if you're going out, could you buy some apricots?'

'Of course. I'll be half an hour.'

M. Dague was still rifling through his wallet for a note as Ralf pushed out into the sunshine and the crisp air. He didn't even need a typewriter ribbon, when it came to it. Just a couple of new pencils and a lot of paper. The idea of having a surplus of paper was a comfort, though it was no longer rationed. He liked having enough to last him some time. One never knew what the future held.

Ralf walked past the grocer unloading boxes of vegetables from the back of a van. He would get apricots on the way back.

'You!' a woman shouted at someone over the road. He could only see an innocuous man walking past in the opposite direction, holding a paperback open with his thumb as if scouting out somewhere to read the next paragraph.

'Come back here!' shouted the woman again, closer this time. Ralf turned to see what the grievance might be, and who causing it, in time to see Elsa striding over to him. 'Where were you?' She shoved him.

'I was there!' Ralf protested. 'I couldn't see you.'

'Were you really?'

'Yes. I had to cycle across the city to make it in time. But I couldn't see you anywhere.'

'That's sweet of you. I wasn't there. I got held up.'

Ralf laughed at the cheek of it.

'Do you have my hat?' he asked.

'Oh, that. No, I didn't think I'd see you again so I threw it on a lamp-post.'

'But I need it,' said Ralf.

'No one wears hats any more.'

'I suppose an apology is out of the question?' Ralf asked.

Elsa took his arm.

'I wouldn't accept one,' she said. 'You have to make it up to me by accompanying me to the Gare Saint-Lazare.'

It seemed futile to object, and although he was now convinced she was awful, she made an interesting case study. So they walked the entire length of the rue Réaumur, the Métro apparently violating some invisible criterion in Elsa's esteem, and, forty minutes later, arrived at the station. A train was just pulling in, steam from its engine billowing up and obscuring the metal struts of the roof.

Elsa took him to the desk and bought two tickets for the next available train, which was bound for Deauville.

'I suppose you're going to ask me to accompany you to Deauville, now?' asked Ralf.

'It will do us both good,' she said.

He studied her. She looked serious.

'Come on,' she said. 'When was the last time you escaped the city? Look at you. You need some fresh air.'

Ralf didn't know what to say. It was true that he hadn't had a holiday in some time.

'The train is leaving in five minutes. Are you coming?'

'Yes, well, why not,' he said.

Elsa smiled without revealing her teeth.

They shuffled along past strapped-up luggage and dark green carriages, reading the plaques, rushing on when they spotted an empty compartment. They slid open the door and sat side by side, Ralf suddenly aware of their bodies as the doors were slammed and the train rolled off. Elsa took off her coat, throwing it with her bag in a heap on the seat opposite. She was wearing a rayon blouse with little blue cornflowers on a white background. It looked like indigo carmine.

Elsa shuffled across to the window, pressing her temple against the glass. She reached back and took Ralf's hand in her own.

'I love nature,' she whispered as the train ran through a patch of trees. 'People always seem afraid of forests. To me they feel safe.'

She closed her eyes, and they listened to the rhythm of the wheels over the joins in the track. He watched as a tear formed between her eyelids and caught on her lashes. Ralf pulled her head onto his shoulder. She put her arms around his ribs. Tentatively, he pressed his lips to the top of her head, her hair like fine silk.

'Oh, fuck,' she said. 'I don't even know you.'

She pulled herself away, putting a hand on his thigh to stabilise herself and turning back to the window.

'Don't think this makes me weak.'

She dabbed at her eyes.

'I don't,' Ralf said.

'It will be nice to see the ocean,' she said. 'I don't often have the opportunity.'

When the ticket inspector came, he looked from Ralf to Elsa and asked her whether everything was all right. She passed over the tickets in silence. Ralf suppressed the obvious questions – why leave Paris? Why now? Why him? – for the rest of the journey, sensing that it would violate their unspoken game.

It was out of season, and the town was quiet. Elsa's skirt

flapped, the wind pulling the material tight against the backs of her legs. Something about the suggestion of her underlying body made him feel sick. She had the solid calves of a Parisian woman, used to tramping up endless stairs. They walked straight along the marina towards the open water, listening to boats straining at their moorings and a sound like cow bells. The boats bobbed so calmly they seemed to be breathing: in, and out; filling, and emptying. At the end of a long groyne they could see a lighthouse.

Some of the shops were closed. Sand gathered at the edges of the roads, and rounded off the inside corners of buildings. They started down a long, straight boardwalk which stretched into the distance, continuing on the same trajectory even as the depth of the beach on its right diminished to nothing. Where there were parasols, they were wrapped tightly to reduce their wind resistance.

'Would you and your wife like a picture to take home?' asked a man on the boardwalk, straightening his waistcoat behind a camera and flashbulb.

'Yes—' said Ralf.

'I'm not his wife,' declared Elsa.

'—we would.'

'She's a regular de Beauvoir, isn't she?' said the photographer, squinting into his camera. He looked up and positioned them in front of a patch of beach free of parasols.

'Smile.'

Elsa preened, adjusting invisible strands of her hair.

As he heard a brief click, Ralf thought about what had happened in that moment which had already passed. For just one hundredth of a second, the shutter had opened and photons had flooded into the dark box. They did not move in lines but everywhere at once, so that some might have travelled from Ralf's face to the end of the beach and back. They went so quickly that, from the perspective of light, the rest of the universe remained at a standstill. For Ralf and Elsa, time was slipping by irrecoverably, but for that single hundredth of a second, the celluloid recorded its bombardment, like the sooty negatives of objects and people, scorched onto the façades of buildings in bombings. The celluloid had ceased to interact with the world, a carpaccio of time, a leaf of the past brought into the present, where Ralf and Elsa stood together, still.

'That's my studio, down there,' said the cameraman, pointing down the boardwalk towards the hotels. 'You can pick it up tomorrow morning.' Ralf took his card.

'Why don't you get a Polaroid?' asked Elsa.

'Because I am a photographer,' the man replied, winding the film.

They continued on until they arrived at a row of beach huts, where Elsa took her shoes off and they sat on some steps, looking out to sea. It could only be perhaps four o'clock, but the moon was out.

'I wonder if it's waxing or waning,' said Elsa.

'Waxing,' replied Ralf.

'How can you be sure?'

'It moves across the sky from left to right, but it waxes right to left. That's a waxing gibbous.'

'When will it be a full moon?'

'I guess about three days. Four days. I don't know.'

They listened to the waves hush their way along the shallow sand. It was the sound of tiny grains rubbing together, the inaudible event amplified a billion times as it repeated across the beach. The lone voice, heard only in chorus. 'My father once took me to the observatory in his university. I only went there the once before we had to leave.'

'Is it one of those terribly sad stories?'

'Yes.'

'Then I don't want to hear it. Not now, when I'm having such a nice day.' She blew into her hands. 'I almost wish I'd brought my bathing suit.'

'Well, we have the beach to ourselves,' he said. 'We could swim in our underwear.'

Elsa stared at him. He looked down, smiling.

'Do you want to see how far my legs go, Ralf? Do you want to see my tits?' Ralf didn't respond. 'I really did think you were a gentleman.'

'Do you find yourself deceived?' he asked, measuring his words to hide his embarrassment.

She stood up, brushing sand off her calves.

'No, I think you're quite sweet. Come on, then, let's go back.'

They flirted with the sea's edge, walking in up to their ankles and threatening to push one another over, marvelling at the cold shock of it, the sheer mass of water, the irregularity of the waves. Occasionally two currents would conjoin and swell, and the water would splash up onto Ralf's rolled-up trousers.

Ralf had begun to suspect that they would not get back to Paris in time to buy apricots. He didn't know when the last train went. They stopped for coffee and a pastry, and sat on wicker chairs waiting for their feet to dry so that they could rub the sand off and put their shoes on. So many of Ralf's days were indistinguishable from one another, but the particularity of each minute he spent with Elsa made this day impossible to forget. He wondered whether he would ever know enough about her to stop noticing everything. He wanted to tell her how much he had been thinking about her, but that kind of sincerity somehow didn't feel very modern.

'It's a shame we won't be here to pick up our photo,' said Ralf.

'We can be,' said Elsa. 'I don't want to go back to the city. It's full of people I know.'

The nearest place to stay was the Hôtel Normandy, which

looked a peculiar sort of building, a little like those that used to be found in Hamburg, but of a size and proportion never built in the times when wooden beams were popular. Ralf was quite aware that they would take his details in advance, and the opportunity to run away in a town such as Deauville was limited. He was nervous about suggesting that they find somewhere more modest, but in the event they found a cosy guest house with high chimney stacks, putting themselves down as Dr and Mrs Wolfensohn, and Elsa seemed happy.

The door had a simple bolt, and the bathroom was shared with two other guest rooms, which were unoccupied. The lampshade, the curtains and even the vase were printed with flowers. Elsa pushed aside the frilled net curtain, opened the window and stood with her eyes closed, gently conducting the muted choir of sea and sand. Ralf sat at the dresser to remove his shoes and then joined Elsa at the window. She opened her eyes and stroked his cheeks, still conducting, the backs of her fingers on his right cheek, the pads of her fingers on his left. He could feel his nerves firing wherever her fingers were or had been. He caught her hand and brought it down to their side. She kept her eyes open when he kissed her. He must have too. For the first time, she looked at him with great affection. He traced the tendons on her neck. They sat on the edge of the bed. She lay down on her back and he kissed her again, her skirt folding as he moved his hand up her leg. He wanted to break the skin between them. He could not bury his face in her neck; there was almost nothing of it. He kissed her delicate collarbone, and her soft throat. Her mouth parted slightly and as he pulled his head back he saw her undo the last of his shirt buttons. He pressed his body onto hers, blurring the distinction between them. Her fingers were small and slender. Her hips were sharp. Her eyes, up close, seemed to Ralf the coldest and most beautiful features he had ever seen. Her movement spoke of passion but her eyes gave nothing, only watching.

She pulled him to her urgently. She dug her long nails into the soft flesh around his ribs. He found himself helplessly caught up in her, in the pleasure and the struggle and the undercurrent of real violence, which he had never felt before. He shielded her body in his own, even as she clawed at him. She held him tighter than he thought possible, biting him on the ear. He felt something very like anger welling up in him, as if he could tolerate no more baiting, and he held her against the bed as his body roared.

Afterwards, he lay on his back with one arm still around her. He had never been so forceful with a woman before. He wondered whether they had done what she had wanted. She said nothing. After a minute, she turned away on her side, putting an arm around her own waist. He moved to bring his chest to her back, but she pushed him gently away.

'Please don't,' she whispered.

Ralf sat up, noticing the rusty spot on the bed cover.

'Did I hurt you?' he asked.

'Don't be tedious,' she said.

'I did, then.'

She turned her head to glare at him.

'Do you really think you could hurt me? Would it make you proud?'

Ralf went cold. Their openness shrank back. He was already nude, but now he felt naked. It was only through an effort of will that he did not cover himself.

'That's not what I meant.'

She turned back to face the open window and he put his hand on her bare shoulder. She did not acknowledge the contact, nor did she move for a minute. Then she silently got up and retrieved her clothes. Ralf followed suit, and sat at the dresser staring at the shallow creases in his forehead and between his nose and the edges of his mouth while she went to the bathroom.

She had been in there for fifteen minutes, and Ralf was

beginning to think he had to check on her even if she wanted to be alone, when she returned.

'Why don't we go for a drink,' she said, hovering in the doorway with a brave smile. 'I'm going to have a quick shower. I'll see you in the bar on the corner.'

She took her make-up bag and disappeared. Seeing no point in hanging around, Ralf put on his shoes and went down past the lobby, ignoring the landlady. It was dark outside, with no clouds to keep the heat in. Ralf looked every bit as if he had just stepped out to pick up the morning paper, which was not far off the truth.

At the bar, Ralf ordered a beer and sat in a quiet corner, sipping slowly, listening to the almost inaudible popping of the foam. Before long, Elsa came in. She knocked back two brandies at the counter before coming over to Ralf, and the waiter avoided their table for a few minutes, before Elsa shouted out an order for a Pernod. They watched the waiter pour the water into the Pernod in silence, the liquid in the glass turning a cloudy green. She immediately drank a mouthful.

'Slow down,' Ralf said.

'Why should I?'

'Because I don't want to have to carry you.'

'What gives you the idea that I'm going with you? I might go home after all.'

Ralf laid both palms flat on the table.

'I can't understand it,' he said. 'It was you who dragged me here.'

Elsa kept her eyes on the candle flame between them, swiping her fingers languidly through it, watching her fingers turn black.

'If you think an apology is necessary, then I'm sorry,' he said.

'No, it's not that.' She was far away, unfocused, firewatching.

'What, then?'

'Of course you won't understand, and it will seem terribly

haughty, but I'm worried you're going to get attached to me.'

'It's true that I don't tend to run off to the sea with people I dislike. And in the hotel I rather got the impression that you liked me too.'

'I don't mean that.' She looked around her chair for her fallen coat, fished around in her bag and put down a thousand-franc note. He wondered what her living arrangements were, and whether a friend might be waiting up for her.

'Please, let me,' he said.

'I may as well,' she replied. 'It's not mine.' She upturned her glass, the tip of her tongue darting out to catch the last drop from the rim, before placing it on top of the note. 'Let's stay the night. You can pick up your photo in the morning.'

At that hour, the image would still be developing. Surfaces would have no texture. The clear line of the horizon would appear clouded by an ocean mist. There would be two faces in the centre of the picture, but they might be anyone.

In the two weeks since they had parted at the train station, it had not stopped raining. According to the radio, it was the worst flooding since 1939, and already the fourth worst this century. Ralf sat in his apartment and smoked, using a towel to mop up the moisture which seeped through the shutters and occasionally going to sit downstairs with M. Dague, who could always be relied upon to buy *Le Monde* in the morning, but who had, therefore, a number of opinions on current affairs.

The news was all depressing. The police had gone as far as to suppress the latest issue of *France-Observateur*, which had been planning to publish a report on the use of torture in Algeria – in its place was a complaint against censorship by the editor. Still, there was a duty to talk about it when one could, and to protest in solidarity – weather permitting.

Ralf kept examining his barometer, the dial falling steadily until it dropped below 970 millibars. As the pressure fell, a cold draught came in round the door, which did not sit flush with the frame, and he sealed it as best he could using an old jumper. Naturally, the two tutorials he had planned for this week had been cancelled. He could not even go out to bathe or do his laundry since some of the roads were shin deep in water. He was reduced to washing in the sink on the landing with a bar of hand soap.

He was surprised to find himself missing Jacques. He yearned to be at the bar with a glass of wine or a beer, where doing nothing seemed like its own reward. With each hour in his apartment, he could feel the retreat, first from noise, then from company, and finally into unshared memories. The bookcases which covered his walls took on an oppressive aspect. He needed a sound, an anchor.

He switched on his transistor radio, which he had moved from the windowsill to the table. Buying it had been an extravagance, but one that he justified by using it constantly. Barely the size of two hands, he had removed the back the day he bought it just to stare at the little cylindrical transistors, almost unable to believe, as a radio operator, that there were no tubes at all. It was a miracle of miniaturism, and he still took pleasure in tracking through the dramas and crooners and Sisters and Elvis (endless Elvis), to find a frequency that resonated. He made forays into current music – he liked Miles Davis, who brought the beat to life, and Georges Brassens for his cheerful anarchism – but he found he settled back on old favourites. Privately, he enjoyed the little French music he remembered from his childhood: Trenet, Chevalier. To him, the older generation seemed so much more heartfelt than the new popular music. Old songs were about real struggles, he thought, as he examined the first intrusions of baldness into the corners of his forehead.

After what seemed like an hour sat staring at a back issue of *American Scientist*, he succumbed and went downstairs, taking care not to step on the loose board.

'Constitutional reform again!' M. Dague said, folding his paper. 'They are impotent, the lot of them. The police themselves have been out protesting on the streets. We must be firm. There's no question of compromising Algeria with so much oil under the Sahara.'

'Did you hear about the way the army has been torturing insurgents out there? Apparently there were rebels hiding in caves, and the army didn't even go in and shoot them, they just bricked up the entrances. It's barbaric.'

'Perhaps they shouldn't be setting off bombs all over the place, then,' retorted Dague. 'We are a nuclear power now, the Americans and the British have to respect our interests. But what is one supposed to do with a coalition of socialists and conservatives? If only de Gaulle were here, he'd exercise some discipline.'

'Whether we wanted him to or not. No customers?'

'Not a soul for days.'

Ralf probed the corner of his forehead, wondering whether he was receding or paranoid.

'I could probably do with a trim,' he said.

M. Dague broke into a boyish smile.

'But of course – please.' He indicated a chair and pulled out a fresh towel with a flourish as a wave of rain strafed the shopfront. 'I have stropped all my blades and scissors. They are sharper than my wit. Shall I go for the usual?'

'Do you know any other cut?' asked Ralf.

'Your usual, then.'

M. Dague picked up an old Stopette bottle, which had been refilled with water, and began to spray Ralf's hair. Ralf felt universally cold and wet. M. Dague combed Ralf's hair onto the top of his head, exposing the horseshoe of shorter hair on the back and sides, and got to work.

'I'll just take off a little.'

'Am I thinning?' Ralf asked.

'It's cold, that's all. I'll only take off what's necessary.'

He worked around the edges of Ralf's left ear, tracing a line down his neck, across his nape and then meeting the line from the right ear.

'Now, with the top,' said M. Dague.

'Yes?'

'Will you still comb it back?'

'I thought I would.'

'Very good.'

'Why?' asked Ralf, turning in the chair. 'Shouldn't I?'

'No, no. It will look very nice with pomade.'

'Right. That's how I—'

'All the same. Some of my customers prefer ... Well, it's decided.' M. Dague began taking length off the back. 'You will look very handsome. I expect you're fighting off the girls.'

'That's not far off the truth,' Ralf said. 'I caught a nasty bruise from one a few weeks ago.'

'Love is a dangerous sport. Is this the lovely Marie?'

'No. I don't see Marie any longer.'

'More's the pity.' M. Dague snipped the air twice to free his scissors of hair, and pointed them at Ralf in the mirror. 'She was a nice girl. Dependable.'

Ralf had broken off with this last intrigue at the start of the year, citing his inability to provide for a family, which was true even if it wasn't the reason. He had not intended to lie to her but the truth, that he found her boring and a little prudish, would have hurt her deeply. He suspected this was how people's worst faults weathered the decades.

'There's only one way to find out what you can't live with,

and that's to attempt to live with it,' said Ralf.

M. Dague chuckled.

'Perhaps that's why, in my day, one had to marry before all else. There's too much choice, these days, and choice corrupts one's certainty of happiness. Give me a set menu any day.'

Ralf wondered how much his obsession with Elsa had to do with the life with Marie he had wanted to escape: the polite dinner dates, which always ended at a reasonable time; the routine questions; her maddening habit of wiping his mouth with her napkin; the formal meeting of the parents, who were at pains to imply that they approved of him, though they only offered him one glass of wine. The relationship with Marie had had an uncanny aspect, as if he were stepping into a role, or filling in for someone absent. The weight of expectation that he would use the word 'love' after three months and a day had ended all possibility that he might ever say it. Now, he could see he was reaching for someone rude partly to spite a woman who wouldn't dare offend, someone sharp as bone in response to Marie's pillowy, maternal safety. Elsa was insolent, even untrustworthy. He could see how much she embodied a rejection of Marie's cloying domesticity. So if he knew this – if he could understand the mechanism of his decisions and tell himself it was so – why did he feel the fish-hook digging into the soft pink muscle of his heart? How was it happening to him, this thing he had never really believed he had the constitution for? He could feel it literally and physically, too far in to be touched by logic. The ache was greatest below his heart, in fact, in his solar plexus, just behind and below his sternum. There anyone might be winded and doubled up by a single thumb pressed with conviction. When they were apart, he could think of any number of good reasons why he must not lose a sense of proportion. Yes, it was good to have met her. He wanted to know her better. But then, when Elsa was in front of him, he felt certain that this was where he was supposed to be. It was a certainty he had never felt before, not in the precariousness of his childhood in Hamburg, nor the London winters, nor the amiable indifference of Paris up to now.

Ralf saw that M. Dague had suspended his scissors in the air, and was looking at him expectantly.

'I said, shall I blend with the top?'

'Yes – thank you.'

'Don't want you looking like Hitler.'

Ralf smiled weakly. M. Dague began combing out and feathering the hair, working his way round from Ralf's crown to his parietal ridge.

'And how is Mme Dague?' Ralf asked.

'I'll never understand her.' Seeing that Ralf would prompt him no further, he continued, 'She's gone machine crazy. She thinks machines will save the world. A machine to wash clothes. I said to her, if a machine is washing my clothes, what will you do? Sit there and watch it? And do you know what she replied? My darling, she said, that is why we must get a television.'

'She's clearly thought it through,' said Ralf, listening to the scissors' sharp, birdlike snips next to his ear.

'And a refrigerator, too! Must we now buy these grotesque quantities of food simply to have enough to fill a refrigerator? I asked her what was wrong with buying the amount of food that she wanted to eat.'

'At this exact moment, I can see the appeal. I'm reduced to eating chocolate and anything that comes in a tin.' The rain was falling steadily now, a dull static like a disused radio frequency. 'I wouldn't go out there even if I had to eat the old beef at the back of my cupboard.'

'But can you honestly say you would buy a refrigerator?'

'Probably not. Wouldn't get it up the stairs.'

The wind picked up again, rattling the door so hard that it flew open.

'I've only just bought a new handle for that, and the bloody thing – oh, excuse me, madame. Are you here for an appointment?'

Elsa stood, her face obscured, in the blue-grey light of the doorstep.

'Hello,' Ralf said, studying her perfect symmetry in the mirror. Elsa sat down in a waiting chair.

'I'm here to visit Ralf,' she said. 'Please, do continue.'

'Oh, I see,' said M. Dague. Then, after a pause, 'Because I was going to say, I think your hair looks very chic as it is, and I can't see how I could improve it.'

'Thank you.'

Elsa removed her gloves, putting them down with a solid thud, twisted her hair into one long rope and began to wring it out on the floor.

'I can shave later,' Ralf said. 'If you could just finish it up. How much do I owe you?'

'Not a centime.'

'I insist.'

'Nonsense. I won't take it. But you must introduce me.'

'Oh! Of course. Yves Dague, barber, landlord and amateur raconteur. This is my friend Elsa.'

'Elsa . . .?' he asked, sustaining the sentence so as to prompt her surname.

'Delighted to meet you,' she said, holding out her damp hand.

Now standing in the middle of the room, M. Dague looked between them for a little while, apparently pleased.

'Well,' he said after a time, 'I must get off. I'll set up at d'Aligre tomorrow if the market's on, so I may not see you.'

They excused themselves and walked up together. Ralf was disconcerted to be bringing her into his home so suddenly, and with such little fuss.

'How did you find my apartment?' he asked.

'I knocked on every door in Paris,' she said.

At the top of the stairs, he saw the yellow tint around her right eye. A punch would normally be on the left. The bruise was not the straw blonde of her hair, but a sickly, urinous yellow, which meant it must have been healing for a week or more, not long after their return to Paris. He moved to take her coat, and she grabbed hold of him, hugging him tightly.

'How did it happen?' he asked.

'I was taking a jar off a high shelf, and another came down with it. I didn't think you'd notice. I've been rubbing it with parsley.'

'It doesn't look so bad.'

'I was lucky it didn't smash when it hit me. At first I was so shocked at the pain that I worried I might have glass in my eye. I was finding little shards of it all round the kitchen for days.'

He held her face in both hands, turning her eye towards him and gently kissing the bruise, feeling the downy hair of her eyebrow under his lips.

'Gently,' she said.

'Does it still hurt?' he asked.

'No.'

He kissed her forehead, between her eyebrows, and the lateral crease of her nose. She pulled awkwardly away, freeing her arms from around his and kicking her shoes into the corner.

'Don't kiss my nose.'

'Why not?'

'It's greasy. I hate it.' She wiped his lips with her fingers and he pulled her to him again. Her dress made the front of his shirt wet.

'A falling jar?'

'A falling jar.'

She didn't blink.

'Talk to me.'

'I can't,' she replied.

'You don't trust me?' he asked.

'No one is kind without expectation. If I don't ask for your kindness, you can do nothing to disappoint me.' She broke away, took a book off his shelf and flicked through it absent-mindedly. '"Dice thrown never annul chance,"' she read, snapping the book shut and replacing it out of order.

He found a matchbook next to his cigarettes and went to the hob. He lit the four corners of the closest ring, and beckoned Elsa away from the bookcase.

'Take off your clothes,' he said. 'I'll dry them.'

'Don't you have a towel?'

'None that are dry.'

'Fine.'

Elsa stared at him as she reached back to unbutton her dress. Thrilling at his own audacity, he turned her gently by the waist and helped with the buttons farther down her back. Curling out like the season's first tentative petals, the two halves peeled back over her shoulders, revealing her smooth, pale back between the wet strings of her hair. She let it drop and stepped out, crouching to pick up the dress and hand it to Ralf, who put it in a wide saucepan. He turned the hob down until the little ring of flames retreated almost into the vents and placed the saucepan on top.

'It's not synthetic, is it?' he asked.

'No.'

'Good. We'll need to keep stirring and removing it from the heat or it'll burn.'

'Would you like me to chop some garlic? I worry it might turn out a little tasteless.'

'Yes, very good.'

'And why must I remove my dress while you remain clothed?'

'I'm already dry, apart from the front of my shirt.'

Elsa took a glass from the draining board and filled it with water.

'You wouldn't,' he said.

'I seem to remember you threatening to push me in the sea,' she said.

'You wouldn't dare.'

'I've done worse.'

Ralf didn't have an answer for that. Elsa smiled wickedly and flung the water in his face. He inhaled sharply, opening his eyes to find that she had not, as he expected, fled the scene. She stood exactly as before, holding the empty glass. Privately delighted to have pushed the boundaries of their intimacy and met no resistance, he wiped the water off his stubble and flicked his fingers at her, before lightly tossing the steaming dress and turning off the heat.

'You will live to regret that,' he said.

'No,' she said, unbuttoning his shirt. 'If I started with regrets, I might not live at all. Life is such a vague art. One mustn't keep a scorecard. Do you not have any brandy or anything, to warm us up?'

'Brandy will only dilate your blood vessels and make you colder.'

'A little glass to help me care less, then.'

'All right,' he said, taking down a glass. 'But it'll get dangerously cold now we're both drinking without our clothes. It's imperative we stay warm.' He glanced over at the bed in the corner.

She motioned for him to lead the way, her breasts rounding as she held her arm across her body. They put their snifters down on his side table and he pulled back the bedcovers, which were so cold they felt damp. He felt silently ashamed that he had a rare guest on the rare week he had no clean linen. The rain had steadied now. They tucked their legs into the sheets. He drew her towards him, and she laid her head and hand on his chest. They lay at peace like that for some time, their backs gently filling out and deflating, listening to the excess drops as they hit his windowsill with little tapping sounds. There was a certain size that a raindrop could be, beyond which it could not hold itself together. Each drop was composed of a million droplets of cloud vapour. It might reach half a centimetre in diameter before the surface tension failed and it split in two, or shed water. It was a limitation of its structure. He imagined the rippling pregnancy of the falling drop, a perfectly round little pearl held together by an imperceptible skin, fragile but stable until it crashed and atomised on the sill.

Elsa drew her head back. He kissed her, and she reciprocated for a brief second.

'Do you mind if we don't—' she began.

'Elsa,' he said, more forcefully than he intended, 'it's all right. It's enough to have you here with me.'

'But that's just it. I know you think there will be a day when I open up and give you everything. But it won't happen.' She saw his expression. 'It's not you. Perhaps other people can bare themselves like that, but I never have, and I don't believe that I can.'

'I don't mind waiting. Perhaps it will take time, but that's all right. You are safe with me.'

'For now, just be a body.'

Threading her hands under his arms, where he was warmest, near his heart, she kneaded the muscle, and he breathed back the damp smell of her hair.

He woke to drizzle, the receding creak of floorboards and the popping of air through pipes. Next to him, the pillow was shaped in a negative of her body, giving back her heat. He watched Elsa return looking adorably small in his dressing gown. Now that she was no longer wearing make-up, he could see that the bruise was worse than it had appeared. When she got back in the bed, her shins and feet were cold against him.

'I'm freezing. Can we make a fire?'

'Where? Out of what?' he asked.

She propped herself up on her elbows.

'You don't need both those chairs, do you?' Ralf got out of bed and went to put the moka pot on, there being no fresh milk for *café au lait*. 'How can you even walk across the floor without clothes on? It's too cold in the bed.'

'I am a caveman. A modern brute.'

'Hardly.'

Ralf filled the base with cold water up to the safety valve.

'Am I not the very essence of masculinity?' he asked.

'Less so than average.'

She watched him for a reaction. Ralf spooned coffee into the filter basket. He did not want to risk laying himself bare, for fear of altogether ruining their day.

'Or, at least, my average,' she reiterated.

'Do you want coffee?' he asked, screwing the top on tightly.

'No. I'll have some of yours.'

He folded her dress over the back of one of the chairs and pulled open the shutters to peer out into the morning. The sun had yet to rise above the rooftops, and the shorter wavelengths of violets and blues had scattered long before they could reach Paris, only reds, pinks and oranges surviving the journey for now. He watched a passenger plane far off in the sky, judging its vector, though there hadn't been bombers overhead for more than a decade. He could hear steam rising through the funnel, coffee bubbling out into the top chamber, and listened for sounds of its sputtering as the last water filtered through. The reaction was what she wanted. It was a perverse kind of test. A test of worldliness or coolness. Of vulnerability.

He poured the coffee and brought it over to the bed. She went to take it from him immediately, and drank a quarter while it was steaming.

'It's not raining any more,' he said. 'We should do something.'

'Mm,' she said. 'What about the cycling? We could go to the Vélodrome d'Hiver.'

'No,' he said.

'Why not?'

'I don't go there.'

'You don't like cycling?'

'It was a detention centre.'

She looked at him with something like scorn.

'That was a long time ago,' she said. 'People go there to watch the cycling.'

'I don't care what people do there now.'

He ran his hand over the back of his head, over his freshly cut hair, feeling the nap: rough up and smooth down; rough up and smooth down; smooth down.

She softened, less as if she were backing off than registering the ability to hurt him should it prove useful. She seemed to be sorting through the silences. Then she handed him back the cup by the handle, got up and put on her dress.

'The collar is still a little damp,' she said. 'No Michelin stars for you.'

'You're not going, are you?'

'You don't have any food or central heating.'

'Coffee is the answer to both.'

She smiled and ran her fingers along the dust on his books with a rail-track sound. In the pink and orange light, she seemed unreal, her outline half blurred. He put his trousers on and buttoned up a shirt.

'You have a lot of books on genetics,' she said, prodding one as if to make it flinch.

'They're my father's,' he said. 'Were my father's.' It was a subject he almost never spoke about, but their dressing gave an impression of finality, of intimacy replaced, and he had the impulse to make a grand gesture that might bind them.

'What happened?' she asked, bringing one of the volumes over to the armchair and setting it in her lap like a kitten.

2

EMIL, *Hamburg, 1899–1933*

)

Sat out in his garden, looking around at the wildlife for the last time, Emil considered that he had had a happy childhood. He had grown up a proud subject of the German Empire; it had been in the first days of the Weimar Republic that he had met Therese; but what was coming now was altogether different.

He had spent a lot of time in his father's garden, as a boy, running around in his clogs catching grasshoppers and following ants' trails through the grass. He had sometimes gone next door to watch the butcher's son killing chickens, holding one wing in his hand, one between his knees, catching the blood which spurted from their necks in a bucket. Emil's father was a breeder of dogs, and Emil grew strong wrestling them to the ground. The dogs would catch his arm in their strong jaws but always held back from clamping down.

Emil was fifteen when the war began. He came in one day from feeding the dogs and was savouring the smell of rabbit stew, mixed with burnt wool where he was standing too close to the fire, when his father came in and announced that he was going to war.

'It's better that I volunteer than wait to be conscripted,' was all he said.

Emil looked after the dogs and studied hard, but he knew that his duty lay in following his father to the front. His mother didn't want him to go – she spoke often of his studies and wondered aloud what she would do with the whole family gone to war – but as Emil's class size dwindled, and the government began to speak of a 'Jewish statistic' to assess whether Jews were shirking their responsibilities, he saw what he must do. He felt none of the excitement that had drawn his friends to volunteer, but he didn't feel afraid, either. He had seen animals die. They only struggled when they still believed they might live. Once it was settled, they laid their heads down quite peacefully in the dirt.

Before going out, prayers for victory were called out in German, Latin and Hebrew. Emil was made a gunner. A few months later, under artillery fire near Fort Douaumont, the rest of his regiment fell back and he held the trench for a whole night single-handed, shooting several Tommies who believed the trench abandoned and tried to pick their way through the gap. He got an Iron Cross for it, which he kept in a drawer at home. On reflection, he would rather have been one of those who quietly carried their guns unloaded and who didn't kill a single person in the war.

Jobs were hard to come by in peacetime, so he went back to work feeding the dogs, cleaning out their kennels and taking them for walks in big, half-wild packs while the family waited for news of Emil's father, who eventually returned home six months after the war had ended. He was quieter than before and wouldn't explain what had happened, except to say that he had tried to write home, and was prevented. For some weeks he kept a loaded revolver under his pillow, a Webley Mark IV, until Emil's mother asked him to get rid of it, and it disappeared for the next few years.

The shop girl, whom Emil recognised from the butcher's, stopped to say hello one day while he was out walking the dogs. The dogs went wild with joy when they saw her on the street, thinking they were about to get scraps. They bounded over to her, dragging Emil with them, and one of the big Weimaraners knocked her over. Therese blushed furiously as Emil helped her to her feet.

She began to join him on his walks, sometimes bringing bones for the dogs. They would talk for hours. She told him about everything that had happened in Hamburg while he was at war: the Turnip Winter, the coal carts pulled by elephants and trained bears borrowed from the Tierpark Hagenbeck, since all the horses had gone off to war. The two of them would go for walks along the Elbe, taking far longer than they were supposed to. They would sit down on his coat and let the dogs go off, running along the sand and snapping at the waves.

They found themselves in a scandalous position. Therese's family saw Emil as a Jew, since he had a Jewish father. As far as Emil's family was concerned, he had never been Jewish, since his mother was German. In short, he was not German enough for the Germans, nor Jewish enough for the Jews. Emil's father, however, was deaf to all complaints and offered to put up the money for their wedding himself. He had always been reserved, but since his return from the war, he had become quite senti-mental. When doors were left ajar in the evenings, he could be heard muttering in his chair by the fire that the couple would have beautiful children, and just think of Therese with a broad belly – she was so gentle with the dogs.

Soon after they were married, Emil discovered that the city was amalgamating a number of institutions to found a university in Hamburg, and he was one of the first to sign up. The family was not well off, but having done well in school and worked for some time with his father, Emil had enough knowledge and experience to begin a degree in the natural sciences – and even without any other commendation, he was a decorated veteran. Emil's father, though not an educated man, respected education a great deal and, after a long and fraught meeting in the Warburg bank, secured a loan to cover the cost of Emil's studies.

The principal lecturer was a well-known and ferociously intelligent professor called Wilhelm Cassirer, who took Emil under his wing. Emil worked hard and excelled in his degree, beginning to specialise in breeding and eugenics; Cassirer, who thought it faddish, tried to warn him off it. In the tradition of Darwin, Emil submitted a study on selective breeding problems in dogs, the conclusion of which anticipated theories of hybrid vigour by thirty years: that in-breeding can achieve specific goals, but tends to amplify defects, and that the most resilient breeds come from heterogeneous parents, which is to say, the healthiest dogs are mongrels.

Cassirer saw what he was trying to do, and in one of their supervisory meetings explained that the paper would be received poorly, both by the Jewish intellectual community in Hamburg and by the most important eugenicists. Nevertheless, Emil sent the paper to the *Archive for Race and the Biology of Society*, provoking a furious rebuttal from its editor, Fritz Lenz, who saw the study as a direct attack on his research into racial hygiene.

Therese had fallen pregnant during this time, and Ralf was born in 1927, the same year Eugen Fischer was appointed director of the new Kaiser Wilhelm Institute of Anthropology, Human Heredity and Eugenics, and the year that one of Hamburg's lecturers, Siegfried Passarge, presented a lecture series based on his new paper, 'The Racial Science of the German Volk and the Jews'. Certain students had begun to shave the back and sides of their heads, scraping their hair across their foreheads. Cassirer accepted Emil's application for a doctoral thesis and offered him a few classes in order to pay his way through the research, though hyperinflation made money next to useless. By that time, many poorer parts of Hamburg had reverted to a barter economy.

Those years were difficult for everyone. Staff at the Warburg bank started carrying guns to protect themselves. The port had never really recovered from the trade blocks, and many were afraid Hamburg would see another Turnip Winter. Emil and his family ate mainly bread and potatoes. Still, in his thirty years of life, Emil could hardly think of a time when there hadn't been a crisis of one sort or another, and all political groups seemed broadly as bad as each other. Anyone marching through the streets of Altona was prone to being pelted with potatoes, whether Sozi or Nazi, and since the brownshirts seemed to be catching the worst of it, it hardly seemed a cause for concern.

At home, life was peaceful as ever. Therese devoted herself to Ralf. They took a trip to a beach in the bend of the river, Emil piling up castles while the little boy clawed the sand, Therese hoisting him up away by the armpits to wash him in the water when he wet himself. Far off, the horn of the Hamburg–America ship sounded, so deep and loud it could be heard anywhere. Ralf began to cry. The child's sensitivities irritated Emil, but he made an effort never to show it. To Emil, that was where morality truly lay – not in the kindnesses that were instinctual, but those that were bloody-minded, that took an effort of the will. He bent down and kissed the boy on the cheek.

Emil spent the rest of the year tracing all historical records of the Habsburg family, gathering data to show that decreasing the randomness of sexual partners – that is, in-breeding – made each successive generation weaker, amplifying genetic flaws which would otherwise be written out of the bloodline, or at least retained as recessive characteristics. The Habsburg jaw was so pronounced in Charles II of Spain that he had trouble chewing food. He did not speak until he was four years old, and was infertile. He died at thirty-nine, and the coroner reported that his body 'did not contain a single drop of blood; his heart was the size of a peppercorn; his lungs corroded; his intestines rotten and gangrenous; he had a single testicle, black as coal, and his head was full of water'. Emil concluded that, in humans, variety was essential to the success of a bloodline, cancelling out anomalous traits and encouraging natural vigour. He submitted the paper to various journals, not entirely hopeful of a response.

Ironically, there was little call for specialist breeds in those straitened days, and so Emil was called from his breakfast one Saturday by his father, stood at his front door with the old Webley, crying. He could not afford to keep all the dogs, and no one would buy them, and he could not let them starve. He had tried to give them away but no one wanted an extra mouth to feed. He had tried leaving their kennel doors open, but the dogs wouldn't go. He had to prevent their long suffering but he could not do it himself. Emil snatched the gun from his father's hand, and pointed it up at the ceiling or God, and said, 'Do you think it might hurt me less?'

'I don't have the courage,' the old man sputtered.

'Killing is not born of courage.'

He walked out, leaving the front door open, and spat softly in the gutter. He checked the chamber. 'I am going to need more bullets than this.' His father nodded, and they walked back together in silence. Later, it became clear that Emil had kept the gun.

A year later, things were not going as well as had been hoped. Emil's study of the Habsburgs had not been published, an unfashionable study being less use than a careless one. A synagogue on the Marcusstraße had been desecrated. The SA had started recruiting from the masses of unemployed, and eighteen people had been killed on their latest march through the Marxist areas of the city.

There was a rumour circulating that Hitler was coming to

speak at the Tierpark Hagenbeck. He had already lost the vote to Hindenburg, but thirteen million people had voted for him, and it seemed he wouldn't take no for an answer. Whether pleased or otherwise, the whole university was in a state of excitement and couldn't talk about anything else.

Why had he chosen the zoo? There were a number of possible answers. Chiefly, there was the issue of capacity. It made a bold statement about the kind of crowds that were expected. But a zoo? Some said that was the best place for brownshirts, and pointed out that the collection was always expanding. They were probably delighted to welcome a pack of hyenas. Others thought the address would be made within earshot of the human exhibits of Samoans, Laplanders, Inuit and Nubians, in order to drive home the point about German superiority, though someone else was sure Hagenbeck the younger hadn't set up any new human shows since *Kanaks of the South Pacific* last year.

For Emil, the zoo was the proper domain of Darwin and von Humboldt. Each animal was a spring shoot on its small branch of life. Despite the dazzling variety of their shape and colouring, they had stomachs, skulls and spines, hearts and veins. They had grown apart over thousands, perhaps millions, of years, but every generation of their ancestors had survived to breed.

That night, while preparing for bed, Emil told Therese that he wanted to attend the speech. When she realised he was serious she told him flatly that she did not think it was a good idea. They broke off to brush their teeth, rolling up their tube of Doramad Radioactive toothpaste. When they were back in the bedroom, with the lights turned out to save energy, he explained that they were going to escape: he had applied for a teaching post in America.

Europe, he explained, was decaying. Wages were being cut everywhere, the retirement age raised. They were still on rations fifteen years after the war. America was different. Universities were more open there, the people more welcoming of plurality.

'But the crash,' Therese said. She did not like the idea of leaving – she never wanted to leave anywhere, even if she didn't like where she was. 'The crash,' she kept saying. 'The crash.'

'Promise me you will think about it.'

She said nothing but held him in the dark.

At dawn, there was a light knocking near the bottom of the door.

'Come in,' called Therese.

Ralf opened the door and climbed onto the bed. At five, he was ruled by curiosity and wary of being left out.

'Would you like a glass of milk?' asked Therese. Ralf nodded. She separated the bedsheets from her nightdress and went downstairs. Emil was asleep on his front, his powerful arm wrestling the pillow as if it had tried to escape in the night.

'Good morning, Father,' said Ralf. Emil opened his eyes and fixed them on his son.

'Mm.' He turned over and rubbed at his eye with the ball of his thumb. 'It's going to be an exciting day today. How would you like to go to the zoo?'

They caught the tram early, beating the crowds, and walked through its beautiful art nouveau gates, past the life-sized dinosaur statues, to look at the animals while the stage was set up. This was the first zoo to keep its animals in open enclosures, using moats to separate the animals from the visitors. When Ralf saw the lions on rocks just metres away, he cowered behind his father, but they were a dented pride, and they were fed, so all they did was lie splayed across the stones, casting their eyes disinterestedly over the other animals.

The gorillas were in a glass enclosure, presumably not trustworthy enough to be separated by a moat. The zoo was beginning to fill up now, and other children laughed and shouted, making faces or banging on the glass to provoke a reaction.

The silverback sat on his own, high up at the back, glowering. One of the smaller gorillas, a youth or a female, came over, its black eyes level with Ralf's, and placed a hand on the glass. Ralf copied the gesture, and they stood like that for half a minute or so, before someone made a loud noise, and it moved off.

A huge area had been cordoned off, with rows of stormtroopers manning the perimeter. Ralf kept asking to be picked up. Emil looked over at the stage, where various men in uniform were taking seats behind a lectern, and held Ralf's hand tightly.

'Now,' said Emil, 'if we are separated, you are to meet me by the main gates. If you are lost, you are to ask a member of the zoo staff, or a member of the public, but – Ralf, listen – you are not to ask anyone with a red armband. Do you understand?'

'I don't want to be separated,' Ralf said.

'Hold my hand and you won't be.'

Just when it seemed that the crowd could not be packed much more tightly, and they had played the national and party anthems, Hitler came on stage, and there was a great deal of noise – whether supportive or not, it was hard to tell. Ralf stood among legs like a dog in a wheat field. A voice blared through the address system, loud, clear and emphatic, as if it were resolving an argument between two stupid people by leading them through the answer.

Internationalism and democracy are inseparable conceptions. Democracy denies the special value of the individual and puts in its place a purely numerical value, so it proceeds in precisely the same way in all peoples and should result in internationalism. Broadly it is maintained: peoples have no inborn values, but, at the most, there can be admitted perhaps temporary differences in education. Between Negroes, Aryans, Mongolians and Redskins there is no essential difference in value. This view, which forms the basis of the whole of the international thought-world of today and in its effects is carried to such lengths that in the end a Negro can sit as president in the sessions of the League of Nations, leads necessarily to the point that differences in value between individuals are denied.

The crowd jostled around Ralf and Emil, and beside them emerged an old man Ralf had seen several times at their kitchen table, smoking and chatting into the night with his father. Cassirer greeted Emil, and Ralf listened as they started up a running commentary on the speech.

'You've missed some fascinating revelations,' said Emil. 'Hitler's standing up against the stupidity of the collective.'

Cassirer smiled and turned to watch.

This whole edifice of civilisation is in its foundations nothing other than the result of the creative capacity, the achievement, the intelligence, the industry, of individuals: in its greatest triumphs it represents the great crowning achievement of individual God-favoured geniuses. So it is only natural that when the capable intelligences of a nation, which are always in a minority, are regarded as of the same value as all the rest, then genius is slowly subjected to the majority. This is not the rule of the people, but in reality the rule of stupidity, of mediocrity, of half-heartedness, of cowardice, of weakness, and of inadequacy.

'Have you noticed,' asked Cassirer, 'how Hitler pronounces the start of his words? He says "st", as if he had lived all his life in Hanover or Hamburg. It's almost desperate.'

'He's been practising in front of the mirror,' said Emil.

Such a conception as that of private property you can defend only if you admit that men's achievements are different. Thus it must be admitted that in the economic sphere, men are not of equal value or of equal importance. And once this is admitted it is madness to say: in the economic sphere there are undoubtedly differences in value, but that is not true in the political sphere. It is absurd to build up economic life on the conceptions of achievement, but in the political sphere to thrust into its place the law of the greater number – democracy. In that case there must slowly arise a cleavage between the economic and the political point of view. And so in the economic sphere communism is analogous to democracy in the political sphere.

'If you're Austrian, you're Austrian. There's no shame in it,' said Cassirer.

'Tell that to Freud,' said Emil.

'Will you shut up?' said a man next to them. 'Have some respect.'

To sum up the argument: I see two diametrically opposed principles: the principle of democracy which, wherever it is allowed practical effect, is the principle of destruction; and the principle of achievement, because whatever man in the past has achieved – all human civilisations – is conceivable only if the supremacy of this principle is admitted.

'I don't have any respect for him,' said Emil. 'He's a damned thug, and his followers are thugs as well.'

'Maybe we need a few thugs around here, to put people in their place,' said the man.

Others had turned in on the group. At first they seemed hostile, but then one of them spoke out in Emil's favour, which caused other heads to turn. Soon, three brownshirts were elbowing through the crowd, and they led Emil and Cassirer off, Ralf struggling behind in their wake terrified he might lose sight of them.

Soon they were back at the entrance to the park, under the sculpted elephant's trunk, where a couple of party members were loitering around rattling collection boxes. One of the brownshirts tried to calm Emil down. He looked like a living poster, clean shaven, with bright blond hair, his uniform pressed and his knife – for he had a knife – strapped impressively to his waist. It was the butcher's son, Hans.

'Please, Professor, it's not safe for you here,' he said. 'You have your boy with you. It's best if you leave.'

'Thank you. We'll go,' said Cassirer quietly, turning Emil towards the exit. In the distance, the speech had risen to high fervour. The brownshirts walked back towards it, three abreast, just as Emil, Ralf and Cassirer walked out into the deserted road, three generations side by side.

At the start of 1933, Emil received a polite reply from the selection committee to whom he'd applied in America, to the effect that they would prefer to welcome a representative of the New Germany. They enquired whether he was a member of the National Socialist Party, or had the intention of applying for membership.

Hitler's speech had been a qualified success in Hamburg. Most Hamburgers tended to think of politics as something that happened to other people. It was understood to be necessary but certainly not discussed in polite company. Hitler was hardly a sympathetic character, but he provided certainty, which was sorely lacking elsewhere.

Emil and Therese had, up to that point, managed to convince themselves that support for Hitler was waning because of the way his supporters bullied others. Then he was appointed Chancellor, but even then, they would talk in low voices at the table, telling one another that the majority of people in government were conservatives, that he would find little support for his programme. Things seemed to snowball, however. Another vote was declared. The front page of the *Hamburger Echo* asked, *What lies behind it?*, with a photo of the Reichstag on fire. According to some reports, it was Jewish Marxists; according to others, Jewish capitalists. Hitler pushed through emergency measures giving him carte blanche to arrest whoever he wanted in the days leading up to the vote.

By the end of March, Hitler had passed the Law to Remove the Distress of the People and the Reich. Within days, a new rector of the university was appointed. On boycott day ('Germans do not buy from Jews'), the caretaker replaced the portrait of Albert Einstein with one of Hitler. Cassirer saw it happen but didn't complain – on the contrary, all his fight had left him. When he told Emil he was leaving the country, Emil was speechless. At every stage, Cassirer had been the one he relied upon to make difficult, honourable choices. He had only come this far in his own career because it seemed somehow achievable in relation to Cassirer's own, greater, more daring achievements.

The next week, the motto on the university crest changed from 'The Living Spirit' to 'The German Spirit'. Cassirer had his books and papers sent on to his house in Switzerland. Emil walked to the train station with him, they shook hands, miserably, and Emil left him waiting on the platform. He had no allies left in the university, nor any prospect of work elsewhere. They didn't have the fare for America and, regardless, it didn't seem at all clear that there would be any prospect of work at the other end.

On 10 May, the Nazis staged a book burning in Berlin. Emil did not subscribe to the idea that books were somehow a sacred vessel, that text was word. Enough was printed that he considered utter idiocy – indeed, the Nazi propaganda was evidence enough that words were not, in themselves, sacred. Nevertheless, the burning of books, for Emil, marked the true death of the Weimar Republic. People were tired of arguing. They wanted the truth to be simple. By burning the evidence of dissent, they were attacking the possibility that there could be more than one interpretation of events. In order to maintain the possibility of alternative truths, one had to have respect for one's opposition, and there was no respect left. The public didn't want understanding, only certainty.

That weekend passed slowly. There had been a press notice that the same was to happen in Hamburg, and everyone was on edge. Nothing happened on the Saturday night. Sunday was quieter than usual. Emil's neighbours gave him a quick nod, no more, as if afraid of being seen.

Emil woke at the normal time on Monday morning, ate his breakfast, and walked to the university alone, shutting himself in his office. He had intended to turn to the problem of producing a piece of work sufficiently uncontroversial to secure his post without the protection of Cassirer.

At 9.30am, several lorries arrived at the main entrance, carrying a hundred students and a brass band. They unloaded and began to spread across the main building, as if they were practising manoeuvres, while the band started up. Down the corridor, he could hear them stamping along. He sat at his desk and waited.

Soon, someone began kicking at his door. He told them it was open. There was a splintering sound, and a final kick took the door off its hinges, kicking up paper everywhere as it landed. Two students came in and began taking books down off his shelf. One of the students leaned over the desk and spilled the ink bottle over his papers. The other took a dictionary from a low shelf and threw it through the window behind Emil. Before the two could come to blows, the butcher's son, Hans, marched in, his demeanour calm and resolved as he explained they were searching for dangerous works.

In the quad, stormtroopers stood with guns, presiding over a growing pile of boxes and stray books. The stormtroopers did not wait until dark to start the bonfire, as they had in Berlin. The usual long speech was made by a local party leader, and the gathered crowd sang the Horst-Wessel. A few of the other faculty staff were out, watching. Presumably only certain offices had been targeted. Emil's was almost empty of words. All his neatly archived notes, the marked-up copies of books he had been collecting for over ten years, his draft papers, thousands of hours of his life sat on the pyre.

A torch was brought, and loose leaves of paper crunched up to get the fire going. Emil stayed to watch, his face warmed by years of learning. Some of his colleagues stood sentinel, tight-lipped, others left as soon as was polite. One or two stood with their hands to their hearts, the Hitler Youth straight-backed, at ease. These people wouldn't listen to Emil because their argument was based on a deep suspicion of his motives. Worse than their hate, worse than their ideology, were those who watched without conviction, who were not convinced of the need for purification, but who watched it go unchallenged. By now, nothing he could say or write would make any difference. It was for the trusted, ordinary public to defend him, and they hadn't, and they wouldn't. There could only be one truth in a war of absolutes. By silent, mutual agreement, Emil was being written out of history.

The last day of Emil's life was bathed in sunshine. He sat out on a chair in the back garden, his dog sitting with its big head in his lap.

Therese brought out a coffee. Emil sat there for a long time, occasionally taking a sip or settling the dog when it had been disturbed by a crow. Ralf was playing with the ants, blocking up the holes to their nests or squashing one to see what its friends would do.

Emil said that you can't reason with people who don't believe in reasons; he said it had happened because everyone assumed it wouldn't; he said that pacifism was the wrong course; the intellectuals had fallen for their own ideals, and hadn't been prepared to respond or persuade; they dismissed or appeased so that they could ignore the problem; they did not show their own strength, or practise it, and now they had none. They were all dodos, plodding up to greet the barrel of a gun. By now Emil was crying.

Therese stroked his back and told Ralf to go to his room. Having an unformed idea that there was something very wrong, Ralf set about tidying his things away and arranging them in neat rows.

After the grandfather clock had chimed two, Emil asked Ralf whether he would like to go for a walk. Emil would normally point out birds and plants to Ralf as they walked, telling him their names and properties, but today they walked in silence, Emil dressed formally in his felt homburg, Ralf in shorts. The road was deserted.

They passed the tide gauge tower in St Pauli, where a huge ship was pulling in. Emil spoke carefully, not looking at Ralf, but squinting up at the seagulls as they fought for position, or staring out at the docks, the horn of the Hamburg–America ship sounding like a great whale.

'Have you heard of purgatory, Ralf?'

He hadn't.

'Christians believe that you must live as if, when you die, you will have to inhabit every creature you were ever cruel to, and watch yourself doing it, end to end – every little ant, every child in the playground, many more than that when you grow to be my age. And the older you become, the more easily you will understand that sometimes it is cruellest of all to do nothing, to stand by and watch. Cruelty is like fire. It doesn't catch easily, but you must put it out as soon as it begins to flare, because once it begins to spread, it's almost impossible to stop.

'You will see your own cruelty again before you can rest. That is what they call purgatory. When you have seen and understood everything, you will finally inhabit every creature you were ever kind to – every dog you played tug of war with, every person you have kissed on the cheek before bed, or made a present for. That is heaven. You will understand that you are capable of terrible things, and you will see how easily and simply you brought joy into the lives of others, and that is the gift of true understanding.

'I'm afraid we are entering a time when there will not be many opportunities for me to be kind, and far too many for me to be cruel. I was too hesitant, my voice too weak, and the fire has already caught. I have already participated, however unwillingly, too much in the cruelty of the world, and it will be some time before my soul is allowed to be still. I'm afraid I can't prolong it any longer. I want to know that the last person I am ever cruel to is myself. I love you and your mother very dearly. Never doubt that.'

When Ralf and Therese went out later that day to the grocer's, Emil arranged his surviving books in a neat pile on the kitchen table. He had made arrangements for Therese and Ralf to move to London for the time being, some money having been transferred there already through the Warburg bank. In a brief note, he apologised, and suggested that the books be shipped in his name, since there was no way of punishing him further. He went back out to the garden so as not to leave a mess.

3

RALF, Paris, April–May 1958

When Ralf had finished, she sat with her head bowed, and he began to wonder with horror whether she had been listening at all, whether he had committed too much of his trust in her, or whether his past was an unwanted gift, a burden that would sink their young relationship just as it had weighed on him. Her eyes had taken on a glassy quality.

Elsa turned and brought him into focus. They drew close and she stroked his rough cheek, her eyes filled with pity. He flushed with pleasure, seeing that he could captivate her, not just as a companion but as the subject of her interest. It didn't occur to him until later that he had used his father's story to amuse her or to imply depth of character, nor that it might have been wiser to hold back. All he wanted was her undivided attention, her eyes looking to him only, reaching out to show him who he was and why his life had brought him improbably here, in a room with her.

'Have you ever been back?' she asked him.

'Only once, in 1945.'

'Would you go again?'

Ralf considered the question.

'I think it would be difficult. I'm not sure I would want to walk through my memories. My mother still talks about Hamburg a lot. It keeps him present, reopens the wound as it begins naturally to scar over. It's the only way for her to explain the person she is now.'

'And you?' she asked. 'If I want to understand you?'

He reached out to smooth her hair, wondering whether he had earned the right to do so.

'Perhaps we'll go one day.'

She looked at him with a tenderness he had somehow not thought her capable of.

'I'd like that very much,' she said.

It was a beautiful morning, the sort that one remembers years later, the clouds spent, neighbours emerging from their apartments like survivors, people putting out tables for the first time in a week, the city washed clean, absolved. They walked out into the Marais in silence, smiling like newlyweds. Drops of water weighed down the leaves, showering like fireworks when birds landed. It was cool and Elsa stayed close to Ralf, shivering slightly in her damp coat. Without the clouds, the sky had no ceiling, and the world felt vast again, full of possibility.

'It's strange,' said Ralf. 'During the war, I didn't think days like this could exist.'

Elsa nodded. Their steps had converged, and they walked in time with one another, watching their feet.

'The war was terrible,' she said quietly.

An urgent question pushed in on Ralf's thoughts, a question to which he suspected he knew the answer, and which he had avoided up to now. She looked vulnerable, and although he wanted their closeness he knew that this was the moment she might really answer him.

'Were you in Germany?'

She didn't say anything at first, and he was beginning to wonder whether she had heard him, when she said, 'Yes.'

'Where were you? Not Hamburg?'

'No. Out in the countryside, in Silesia. My family were in Berlin.'

'We don't have to talk about it.'

'I was quite young.'

They walked on, and she stopped to get a croissant, which she let flake over her as they walked. Ralf felt overexposed, realising now that he knew so little about her life. He knew he should ask her about it, except that he suddenly didn't want to. She handed him the rest of her breakfast.

'Can I show you somewhere I like to go?' she asked.

'Yes, of course,' he replied, thrown by how quickly their thoughts had diverged. They walked carefully, as if she was leading him blindfolded. They crossed over onto the Île de la Cité and continued down the river.

They walked down through the Square du Vert-Galant, eventually reaching the pointed tip of the island, where the cobbles were shaded by an old willow. This would be the perfect place to watch the sun set, but that was hours away.

Elsa put her coat down – insisted it be hers, since it was already damp – and they sat on the bank together, watching the tourists walk over the Pont des Arts and the traffic along the roads. Elsa waved at one of the passing boats, which seemed out of character, and laid her head on his shoulder.

'I love it here,' she said. 'Don't you?'

'Yes,' he said.

'It's so peaceful. I could sit here for ever and just listen to the flow of the river and the traffic.'

'It's quite a unique perch.'

They sat, contented to watch without joining in.

'I've never brought anyone else here,' she said abruptly.

'No?'

'No. I've always wanted to.'

'I've walked past it countless times,' Ralf replied. 'I suppose it's not somewhere you feel like sitting alone.'

'No, it's not.'

He took her hand.

'There's a march coming past here in a week's time,' he said.

'Is there?'

'Yes. In support of Algerian self-determination. I'm going with my friend Fouad.' She didn't respond. 'Would you like to come?'

'I'm sure they can manage without me.'

'Why not join in, though? Everyone wants to see an end to the war.'

'I've always thought the main purpose of marching was to reassure those doing the marching. The banner is interchangeable.'

'So you don't have any ideals?'

'I certainly hope not,' said Elsa.

Ralf laughed.

'What about love?' he asked.

'I'm not sure I believe in it.'

'But you believe in the trappings. Trips to the sea, romantic walks along the beach. Lying naked together.'

'Perhaps. But those aren't acts of faith.'

'But then what is the point of living? If there are no ideals and we are all clusters of objects? If nothing is important?'

Elsa looked out at the city.

'You're the scientist. You tell me.'

They sat in silence for a minute, Ralf beginning to wish he hadn't told her about his father.

'It's not you,' Elsa said quietly, resting her hand on his leg. 'You're wonderful. Really. I care more for you than anyone I've ever met. I think about you constantly.'

'But you don't love me?'

'If I were to love anyone, it would be you.'

It was so close to what he wanted to hear, and he was so

nearly happy. He kissed her. They listened to the swaying of leaves, the lapping of the water.

Ralf took a deep breath. He wanted to pretend he hadn't asked at all, but it was too late for that. He stood and brushed the dirt from the seat of his trousers.

'Sorry, I had better go.'

'Where?'

'I've just realised the time, and I have some errands to run.'

'We're having such a nice day, Ralf; don't go.'

'No, I had really better. I don't have any food.'

'When will I see you?'

'I don't know,' he said. 'Are you sure you don't want to join the march?'

She nodded sadly.

'I'll see you afterwards, then.'

It took such willpower – it was like pulling magnets apart – but he wrenched himself away, leaving her on the bank, each step getting easier even as the physical tug was replaced by the sensation of being washed out to sea.

It had been a good day's marching, and it was naturally time for a drink. Ralf went to the bar to order, and Fouad started setting up a game of backgammon on the board he left there, the pieces arranged unevenly round the board in twos, fives and threes.

'This is a beautiful game,' Fouad said as Ralf set down the drinks. 'If I win, I can be proud of my strategy; if I lose, I can curse my dice. It has the ebb and flow of life.'

'Funny how you never win when I catch you cheating.'

They rolled to start. Fouad won with a three and played his first pieces by rote, stacking them to create a new safe point and hem Ralf's two farthest pieces in. Ralf shook the dice vigorously and rolled a two and a five, playing it as a seven after some thought.

'The police were rougher than usual today,' Fouad said, picking up the dice and clattering them against the inside wall of the board.

'They're nervous,' Ralf said, watching Fouad's hand. 'After all the violence in Algeria, and now the violence here.'

'No, they've always hated us Muslims. The difference is that now they've understood no one will stop them.'

'No. The violence on both sides is irrelevant. History is only moving in one direction.'

'Violence doesn't feel irrelevant.'

'That's the problem. People are always trying to use it to win their arguments.'

Fouad smiled, his eyes on the board.

'That reminds me,' Fouad said. 'Whatever happened with that delicate boxer you encountered?'

'Ah. Yes, well. There have been further developments.'

'Anything that would make me blush?'

Ralf took his turn.

'I expect so. Not least of which, I think I'm falling in love.'

'I thought better of you.'

'I know. But she's unlike anyone I've ever met. She's honest, and direct, and spontaneous. And she's quick, too – I can barely keep up with her. It's as if she's already studied everything and made a decision in advance.'

Fouad nodded gravely.

'You may not have noticed, as you were busy assessing her many admirable qualities, but she also looks very fine.'

Ralf shook the dice for longer than necessary.

'I wouldn't know about that,' he replied. 'I'll make a point of looking next time I see her. Now, will you have another drink?' he asked.

'I will if you're paying.'

They sipped away while they played. Fouad had all his chips in his home quarter and was picking up, while Ralf still had a chip trapped on the centre of the board, unable to move off until Fouad's pieces had cleared. He rolled a double, but it made no difference.

'Where did you learn to cheat like this?'

'In Algiers.'

'Where you grew up?'

Fouad scratched his cheek roughly.

'From the age of ten.'

'Where did you live before?'

'My father came from Kabylia.'

The bar had begun to empty out. Jacques was clearing broken glass.

'What was it like?'

'Not good. We had nothing there but a few olive trees and a donkey. The government gave us a few litres of barley each month, but it was spoiled in any case. They gave us the grain that the army's horses wouldn't eat – that was my father's joke, that he would take the horse's job if he could get hold of its rations.

'It could have been worse. Most people had a drop of olive oil on their barley cake each day, and some had only water. We could afford more, but we still had to improvise. We would gather thorns and boil them for hours with mallow roots. We sometimes had figs, usually at the expense of something else. At night I dreamed about food.'

'So you left.'

Fouad nodded and flattened his moustache down with his palm. He picked up the dice.

'The winter I turned ten, we were gathering twigs in the snow to make a fire. You weren't supposed to pick up fallen wood. It was bad for the soil. But what good is a forest if everyone has died of cold? Anyway, my father and I were caught with a bundle of twigs and our donkey was confiscated by the forest wardens.

My father was a proud man and he refused to suffer the indignity. We travelled to Algiers knowing that, whatever happened, our circumstances would be equal or better. My game.' Ralf looked down at the board. Fouad had won a double. 'Shall we play another?' Fouad asked.

'No, I don't trust the dice. Come on.'

Ralf drained his glass and got up.

'Where are we going?' Fouad asked.

'Mine. It's just around the corner.'

Ralf went and paid while Fouad put his jacket on, and they walked out, the cool night air moulding itself to their faces and the backs of their hands.

'Did you like Algiers?'

'I came to love it. I remember I cried the first time I saw the sea. Water was something drawn from the ground, wrung out of the fissures in rock. I had never seen a large body of water before. Can you imagine? It was flat to the horizon, without a single landmark, no sign of animal or vegetation, and it shifted nauseously, never resting. Seeing the boats tilting in the marina made me dizzy. It seems absurd to me, now, but the sea appeared monstrous to me then.

'My father said I should learn to swim just well enough to avoid having to save anyone else. I resisted for a long time, but when I finally did learn I started to think of the sea as a heavy kind of air. Swimming still has that surreal quality for me, as if I am in a pleasant dream with the preconditions of a nightmare.'

They crossed the road. Ralf passed Fouad a cigarette and lit one for himself.

'But Algiers itself?' he asked, picking a bit of stray tobacco from his tongue. 'Were you unhappy there?'

'No, no. We were happy in Algiers.'

'It just seems odd to me that you would leave your home behind.'

'I could say the same of you.'

'I don't really have a home. Not since I was six.'

'But you have stayed in certain places longer than others, because there is a certain sympathy there. Algiers was sympathetic to us. There was money, even if we didn't have it. People wore bright fezes and the city was filled with people, Chinese and Negroes, Maltese and Sicilians, above all blackfeet and the French, who would stroll around buying everything. I picked up French as I led people round the Kasbah for small change. A few hours a day, I would stand around with my friends propping up the walls, each of us telling the others stories about France.

'Algeria was the centre of the world. We had Arabs, Europeans and Berbers; ports and mountains; snow and desert. Everything in existence seemed to have its prototype there. A friend once told me there is a piece of rock orbiting our sun called El Djezaïr – Algiers – which was discovered in 1916. People in France look up at the sky and they don't even know it exists. But Algiers was my world.

'Nevertheless, as I grew older, I became aware of a certain distant planet called France. They were our invaders, our oppressors, yes, but we used their own language to curse them, the only language they spoke. And while I heard about the daily injustices we all suffered, the experience on my doorstep was that the French brought money and gave it out readily.

'I had travelled once, and it had shown me the difference between a desert and a teeming city, so it seemed perfectly reasonable to me that all the stories about Paris were true. This was before the war, of course.'

'We'd better be quiet now,' Ralf said. 'I don't want to have to deal with the landlord in the morning.'

M. Dague's shop was shut up for the night, its wooden shutters bolted, its door boarded and barred, so they would have to go round. They approached the door for the court, Ralf occasionally glancing behind to check that Fouad was following. His footsteps were eerily silent. Not that he believed Fouad to be dangerous, but there was a cut-throat sort of intimacy to this empty street. Ralf felt for the right key, and Fouad stood patiently beside him, his thick eyebrows making shadows of his sockets, newspaper clutched under his arm, blowing smoke in thick white purls.

They walked up the stairs in single file, Ralf pausing to point out the bad floorboard, and carried their silence into the apartment with them, lest they wake next door's baby. Ralf lit the hob for warmth.

'I'm sorry it's a little cramped.'

Fouad's face flashed with something like contempt, before settling into a weary smile.

'It is kind of you to invite me,' he said.

Ralf opened the cupboard above the hob, feeling the warmth on the underside of his arm, and took out an open bottle of wine. They sat, Fouad in the chair next to the bookshelves, Ralf on the end of the bed, and touched glasses.

'So how did you end up here?' Ralf asked.

'I bought a ticket.'

'I meant to say why?'

Fouad's grin faded.

'After Paris was liberated, people assumed France must now understand the Algerian position on independence. The first time I saw France, I was defending it with a gun, tramping through the woods shooting lost Germans.' He caught himself. 'Did you fight?'

'Yes, with the British. I was in the Royal Armoured Corps, alongside the Canadians.'

'Are you Jewish?'

'No. A little. Not strictly. My grandfather—'

'I understand.'

'And you were with the French.'

'Yes, though we didn't fight side by side – the French were polite enough to let us go first. We spent a month defending a single farmhouse, eating some old woman's eggs each morning, little bullet holes spreading in the plasterwork as if the house had pox. Every morning we had to ask her about the eggs, and every morning she said she'd have to see, as if we were imposing on her hospitality. When we found out it was over, she kissed my commanding officer, a Frenchman, three times on his cheeks and told him he was a credit to France. Not us, you understand. Just him.'

'And you were given leave to remain?'

'No, no, they put us all back on the boat. But the atmosphere was incredible in Algiers, we were dancing in the street, we were reunited with our loved ones. Life was precious again. There was a march in Sétif in 1945, partly to celebrate the surrender of Germany, and partly to celebrate or protest this principle of independence. People really thought France must now understand. We had won victory over Germany together, we had fought together for liberation.

'Well. The police executed hundreds of people, protesters and bystanders. In Algiers, the atmosphere soured, even as the celebrations continued. I followed my father as a cobbler, and was introduced to my beautiful wife, Fatima.'

'What happened to her?'

'Nothing. She is in Algeria.'

'Do you contact each other?'

'I write to her as often as I can. She can't read, so I can't tell her everything that I would like to, knowing it will be read to her by her father, but perhaps that is for the best. My love for her must seem very pure.' He sipped his wine thoughtfully. 'But of course it has become very dangerous in Algiers. The women aren't searched, but they are hardly treated with the proper respect. It no longer matters whether you want to be part of the militias, the FLN or the MNA. The police treat everyone as if they are involved, and so do the FLN. I was held for some time and released without charge. They knew I hadn't done anything, but they wanted whatever information I had. Everyone wants you to pick a side, and I had fought with the French, so naturally they thought I would help them. When I was released, I came here to earn money for a new life, away from the violence. I know it is absurd to escape exploitation by travelling to the country that is exploiting me, but at least the pay is better here than there. I am saving everything I can. I'm not prepared to wait any more. I need to start earning a living.'

This last sentence struck Ralf deeply, though he was at a loss as to how to respond. He topped up their wine.

'Are you going to go back, or will she come here?'

'She is coming to join me in a month or so. But I think she will be very disappointed when she gets here,' Fouad said heavily.

'With the city?'

'Yes, with the city, with everything. With me. I drink, I no longer pray. I've lost sight of God. But yes, the city. A friend is trying to find me a place in La Folie – near where they are building the new university campus, in Nanterre. He has planted a sapling on his road – it's a local landmark, they call it "the tree". I haven't told her this. I don't think she would come if she knew.' Ralf listened to the air whistling through Fouad's lungs. Fouad muttered something in Arabic, or another language Ralf didn't understand. 'Could I have a glass of water?' he asked.

'You're not supposed to drink this water,' Ralf said.

'It's not the water that is going to kill me,' Fouad replied.

Ralf poured him a glass.

'I'll just drink this and let you sleep.'

'Why don't you stay? You can have the bed, and I'll take the chair. It's quite comfortable.'

'No, I couldn't.'

'Please, take the bed, just for tonight. When was the last time you slept on a mattress?'

Fouad gripped his glass of water, holding his breath as if afraid to let the air back into the room. Eventually he seemed to deflate and swallowed without drinking. He went over to the bed and stood looking at it for a couple of seconds before sitting down.

'One day, I will return this kindness,' he said.

'You don't owe me anything.'

Fouad lay down, facing the wall.

'Nevertheless. You are a Jew and I am an Arab.'

'Well. We are all in the same position eventually.'

Ralf switched off the light and padded over to the chair and then, thinking better of it, folded his coat and laid it on the rug as a pillow.

'That is why Camus will never solve Algeria's problems,' Fouad replied, his voice resonating strangely against the wall in the darkness.

'What do you mean?'

'"If I am forced to choose between justice and my mother, I choose my mother." It sounds so reasonable, so understandable. But really what he is saying is, "I value one life over another, one life is more deserving than another, I reserve the right, as a human, to be partial." It is cruelty masquerading as kindness. But you have given me your bed. So no, I don't owe you anything. But everything I have is yours.'

Ralf lay staring at the sloping ceiling for some time, watching the moon's weak shadows creep across it. Fouad's breath slowed and became curiously shallow, as if he were aiming to displace as little of the world as possible, becoming like the wood of the bed and floors, an object that didn't project the past or future. Perhaps his lungs hurt, or perhaps it was a way of staying warm when sleeping out of doors.

Feeling that he might not sleep, Ralf considered playing his Long Game, picking a single moment and thinking back a year, two years, four.

This time last year, there had been political deadlock among the socialists; crisis in Algeria; strikes in Le Havre. Last year's newspaper could have been today's, if you changed a few of the nouns. For some time now, everything had seemed stuck in a holding pattern. It was as if all France was waiting for something to burst, some skin to break.

Tonight, he felt balanced on the very fulcrum of his life, so that, if he took a single step, the balance would shift, the past would rise up steeply behind him, and the future tip down ahead to meet the earth.

'Shall we go out tonight?' asked Elsa, as they sat having coffee the following Saturday.

'If you like.'

A butterfly had landed on the floor by Ralf's foot. The poor thing must be lost: there were no flowers here, nor any of the light green leaves it emulated. There was a little brown spot on each of its four wings in imitation of necrosis, but they were too symmetrical, and the leaf colour too bright, as if the patterning was governed not by evolution but by an artistic impulse to over-represent. It turned its back to the prevailing breeze, keeping the backs of its wings flush with the floor to prevent uplift.

'I can't imagine you dancing,' she said.

'Neither can I,' he said. 'Will you teach me?'

'I can try.'

The wind direction changed, and the butterfly shifted position.

'Would you like another coffee?' he asked, examining the syrupy dregs of his own.

'I'd like a Coca.'

'I don't think they serve it here.'

'Shall we go somewhere they do? I know a place nearby with a good jukebox. Don't look at me like that.'

'Like what?'

'Like I've said something disgusting.'

Elsa uncrossed and recrossed her legs. The butterfly took to the fickle air. Ralf looked behind him, and Jacques held up a bottle of wine. Ralf held up a hand to stop him.

'What about a jazz club?' she said.

'I didn't mean to offend you. We can go to the other place.'

'No.'

'I can't bear it when you sulk,' he said.

'Shut up, will you.' She rifled through her bag for a pen. She laid his hand face up on the table and wrote the address on his palm – 5 rue de la Huchette – the nib scoring his flesh. He knew the place – it was a little touristic but it had had its fair share of the world's greats on its tiny stage. He watched the ink diffusing down the lifeline of his palm. 'Try not to dress for the library. I'll be there at eight.'

She left without kissing him goodbye. He tried to feel the breeze on his hot face, tried to judge its direction as he watched the spot where she had disappeared. He knew there was nothing she could do or say which might cause him to turn from her, that she might treat him like a dog and he would only gaze up at her pleadingly. This love had no dignity attached. It was voracious and miserable in the vast stretches of time that elapsed between the perfect moments that sustained him. Impossibly, he wanted to know how she behaved when she was not watched, as if it were all a performance, a construct of attractive clothes and behaviours and associations. And yet he found himself believing in the image and making it real. Perhaps everyone was image and there was no substance, he thought as he returned home. What we called people were only an aggregate of behaviours and clothing. Really, that was the evidence of a person.

Back at the apartment that afternoon, Ralf shaved carefully, holding up his mirror. He could feel the beginnings of a slackness in the skin around his jawline, and couldn't help imagining himself with the jowls of a bloodhound.

He pomaded his hair, brushing it backwards and trying to flatten out his cowlick to prevent the hair curling back onto his forehead. His hairline did look more pronounced this way, but it was nothing more than a slight widow's peak, and there really wasn't a better option. He wished that Elsa could have met him when he was young, unblemished, unlined, elastic. When the whites of his eyes were white. There was a time when he had thought of health as a store that could be depleted or refilled, whereas now he saw that it was more like flight: the wonder of it was equal to the inevitability of hitting the earth.

He deemed this evening significant enough to use a little cologne. The bottle was a quarter full, and that was the last of it. They didn't make it any more; its popularity had been too steady. Somewhere, a capitalist had made a quick experiment in planned obsolescence and, in doing so, had inadvertently broken off a little piece of Ralf, to sink and rest among the sediment of time.

He tried on a number of ties but couldn't find one that he was sure she wouldn't hate. She was like the first steps in a foreign country. He rubbed his neck where it met the coarse wool of his jacket. Perhaps it was still too formal, but since he only owned one jacket, it would have to do.

It didn't take long to walk to the club. The sun was down, and neon light slid along the heavy chrome bumpers of parked cars. As he approached, he recognised the all-but-permanent banner advertising Maxim Saury and his New Orleans Sound in cartoonish block capitals, with a poster of the man himself grinning and wielding his clarinet like a cheerful thug. They went through the usual charade of asking whether he was a member – some kind of licensing loophole. He ordered two Scotches in the bar, and then followed the stairs, down and right, and the dance floor opened out in front of him: walls of large, rough, irregular stone, hanging lanterns, and a number of large axes pinned to the wall near the band, a little nod to its history as a dungeon. People were dancing to a Dizzy Gillespie number, or something like it. The pianist, drummer and bassist stood on the little stage, with the brass players that couldn't fit standing on the floor in front, all in matching suits with square jackets, white shirts, black shoes and ties. To their left there were a few modern pictures, which he didn't think much of. For him the beauty of an image rested in its preciseness.

He spotted Elsa being spun one way and another by a young man in a chequered shirt, her skirt snapping and fanning out to afford a glimpse of her thighs. He found a table at the back and waited for her to spot him. The drummer went off on a wild roll. Ralf sipped his drink. Elsa danced on. Ralf wanted to lean on the table, but he thought the elbow of his jacket might get sticky. The place was full of students, young women in cute cardigans buttoned at the neck and men wearing tight-necked jumpers despite the heat. When the trumpets gave their last flourish Elsa stopped, flushing around her neckline. Ralf held the spare drink up forcefully, and she looked over. She seemed pleased to see him, and leant in confidentially to the young man in the chequered shirt without seeming embarrassed. The young man held Ralf's gaze before going to join his friends by one of the archways.

'Shall we join your friends?' Ralf asked.

'Oh, I don't know them,' she said. 'We just met. They're Americans. I think they're all called Sam.'

Ralf sipped his drink.

'I didn't think you'd come,' she continued.

'We arranged to meet.'

'I thought you might be afraid of the youth.'

'I'm not much older than you.'

'A few years, but a whole generation.'

'I got you a Scotch.'

She smiled devilishly and rattled the cubes against the glass.

'You look very beautiful,' he said, trying to draw her out.

'Don't I always?'

'You do.'

She took a quick sip.

'I want to dance.'

She took his glass and put it down with hers. Moving to the centre of the room, he held her waist just above the hips, his thumbs resting in the dip between her stomach muscles. He could feel the hand that had been holding the glass thawing against her body. Mere threads separated his skin from hers. He thought of the two time signatures, the music and her pulse, beating at odds, confused, but converging on the beat, the single beat, when they would strike in unison. It would pass unnoticed among the other dancers, that moment of perfect synchrony, but she would feel it. And the one beat would slur, separate again, but this time it would sound and feel like cell division, one mass growing bigger than itself, pulling apart, growing two skins. And the two beats would separate, but this time with the knowledge that they had been together once, were one once, and might not be again.

She was laughing at him. He had never been much of a dancer, but he had never been watched either, and so he had got by when necessity dictated by being inconspicuous. Now he felt he had lost his rhythm entirely and couldn't account for the lag time in his feet as he tried to fall back into step. He recovered just as the song drew to a close, his neck and forearms prickling with heat, his shirt damp along his back and armpits. His wool jacket was the cause, and it would have to be the solution.

'Where are you going?' she asked.

'To get my drink.'

'We've only danced one song.'

'I'm hot.'

Reaching the table, he threw back a mouthful of whisky and melted ice, his tonsils and soft palate turning numb. The cold spread a little way down his throat and combined with the sweat and surface heat to make him feel feverish around the front of his skull. He put one hand on the table. He turned around to see Elsa dancing with the man in the chequered shirt again. Ralf stood without moving, watching blankly, as he did whenever a situation came along both without precedent and without the assurance of allies. He had nowhere to turn so he did not turn. She abandoned herself to the dance. He saw everything. The snap of her dress as the man in the chequered shirt caught her waist. Her eyes, which never left her partner. Her unapologetic, reckless laugh as she barrelled into a fellow dancer. He had dared to believe that she might love him, but she seemed to forget him when he passed out of her view, whereas he had only to close his eyes to see her face.

The couple were dancing in double time, her short heels barely touching the floor. The man's expression was laid back, even indifferent, but his body was excitable, barely constrained, each little movement reaching for connection and exclusivity. To cut in now would be inelegant. He would wait until the song was over. He sipped his drink. She showed no sign of running out of breath. The trumpeter played on hysterically. The whole room pulsed with movement, frenetic bodies like molecules on the boil, or like a dancing plague, the musicians hired to exhaust them, each of them convinced they couldn't stop. Elsa had kicked off her shoes and was holding the man in the chequered shirt close now, his thigh subtly interposed between her knees. Ralf felt a hot panic as he tipped his empty glass. He thought of

visiting the bathroom, or of leaving. He had to wait for the song
to end.

He started on Elsa's drink for something to do. Some had
noticed, but no one cared, that he was alone. Elsa had the man
by his shirt and was tugging each shoulder in time to the beat.
The man raised his eyebrows. Ralf looked around for a seat.
One of the man's friends put two fingers from each hand in
the corners of his mouth and whistled, not at Ralf, as he'd first
thought, but towards the stage, as the exhausted brass blew a
tremulous coda, the dancers' hands high and joined, in victory,
prayer, union. Ralf bit down on an ice cube and walked over.

Elsa stood in the glare of a light, which caught the gaudy red
of her lipstick. The man in the chequered shirt held his hand out
to Ralf as he approached.

'Ralf?'

'Yes,' Ralf said, gripping the man's hand firmly.

'Jimmy. Jim.'

'Right.'

'I'm getting Elsa a drink,' Jim said. 'Would you like anything?'
He spoke correct French with a laboured accent.

'No, I'm fine.'

'Nonsense. I'll get you a beer.'

They stood with Elsa's new friends while they had their drinks.
As it turned out, the whistler was called Danny, and the other
was indeed called Sam. Danny tapped his foot compulsively, evi-
dently much taken with the music, and sometimes clicked his
fingers inaudibly. 'Do you like jazz?' he asked.

'I like the slow numbers. Miles Davis. Duke.'

'Did you hear, Miles did the score for the new Louis Malle
picture?'

'Right.'

'It was phenomenal.' He made the *phenomenal* sign, creating
a circle with his thumb and forefinger. 'It might still be on.'

Jimmy/Jim continued his conversation with Elsa. Ralf could not tell whether he was being included or humiliated. Danny kept asking questions about the Parisian music scene and making self-conscious references to the existentialists. He seemed to have travelled here in the hope that he might benefit in some unarticulated way from proximity to them. Given the freedom of an open field, most will take the footpath, thought Ralf, and why shouldn't they. Elsa raised a hand to her mouth and swallowed before laughing at something Jim had said.

'What's that?' Ralf asked, cutting Danny off.

Jim looked to Elsa for a cue.

'Oh, nothing,' she said.

'Come on,' Ralf said. Danny and Sam were watching him.

'It's too long-winded,' said Elsa.

'I'm curious,' said Ralf.

'My French is not perfect and I accidentally said something rude,' said Jim.

'What was it?'

'I wouldn't like to repeat it now I know what it means!' Jim said, prolonging the laughter.

'We can speak in English if you prefer,' Ralf said in English.

'No, I have to practise. I am hoping to buy a place here, perhaps to meet a girl.'

'Yes, well, I hope you are as lucky as I am.' Ralf put his arm over Elsa's shoulder and she tensed, though she did not shrug him off. Jim nodded and looked at Elsa in genuine appraisal.

'I have a place in mind,' he said. 'But you don't get much for your money here. I told the estate agent there was no room to entertain, and do you know what he said? "There is a great café around the corner."'

Elsa smiled.

'If you don't like it you can leave,' Ralf said.

'I like it fine,' Jim replied.

Elsa dug him hard in the ribs.

'Ralf,' she said. 'You're being rude. Don't you think you should apologise?'

'Would you excuse us for a moment?' Ralf asked Jim.

Jim looked at Elsa.

'Don't look at her,' said Ralf. 'She's not asking you. I am.'

Jim kept looking at Elsa.

'Well, I'm going to dance. I don't want to talk, especially if you won't apologise,' she declared.

Jim smiled. In his large, open face, Ralf saw everything that he hated in Elsa. Every quiet slight, every thoughtless flexing of power, every glossed-over hypocrisy. He could see that Jim believed in appearances. He preferred looks over substance, and not just preferred them but thought they were better, and he would go through life assuming he was right and persuading others of it, this creed of deceit and appearance and hedonism over utility and resilience. If anyone contradicted him, he would simply move on without troubling to learn the causes, and would take his ability to do so as proof he was right.

Jim led Elsa by the hand onto the dance floor. Danny was no longer making any effort to engage Ralf, and had gone back to watching the band, exchanging occasional comments with Sam. Ralf put down his empty beer. Next to it was the ashtray and a Scotch glass. Danny tapped his feet and the stone walls sweated. Ralf could feel his heart pumping blood furiously around his body, charging his extremities. Smoke hung under the stone arches like a fine mist. He had, after all, tried talking and being reasonable, but she didn't respect him for that. He felt the thinness at the top of the Scotch glass, and the solid heaviness along the base. Jim did not understand what it meant to humiliate him in front of Elsa. He tipped the meltwater on the floor. It was dark in here, and the noise pressed in at all angles. He would be grateful for some air. He pushed through the dancing crowd, making no attempt to match their rhythm. When he reached Elsa she stopped dancing, and Jim turned around to see why. Ralf's trapezoids tensed as he made sure of his grip on the glass and glanced briefly over his right shoulder for space to move. Glaring into Jim's uncomprehending eyes, he swung the glass tightly round like a hook punch, aiming for the sphenoid bone between ear and eye. Ralf caught him plumb with the heavy bottom corner. Jim's face went slack and his ankles and knees gave way. Ralf grabbed Elsa by the forearm and she put up no resistance as he pulled her towards the stairs. As he left he saw that a radius of shock had opened around the body, those closest bending down to him, the women with their hands on their mouths, and those farther off still dancing, unknowing or unwilling to know. At the top of the stairs, he put the glass down on the bar. The band played on.

They left the place walking. They had the advantage of confusion and the night soon closed behind them. Ralf's hand hurt. The glass hadn't broken but the rim had bruised a line along his fingers, and flexing the joints was painful. A G7 taxi cruised passed them slowly, the driver peering out of the side window, but there was no one else. Ralf thought his hand might be bleeding under the skin. They crossed the river and turned down a cobbled side street a few roads from Ralf's apartment.

Elsa called his name softly and he stopped.

'Do you – do you have a cigarette? Only I've left my bag behind.'

Ralf reached into his jacket pocket for his case.

'I only have unfiltered.'

'That's fine. Thank you.'

She was shaking, either from cold or from the shock. She inhaled deeply.

'What did you think you were doing?' he asked.

'We were just dancing, Ralf. I didn't think you would do that.'

If this was the admission Ralf had been hoping for, it didn't feel like it. He had not thought he would go so far, but he could not allow her to think him weak.

'Let's go,' he said.

Elsa stood planted, unnerved. He began to feel a creeping horror along his spine.

'His head hit the floor,' she said. 'It was like a fruit falling off a table. It wasn't like a head at all.'

'Let's get inside,' Ralf said.

'I don't want to.'

'Come on, there's no sense in standing in the cold.'

She was shuddering deeply.

'I don't want to go with you,' she said. She looked at him without recognition.

'We're two minutes away from my apartment.'

She started walking back down towards the Île de la Cité.

'Where are you going to go at this hour?'

'Home.'

She crossed the road and he followed.

'All right, I'll walk you home.'

She stopped, stricken.

'No.'

'I don't have to come in.'

'You can't come at all.'

'Why not?'

'I don't need you.'

'I'm not going to let you walk home at this hour on your own.'

'I'll take a taxi.'

She kept going, past the Hôtel de Ville.

'How far is your apartment?'

Elsa did not respond. She was striving to stay a couple of paces ahead of Ralf, who noticed she was still barefoot.

'It would be nice to see where you live,' said Ralf.

'Well, you won't,' she said.

'I don't care where you live. I won't love you any less.'

'That's very magnanimous.'

Elsa flagged down an approaching taxi.

'I didn't mean to hurt him badly.'

'It's not about that.'

Elsa leant into the car.

'Can you start off towards the ninth, and I'll direct you from there.'

She got in the back.

'I'm sorry if I gave you the wrong impression,' she said, closing the door.

The driver looked pityingly at Ralf before pulling calmly away.

And she was gone, and time sped up again. Ralf knew he wouldn't sleep now, so he went down to the river. It was not yet the hour of the dispossessed, not quite. Fouad might still be at Jacques'. If not, he, too, would be on the streets, trying to stay out of trouble until the time came to start work again. A barge was moored loosely below Ralf. He could hear the water slopping between the hull and the river wall. He wondered how deep the water was, and whether the tide ever dropped low enough for the boat to thud onto the silt. The surface gave nothing; the fish might as well be blind. Somewhere out of the city, the Paris homeless slept in comfortless tents, huddled together on a bare patch of earth like saplings after a forest fire. Farther off, in Bercy, the dockers would be out by now, shifting crates down streets named Médoc, Mâcon, Chablis, Beaugency.

Ralf ran his hand along the smooth stone of the wall. An earworm of jazz echoed around his head where the trumpeter had lingered jarringly on an accidental. Danny had kept tapping his foot and the band had played on. That was life – one improvised. The cruel trick of the human species was to have a mind that required a score. He had not heard the glass hitting Jim's skull, but he had felt the shock travel through his hand and forearm. There was no way to know how hard one had to strike a person to knock them out. It was guesswork. Would he be up by now, and have piled into an open-top car with Danny driving and Sam in the back? Or would he be in the Hôtel-Dieu, losing blood pressure? Ralf had called Elsa's bluff, but only now he had won the hand had he seen what they were playing for. When he was six years old, he had been taught that compassion was the only quality of any consequence, and tonight he had tied a knot along the smooth train of his life, and it would trail behind him, snagging over rough ground, staring back at him when he stopped to look, no matter how far he tried to pay it out.

But *it's not about that*. The memory of the phrase began to cool and congeal, though he couldn't make sense of it. He felt he should know her by now, but her mind remained closed to him. The wind blew hard against his ears, and he felt suddenly, dreadfully, that he had to be indoors, had to put a layer between himself and the world.

Ralf sat by the radio with his hand on the volume, ready to turn it off, as he had been for some time. Just ten days ago, de Gaulle had ridiculed the idea that he might seize power by means of a *coup d'état* ('Do people really believe that at the age of sixty-seven I am going to begin a career as a dictator?'). But here they were. The army junta who had seized Algeria had now taken Corsica, and they were pressuring the government to hand power to de Gaulle – not just presidential powers, but unlimited executive powers.

Ladies and gentlemen, I am standing in the courtyard of the Elysée. I can now tell you that the National Assembly has voted

329 to 224 in favour of dissolving the government of the Fourth Republic.

Ralf kept his hand on the dial.

'The French people are threatened by dislocation and perhaps even civil war,' General de Gaulle said in a speech to a crowded Assembly.

Ralf clicked the radio off. He was asking the people to give up their rights, after everything Europe had been through.

These past days, as the Fourth Republic had collapsed, Ralf had wondered what was left for him here. He found his imagination swinging wildly between certainty that his relationship with Elsa must be over and involuntary attempts to picture their child. He felt somehow that the child would be a girl with blonde hair and dark eyes. Ralf's mother was blonde, so half their children would be blond(e). Eye colour was harder to predict. He imagined picking the girl up, his hands under her shoulders. The girl was always four or five years old in these daydreams. He would pick up the girl and she would clamp her little legs around his waist and sit, a little too big, on his hip. Elsa would smile indulgently. That girl would be a manifestation of their love for one another, out and walking in the world, half a measure of Ralf and half a measure of Elsa, poured out and blended.

These idle thoughts were mainly confined to the day, and they ended with the simple image of the child in his arms and the warmth of Elsa's smile, the impossibility of awkwardness or irony, the wholeness of sincerity. But the girl had appeared last night while he was asleep, and as he picked her up the vision mixed hideously with another world, and he saw Elsa smiling anxiously at him, and as he hefted the child on his hip he heard Elsa say, *There is no home for us here any more.* He heard himself respond, *We haven't any other.* And the girl stared up at him stolidly, not reacting, as if she wasn't sure whether the conversation was over.

Ralf could hear shouting in the street, and the rumble of a crowd. The Chant du Départ started up –

live for her

for her

– with many more voices joining in for the chorus. Few seemed to know the words to the second verse.

Ralf finished fixing his tie, pressing a scoop below the knot, and laced his shoes. Downstairs, M. Dague was tending to a customer who looked as if he got his thin white hair cut as an excuse to leave the house. The two continued in obscure reminiscence as Ralf walked past.

'Fraternising with the enemy, Ralf?' called M. Dague after him.

'What?' Ralf turned.

M. Dague leaned out of the doorway.

'An Arab came past this morning for you. I told him we don't allow dogs in the shop.'

'Did he say where he was going?' Ralf asked irritably.

'I didn't ask.' M. Dague turned to his customer in the shop. 'Arabs everywhere. This is what Mendès France has done to our country. Bring back Poujade, I say.'

Ralf continued on through the courtyard and out onto the road, which was a little more crowded than usual, but not by much. The singing must have been coming from the main road.

'Is there a march on?' Ralf asked a passer-by.

'Of course,' the young man replied. 'We're joining Mitterand and Mendès France at the Place de la République. Two hundred thousand, they reckon.'

Well, that explained where Fouad would be. Ralf continued down past Jo Goldenberg's, and found Jacques' bar full.

'What's going on?' Ralf asked, standing by the hinged section of the bar.

Jacques wiped a dark streak across his forehead and pointed to the corner normally abandoned by the regulars, which was occupied by men in loose double-breasted suits with miserly little moustaches. 'The Gaullists are having a drink to celebrate.' He turned back to the rest of the bar. 'And everyone else is having a drink.'

'You'll be serving the drinks at the end of the world.'

'What can I say? It's a disgusting job, but someone has to do it. Not at the end, though. Men should die sober.'

'Have you seen Fouad?'

'Not this week. Last I heard he'd fallen in with some Algerians, was staying on a floor somewhere around the Three Cats. Can't see him missing the action, though, can you?'

'No, he'll be there. Finding him is another matter.'

Ralf left the bar and walked against the current of pedestrians on the pavement, heading down towards the river. A mother ushered along two young boys holding placards saying 'Vive la République!' *Which one*, Ralf wondered. He crossed the bridge, walking over hundreds of little pieces of paper strewn across the tarmac, each about the size of his palm, on which were printed NON in bold caps, sans serif so that every way was the right way up, the type soaking through those that faced down on the wet ground. He could see the crowds now, many people wearing armbands, many holding hands. Two men were carrying a large banner, pulled horizontally between two vertical poles, which declared 'NO to de Gaulle's Fascism'. The people proceeded twenty abreast past a Citroën DS that was stranded in the road, the owner smoking and talking to a policeman who was so short you could see the X on top of his hat. Behind them, two young parents were out strolling with a little boy, seemingly oblivious to the crowd. He felt he had to look at the woman even as he was carried along by the crowd. The way the dress cinched in at the waist.

He was apt to see her everywhere he looked. He found that he could not look away until he was positive it was not her. He considered the possibility that it really was her. He had never seen her in a headscarf; her belt was pulled in to a waifish extreme, perhaps only from this angle; she was walking with a man and child. It was a wide city, but he and those he knew only inhabited a small part of it. They cut channels through the Marais and certain sections of the Left Bank. Ralf could usually be found in one of a handful of places. If the same was true of others, he might live in the city for years without encountering some of its inhabitants, while others would barely pass from his vision.

He craned around a protester. Knowing that it couldn't be her, and yet compelled somehow to confirm it, he edged his way to the other side of the crowd and broke free.

'Where are you going?' asked a policeman, adjusting a white glove.

'Over towards Voltaire's. I need to get home.'

The policeman stared hard at Ralf.

'What is your party?'

'I don't have one. I don't care about any of this.'

'Then if I were you I'd go home and stay there.'

Ralf nodded and walked off with his hands in his pockets, trying not to draw attention. He had seen them take a road to the north-west, probably the Boulevard Saint-Martin. He walked quickly, aiming to close some of the distance, but when he reached the bottom of the road he found himself within twenty metres of them, and he didn't want to be so close that they might turn and see him.

Ralf ducked into a GI surplus shop and stood in the window among heavy cotton shirts. He watched the family through the window until they were a good distance away.

'Can I help?' asked the shopkeeper.

'I'm surveilling someone,' Ralf snapped. 'I hope you have a permit for the resale of military property?'

The shopkeeper blinked at him.

The child had grabbed a fistful of the ruffled skirt at her hip. *It's not about that.*

The child took five steps for every three of his mother's. She seemed not to want to slow for him.

Ralf left the shop and continued on the other side of the pavement. When they crossed to his side, he stopped to ask a stranger for a light, though he had a full matchbook in his pocket. They were heading in towards the Opéra now. The land of milk and honey. A bright red Alfa Romeo parked illegally as Ralf passed.

I'm worried that you're going to get attached to me.

It was the arrogance of what she had said that had got to him at the time, and not the possible truth of it. It had seemed to be a kind of joke, and yet she had seemed genuinely sad.

They were heading into the 9th arrondissement now, and the little boy was beginning to act up. The mother was dragging him by the wrist, holding it up in the air so that the boy couldn't lean backwards. *It was a boy came in.* The child's frame was slight, and if he weren't determined to resist the definition he would look like a smart little gentleman. Perhaps it was the fact he fitted his clothes, which was a rare enough sight for children in Paris, or perhaps anywhere.

Elsa was always immaculately dressed, and when she removed her gloves there was always a light thud. The left glove, presumably, her slipped-off wedding ring hidden inside. That was it, wasn't it? A sleight of hand.

The father stood in front of a smoked glass door expectantly and it was opened from within. He stepped aside and allowed the woman and child to go in first, looking over his shoulder towards Ralf, before stepping in after them.

Ralf stood watching the doorway. The smoked glass was flanked on either side by fussy little pompoms of privet, the pots slowly overflowing with ivy. In the keystone of the segmental arch leered a stone face, its eyes recessed and no doubt inhabited by insects, its hair a thick Medusan tangle. The heraldic shield had been chiselled blank in a revolutionary *damnatio memoriae*. The shield itself was left curiously intact, so that one could see it once stood for something. Now it stood; just stood. Above, tall windows in neat pairs, fenced off by the twisting black vines of balcony railings.

If this were Amsterdam, or London, Ralf might simply look in through the windows, but he could see nothing here except the cool white stone, scrubbed free of soot so as to disown any association with the streets around, the people who drove their own vehicles, the people who couldn't afford fresh air.

Ralf took a seat at a table on the other side of the road and ordered a coffee. The way was unclear. Inside, a man was reading a newspaper while he fed part of his lunch to his dog.

Ralf watched an arm emerge from the shadows on the second floor and unscrew a window lock. A woman appeared, using both arms to tug the lower pane upwards. A car switched lanes, nearly knocking a man off his moped, and the traffic slowed to accommodate their argument. The woman watched before receding into the gloom. Ralf weighed down his bill with a couple of coins and crossed the road without a plan.

Inside the lobby, an older woman sat beside a bell, waiting for Ralf to speak. Her shoulders were slightly rolled, as if she had grown over her desk in the course of many years, and might not balance upright without it.

'I am here to see Elsa,' Ralf said.

'Surname?' the woman asked, making no move. Her tone implied that there was verifiably an occupant named Elsa, but that to refer to her by given name was an impropriety that must not go unchallenged.

'I'm afraid I don't know it,' Ralf said. 'Perhaps I could call up to introduce myself? I was given her address by a mutual friend and I'm afraid we haven't yet properly met.'

'Apartment?'

'I'm sorry, I don't know.'

The woman held the receiver in one hand, her other holding down the button on the cradle.

'Excuse me a moment while I call up and see if Monsieur and Madame Lambert are accepting guests.'

Ralf felt the coolness of marble through his thin soles.

'What is your name, please?'

There was no need to go up now, since he had what he came for.

'Ralf Wolfensohn.'

He was directed up a flight of stairs with a polished brass banister and a fern on the entresol. The door was answered by a maid, who persisted in offering to take Ralf's hat until he relented, before seating him in a drawing room, where he was left alone.

He was making a terrible mistake, putting his hand in the fire to check it was warm. Perhaps, even now, he wanted to believe there was some alternative explanation. A protective brother . . . He'd had no access to her surname, her home or place of work. She had come to him as an apparition, on her terms.

A record player sat with its lid closed in one corner. In another, a sideboard with a couple of crystal decanters. Over by the fireplace were two stone lions in the Chinese style, with flat, snub-nosed faces. Next to the sideboard, by the window, a Lear's macaw stood in a large, domed cage, occasionally shifting on its perch, its head snapping round and angling at any noises from the corridor or the road outside, its lizard eye keeping Ralf in sight.

Ralf sat on their sofa in his hairy jacket feeling like a stray, and half expecting the maid to come back in and sweep him off with a broom.

Presently, he heard clipped heels in the corridor, and straightened his back in anticipation of Elsa. A young man swept in, wearing patent-leather shoes, a slim navy suit and a thin red silk tie. Ralf remembered himself and stood to shake the man's hand.

'Monsieur Wolfensohn.'

'Ralf.'

'Theo. You're here to see my wife?'

'Yes.'

The macaw whistled and began to bounce as the man crossed the room. Theo opened a drawer, removed a palm nut and gave it to the bird, which caught the nut in its beak, manipulating it with one clawed foot and a yellow and black tongue.

'Can I offer you a drink?' Theo asked. 'I'm having a whisky.'

He upturned two glasses and unstopped a decanter.

'Thanks, I will.'

Ralf's leg was trembling, and he tried to focus on it consciously to overtake his sympathetic nervous system.

'So you're Elsa's latest enthusiasm.'

Theo poured out the drinks.

'Excuse me?'

'I assume that's why you're here.'

Theo stood holding the rim of each glass by the pads of his fingers, and Ralf had a momentary impression of glass on skull.

'What is it that you teach? As long as it's not primitive art.'

'Language. English.'

'She already speaks English.'

'One can always improve.'

Theo handed him the glass.

'Spoken like a paid tutor.'

The man hitched his trouser legs with his free hand and sat in the chair facing Ralf. He was young, perhaps only in his mid-twenties, and clean shaven.

'I hope I'm not intruding.'

'No. Elsa will be through shortly. She's just supervising lunch. If one leaves it to the maid all one ever eats is cold ham.'

'Do you mind if I smoke?'

'Not at all.'

Ralf took out his case and fumbled it open.

'I have cigars, if you prefer,' said Theo, indicating a walnut box on the sideboard.

'No, thanks.'

'Just as well. They're Havanas. If Batista doesn't wipe out those damned communists soon they'll be collectors' items. No more rum, no more dancing. No more fun, in all likelihood.'

Ralf looked over towards the hallway and shot his cuffs nervously.

'So how did you come by your fluency in English?' Theo asked. 'Were you a spy?'

'My mother and I left Germany when I was six and settled in London until the war.'

'Did you fight?'

'British Royal Armoured Corps.'

'And you stayed on here?'

'It seemed like the thing to do. The atmosphere in those days was one of endless possibilities. I felt like studying and I had very little to go back to, no girl, no job. No girls allowed at the École Normale, of course, but I rather thought I'd have met one by now.' Theo was examining his whisky. Why was he telling this to Elsa's husband, of all people? Did he think the affair might seem more palatable if only Theo understood how much he needed her? The man hadn't asked, and plainly didn't want to know. 'So although my academic background is in biology, I speak excellent English,' Ralf finished limply. 'I tutor students and do a little translation.'

'It's not a bad idea for Elsa to learn. We'll be moving around a lot in the next year or two, you see.' Theo carried his glass over to the sideboard. 'I'm working with Bic to introduce cheap ballpoint pens into America. We did England last year. It's the perfect business. People are forever losing pens. We sell them at sixty francs and people buy five at a time. You wouldn't believe what we're shifting.'

'I don't suppose I would.'

'We're manufacturing a million units a day.'

Elsa swept in.

'You're not talking about your fucking pens again, are you, darling? You must see that the reason you're so well compensated is that it's terminally dull.'

She kissed him on the cheek.

'I don't have to be embarrassed about you today because you've already met our guest,' said Theo.

'Hello, Ralf,' said Elsa politely. 'Have you been waiting long?'

'Not too long,' said Ralf. 'I hope I'm not interrupting your day?'

'No, we can have a little chat before lunch. It was so kind of you to come to see me at home.'

'Not at all. It's a terrific place you have here. Very well appointed.'

'There you go, you see?' She turned from Theo to Ralf. 'Theo is always complaining when I replace things—'

'And Elsa points out that I sell disposable goods,' cut in Theo, 'as if that proves nothing should ever last, and our lives should be a parade of novelties.'

Elsa didn't say anything, and Theo crossed the room to fetch a cigar. Elsa nodded for Ralf to speak.

'I came about the English lessons,' Ralf said to her in English.

'My husband speaks it better than I do,' Elsa replied in a warning tone. 'But I can make myself understood.'

'I understand; it is elegance you lack.'

'Perhaps,' she said, reverting to French, 'but I think I may have overstated my enthusiasm when we first met. You might be surprised how busy I am with my family and my household. I'm sure you would be excellent but – forgive me – I don't see how you could fit in.'

Ralf felt his windpipe collapse. No words were possible. Nothing was possible. He looked across at her, but rather than holding his gaze as he expected, she averted her eyes and rearranged objects on the coffee table. Theo turned to face the room holding a cigar cutter, and Ralf imagined inserting one of his fingers, asking Theo to chop it cleanly off before refilling his glass.

'You should think about it, darling,' said Theo. 'Aren't I always telling you not to be rash? I shouldn't want you to be too blunt with one of the American clients. You know how delicately these things have to be handled.' Theo smiled encouragingly at Ralf. 'Good business is really all diplomacy.'

Was it possible that Theo didn't know? Or was he indulging Ralf to torment her?

'In fact, will you excuse me?' Theo said. 'I must quickly use the telephone before lunch.'

'Yes, of course.'

Ralf stood to shake his hand.

And then he was standing in the middle of Elsa's floor. The Chinese lions were looking dead ahead. The macaw preened its shoulder. The bird might be older than Ralf, and he wondered what it had seen.

'How did you find me?' Elsa asked.

'I followed you. I had no illusion that it was a good idea, but I had to do it.'

Elsa nodded, lost in thought. She closed her eyes slowly, her eyebrows sank, and she made a low, agonised moan.

'You understand that you have ruined everything,' she recited. Ralf felt that the opposite was true, but it was impossible to argue here, or at all. She smiled weakly. 'But in the end, I am glad. Now I can begin to hate you.'

'I suppose I am to blame,' Ralf said furiously. 'For this? For your secrets?'

'No, no. It's not a question of blame.' She stood and kissed him lightly on the mouth as he stood there like a pillar of stone. 'Calm down. There is nothing to be done now. I'll visit you soon.'

Part Two

4

ELSA, Berlin, Upper Silesia and Nîmes, 1939–1956

●

Three months into the war, Elsa's father took her to see *Danton's Death*. Rationing had begun already, but the shop was doing well, indeed, had expanded a year before, when they had taken over the adjacent lot, and he decided to take her out for a treat. The theatre was on the Gendarmenmarkt, a grand square south of the Spree. Elsa could not remember having seen it before. It was as if it had appeared that night out of the ground, rising up tectonically, pushing the shops and streets outwards to leave space for wide paths, huge square stones sprouting in the vacant epicentre.

Two identical churches flanked the grand, classical pediment of the State Theatre. Her father held her hand in the crook of his elbow and smiled down at her.

'This way, *mademoiselle*.'

They approached the white stone steps, Elsa wondering who her father really was, that they had access to this place. Inside, she marvelled at the hundred candles of the banister posts and the genteel slope of the staircase up to the circle, as if one needn't exert oneself amid such luxury. Father bought a programme and Elsa traced the radius of the eagle's wings, the long primary feathers, and the beautiful Gothic script, like a tattoo.

When they reached their seats, Elsa had a dizzying notion that she was still on the ground floor, and that the stalls below were a great pit or crater, carved out of the earth. Everyone was chattering excitedly about the Polish campaign, the heroism of relatives. There was not enough to eat, nor enough coal to go around, but their pride kept them warm and full.

Elsa looked up at the chandelier. She had never seen a ceiling so high before, and it raised the question of whether the upper atmosphere of the room counted as the sky. She stroked the plush red seat, surveying Berlin society in its finery. The light dimmed, then went out altogether. Elsa looked up at her father, who raised his finger to his lips. The lights went up on stage, and suddenly the whole vast theatre was an eyeball, the audience its little receivers, sat in the dark, looking through the peephole at Paris.

The men on stage spoke about revolution and the guillotine with great passion. They joked and they talked about beautiful things, they cried out, they shook each other, as if every word was a desperate attempt to change each other's constitution. At the end of every scene, the world spun around to reveal a new one on the other side of it: a drawing room with cushioned chairs and flocked wallpaper; a boulevard in the rain; the Place de la Révolution.

At one point, Danton gave an impassioned speech: *One day, the truth will out. I see a great misfortune overwhelming France. It is dictatorship. It holds its head high, and it marches over our dead bodies.* Certain audience members began to whisper, and Elsa wanted them to shut up, because the monsieur was speaking, and their voices had dragged her back to Berlin. When she looked back at the stage, something had broken; she could see it was only a raised level in the room, and she couldn't help but notice the bright lights in the flies, and the exaggerated gestures of the actor who, after all, was speaking German.

The play went on, but there were no more wide vistas of Paris, only claustrophobic boxes: an assembly room, a cold stone prison. Elsa did not understand why, but she could see that a fine world had collapsed, and she didn't know whether it was meant to be that way, or whether it had only collapsed for her. When the lights went down, and came back up on the actors, the audience sat around her in stunned silence for two or three seconds, before clapping furiously, standing up from their seats so that Elsa could no longer see, and could only hear the applause like a sudden downpour.

They walked home, Elsa asking questions. There were certain things that didn't make any sense – not because of something she didn't know, but because they seemed a nonsense. For instance: *We are all villains and angels, idiots and geniuses, one and the same. We sleep, we eat, we have children. The rest is a variation on a theme.* How could one be a villain and an angel? Her father smiled indulgently and pointed out that she, Elsa, was quite capable of being a villain and an angel. On certain days she imagined she was a little duckling, and she would fluff her yellow hair and quack, and flap her arms like wings. But other times, she would not eat her dinner, would not sit still, would not be quiet. Well, then, depending on her mood, she was a little villain and an angel both. But Danton was wrong about one thing, her father explained. There really are devils and angels out there, and one must not underestimate them.

That winter, they were glued to the radio, as victories followed predictions of victory, smiling at one another as they sat in their coats in the sitting room. Elsa's brother, Wilm, had signed up in August, and wrote marvellous letters about their exploits. Paras had glided onto the roof of a fortress and taken it from the inside without a bullet wasted. They were taking ground as quickly as they could move, with barely time to stop for meals. There was a planned offensive, which he couldn't talk about – in the next letter, it had already taken place, and Wilm's division hadn't even made it to the front in time to see action. He wondered whether he would have the chance to win himself a medal at this rate.

On through Belgium and into France. The opposition seemed to flatten like grass under a wheel. Paris was declared an open city! Elsa imagined the wide streets hung with flags, the soldiers in their smart uniforms, strolling along the river or sitting at café tables, arguing with passion, dedicated to love and ideas. Britain had fled the mainland and would soon negotiate. The war was all but won, and Wilm would be home soon. Elsa only felt sorry that she had so long to wait for her life to begin.

One night, towards the end of the summer, Elsa heard aeroplanes and a crashing. She got out of bed and looked out of the window. She saw a light go on in a window opposite, and dark wisps of cloud drifting against the darker sky. She could make out the sound of guns. She heard the engines overhead for some time longer, receding so gradually that she didn't notice the moment they passed out of hearing. The noise had gone, but the quality of the silence had changed. It was not the same silence that had been there before the planes. It was a crouching, a listening silence. Not the silence of sleep, but the silence of waiting.

Her father was cheerful the next morning. Wilm had sent a pack of coffee home, not ersatz, but real coffee, and her mother brewed it reverently, placing cups in front of each of them. The coffee made Elsa anxious and sick, and her heart palpitated erratically. Her mother switched the wireless on. *If they increase their attacks on our cities, we will erase their cities from the Earth.* It had been an awful, nerve-racking night, Elsa torn between competing desires, first to run into her parents' room, and second, to be brave. How good it felt now, how reassuring, to hear such certainty, to stand behind the powerful. She wouldn't give up that feeling for anything. Because, as her father

said, weakness was contemptible. It didn't matter if a few buildings were bombed, or even if the English had violated the agreement by targeting civilians; *God is with us.* One day soon, they
would bring the whole world into agreement, and there would
be no need to fight. They would take command of nature itself,
bring it to heel and, finally, overcome all limits.

Her father made it sound as if nothing had happened, nothing
had changed, and yet a couple of weeks after the bombing, Elsa's
mother came to her room and sat down on her bed.

'Do you remember your walking trip last summer?' she asked
Elsa, stroking her hair.

Elsa nodded.

'It must have been wonderful to be in the forest with the
birds and animals, and to have had so many other girls to make
friends with.'

Elsa shrugged. She had got into trouble for kicking one of the
others and rubbing dirt on her. She thought perhaps her mother
had found out, but didn't know why she had waited so long to
bring it up.

'Your father and I were thinking,' her mother continued, 'that
you might like to go out to the countryside again.'

Elsa didn't understand. What about school?

'We have found a lovely village where they are setting up a
dormitory for young girls. You'll make lots of friends there, and
the teachers are supposed to be very good. The abbess said they
can even teach you French. Your father and I are jealous – we'd
like to come too, but they told us we're too old!'

Elsa didn't know what was wrong, only that there were great,
unspoken forces at work, and that the only way to live with
them was to watch and stay quiet. Her mother worried about
rations, so she ate little. Her father liked to talk about the future,
and she let him. On the eve of her departure, she wrote to Wilm
on the back of her father's letter, giving her new address and

asking him to tell her about France. She imagined her brother marching down the shimmering boulevards in his uniform, the eagle hanging from the Tour Eiffel. The Place de le Révolution, where they had chopped the king's head off, and then Danton's.

The first nights, Elsa slept on loose straw while her dormitory was arranged. It was more comfortable than the floor, but it pricked at her exposed skin and made her eyes itch. She wrote to her mother to ask for her own bedlinen, but nothing came.

The beds were built. A routine soon established itself: tidy the dormitory; morning assembly; raise the flag; morning lessons; midday prayers; afternoon lessons; evening prayers.

When, several weeks later, the bedlinen finally did arrive, it became a prized possession. In the first few days, one or two of the girls made up some excuse to lie on her bed and read before the lights went out. Then, a week after the package had arrived, Elsa returned to the dormitory to find that her sheets had been taken off, and turned every bed over until she found them, getting half the dormitory into trouble in the process.

It was an older girl, Trude, who took them the second time, and refused to give them back. Elsa waited until everyone was sleeping, and waited longer still, to make doubly sure. Then she slipped out the sewing scissors she had taken earlier that day, padded over to where the girl slept, and stood beside the bed, squinting at Trude's face. She slipped a hand under the blanket and felt the sheets, her sheets. Carefully, she lifted one of the girl's braids, feeling the neat plaits between her fingers, and chewed through it with the scissors. It was like a rope and didn't cut easily. The girl began to wake up. Elsa kept hacking away, finishing as quickly as she could, finally holding the braid limp in her hand like a dead snake. Trude opened her eyes, saw Elsa's silhouette over her, and began to scream. Elsa stuffed the hair in the girl's mouth and pushed and pushed, blanket and girl, until they landed on the floor with a thud. She took up the sheet and the pillowcase while the girl cried on the floor.

Different teachers led prayers. Some had set routines, and would lead them through the Lord's Prayer, or a laundry list of relatives and leaders. Elsa preferred those who left her in silence to compose her own. She would ask God for a letter from Wilm. At first, she simply asked that He keep her brother safe, but she soon started asking for a letter from him instead. A letter not only meant he was safe, but gave her something to look forward to beyond her French lessons.

When, several months later, Wilm finally wrote, it was from Rouen. There was a blank postcard enclosed with the letter in the army envelope. He had been promoted to sergeant, with an increase in pay, and was thinking of using the money to buy prints and woodcuts to sell back home. He had found a wonderful antique bookshop and was pursuing a friendship with the owner, a man he found fascinating, faultlessly polite but incapable of concealing his moods; they passed across his face like clouds drifting in front of the sun. Wilm had questioned him about France and the French, what they thought of the Germans. He had been convinced, at first, that the bookseller hated him, but it wasn't so – the French didn't hate the Germans, he said. *All they want is to be left alone with their constitution intact. Above all, we must not attack their way of life. It is this they have fought viciously for so many times, with the Prussians, the Russians and each other. They would not sacrifice their way of life for anything; for that, they would be prepared to die.* The old man had made quite an impression on Wilm, who seemed almost to have abandoned all thought of the Reich.

The postcard, he said, was of the cathedral in Chartres. In Rouen, they had the Abbaye Saint-Ouen, but he found Chartres superior – it soared like Cologne or Strasbourg. Elsa looked at the postcard and imagined travelling through the French countryside by horse, running her hand down over its smooth, hard shoulder as she dismounted, crossing herself in front of a grand altar. Glancing furtively at the men in their suits through a gauze. Feeling their eyes on her as she exited down the aisle. Putting one foot in a stirrup and sitting astride, the horse flexing powerfully under her. She looked around at the other girls, convinced she had been seen (but doing what? What rule had she violated?). She folded the letter in quarters and tucked it into her diary with the postcard. Later that night, she wrote down an account of what she had imagined, but the idea no longer carried the same excitement, so she tried to convey a little of what she had felt, the strange churning in her gut. Perhaps what she had imagined was really a wedding?

Elsa would sit through lessons about expanding the German Empire to create living space, or sewing while they listened to a broadcast of *Lohengrin*. For days after that, the abbess was in a better mood, and took to calling her 'my lovely Elsa', though she was hopeless at sewing and spent every hour trying to avoid pricking her fingers. In fact, despite being not only unwilling but positively insolent to her teachers, Elsa found herself raised up as an example to the others. When they were sent out for exercise, or a doctor arrived to measure their heads, or there was a parade, her name was called first or she was put at the front. She would often find herself standing next to Trude, her short hair now pinned up. She and Elsa shared something more honest than friendship. Unlike many of the others, Trude seemed to respect Elsa for having taken her sheets back by force. It was rumoured that she was here as an orphan, having denounced her parents for criticising the government.

In the summer of 1941, Trude was appointed head of the Young Girls' League. Elsa was sworn in at a torchlit ceremony, swearing to give her life for the Führer, the people and the Fatherland. They were left to their own devices for whole afternoons, singing songs on route marches, practising gymnastics in gas masks, or sunbathing in the field next to the army garrison in their gym slips. On their marches, they walked farther than Elsa had thought possible. If someone fell, they would all shout until she got up. If someone couldn't swim, they would throw her in the river.

'If you lower a baby into water slowly, it will splutter,' said Trude. 'If you dunk it, it will hold its breath.' They stood on the riverbank watching a young girl splashing around, lifting her chin above the water, pleading in short gasps for help.

'You have to scoop the water with your hands,' called one girl.

'Let her find her way,' said Trude.

And she did. She got out, bedraggled, and they marched on. The girl was shivering, and her friends pulled her up the bank, and soon she had caught up at the back, laughing through her chattering teeth. They stopped to pick mulberries, and Trude showed Elsa the fat caterpillars eating through the leaves.

'Are they pests?'

'No, silkworms. The farmers pick them off the trees when they have woven their cocoons and boil them alive so they don't eat through the thread.' Trude held out her hand for the caterpillar, which she held up for Elsa to see. 'My uncle farms them.'

'Are there never any moths?' asked Elsa.

'Some,' said Trude. 'You hold the fattest back to breed. You don't get the best silk of the generation, but you get the best offspring.'

That winter, Wilm's division was called away from France to join the great push to take Russia. Father had long since stopped talking about Russian alliances and the danger of fighting on two fronts, and had declared in his last letter that they would take Moscow before the winter set in. Indeed, it seemed that way; when Wilm did manage to write, they had taken 480 kilometres in just two weeks. He wrote of the villages which welcomed them with eggs and vodka, of the dead, inhuman expressions of the Russian soldiers. *It's the landscape – flat to the horizon, featureless – it deadens the soul.* He promised to send her back an embroidered skullcap from the local market as a curio to show her friends. Elsa replied that she hoped he had killed a great number of them, and that she wished she had been born a boy, so that she might lay her life down for the Fatherland too.

Trude took her letter as she was finishing. Elsa watched her read. Trude had grown taller these past few months and now had a sprinter's limbs. There was no question of snatching it back. Trude put the letter down on the table.

'If you're a man, you can give the Fatherland a soldier, but if you're a woman, you can give five soldiers. That is your duty.'

Elsa didn't receive a reply from her brother for five months. Her parents hadn't heard anything either. Around her, horror stories circulated in hushed whispers. Someone's father, who had a connection, told stories of marching at gunpoint in -40°C blizzards, sentries whose steel helmets had frozen their cranial fluid, earmuffs frozen to ears. Returning troops whose eyelids had fallen off from frostbite, and who could only stare like ghouls. But even if it were true, which she couldn't credit, wasn't the sacrifice necessary? Theirs was the generation that would be marked out for all history, the selfless, the willing, those who had the strength to suffer.

It wasn't long before the bombers were flying over again. Out here, in the countryside, there was no bunker. There was only a slit trench, a thin zigzag dug out of the field, open to the sky, with a long wooden bench running along its length. Elsa would listen to the younger children crying, and try to understand what it was about the sound of crying, among all else, that she couldn't stand. She thought at first that she didn't like noise, but that wasn't true – she found noise interesting. At a certain point, she decided that she was annoyed at the nuns, whose job it was to keep the children under control. The problem was not that they were afraid, but that they had learned to expect sympathy.

When Wilm's next letter arrived, it was uncharacteristically abrupt. He asked whether she could send him Pervitin, as their parents couldn't find any in Berlin, and asked how her lessons were coming along. He told her he loved her, and couldn't wait to take her in his arms again. *After the war we'll start living,* he wrote. The letter was signed by him, but the body written in another hand.

The world grew stranger with each passing year. They learned how to put out fires, how to dig people out of ruins. Freight trains passed by with human cargo. Elsa bled one night while she slept, and her sheets were ruined with bleach. Whenever any of the girls was derelict in her duty, Trude would punish the whole group, taking them on silent marches or worse. On those days, Elsa nursed fantasies of revenge, imagining what it would be like to stab Trude with a letter opener, or carry the copper pot up the stairs, heavy and wobbling with boiling water.

But then, on her birthday, Trude graduated to the League of German Girls, and spoke of her plans to leave. Sitting down to their potato dumplings one evening, Trude told Elsa about the *Lebensborn* programme, the Fountain of Life. There were camps where the finest girls could go, where they would meet men who were racially and biologically valuable, to produce valuable children, which would be adopted by the Reich. A lot of the men were pilots, since they were fit and had a short life expectancy. The nuns had tried to stop some of the older girls before but she was going to find a way to apply.

'You'll give the child away?'

Trude looked quizzically at Elsa.

'It won't be mine to give.'

Elsa finished her soup, not much more than salted water. She looked over at one of the younger girls, who had received the same portion despite being much smaller.

'Will you do it too?' Trude asked. 'When you are fourteen?'

Elsa suppressed a cough.

'Yes. Of course.'

'Better to be with a German than a Frenchman,' Trude said. She had read the diary. She smiled and got up with her bowl. Elsa waited until she had left the room before going upstairs, retrieving her diary from her bedside, and burning it in the grate.

Wilm had long since stopped writing, and she suspected that he was regrouping in the encirclement outside Stalingrad. Her parents had told her nothing of the sort, but by now she got her news from the radio. On the anniversary of the party's accession, they had tuned in at 11am for Göring's speech, but the broadcast was a confusion of shouting. It sounded very much like an air raid, except that it was the middle of the day. The speech was delayed by the announcer, with intermittent music, for a full hour before being aired, the girls sitting tensely, a nun flitting in and out, suggesting ineffectually that they break off for prayers. When Göring's voice was finally heard, he announced tersely that they had underestimated Soviet capabilities, and that the soldiers serving in Stalingrad would die a hero's death.

The news contradicted everything she had ever known or been told about the war. Germany had never lost a battle as decisive as this, nor given up its soldiers to the enemy. It didn't make any sense.

She ran away, that day, and spent the afternoon climbing trees in the copse nearby, seeing how far she could travel between branches without touching the floor. It felt safer away from the floor. She cried, hunger needling at her stomach. She wanted to be in Berlin with her father and brother, or perhaps to hide here until the war was over and there were no more sacrifices to make. She stroked the rough bark, flaked bits off to see what was underneath. She climbed higher, the trunk and the branches getting thinner. As she neared the top, the tree began to bend with her weight. From there, she could see a field of treetops, a new, uncluttered ground, like the carpet of clouds one saw from the cockpit in newsreels. She got down to look at a nest on the floor among the ferns, thatched prettily together with twigs. She could see no birds. It looked comfortable inside. She picked it up and climbed back up the tree, taking care not to damage it, and perched it in a dip between two branches, then got down and returned to the dormitory. When she got back, her absence had been discovered. All the girls were to be punished by having their post held back for a day. Elsa sat on her bed while the others pinched her neck and arms and pulled her hair, feeling strangely detached, even pleased.

Trude left soon after that. She was going to a purpose-built camp that was next to a boys' camp, and at nights, when the girls had gone to their dormitories and the lights were out, the camp leaders would open all the doors and the boys would run over and find a bed. Sometimes, she said, there were more boys than beds, but it didn't matter because they were all young. If everyone slept with people their own age, there would be no venereal disease at all. Elsa listened to Goebbels on the radio, trying to take it in. *The goal of Bolshevism is Jewish world revolution. They want to bring chaos to the Reich and Europe, using the resulting hopelessness and desperation to establish their international, Bolshevist-concealed capitalist tyranny. International Jewry finds cynical satisfaction in plunging the world into the deepest chaos and destroying ancient cultures that it played no role in building. Eastern Bolshevism is not only a doctrine of terrorism, it is also the practice of terrorism.*

They had their prayers, their parades. She stopped replying to her father's letters. At nights, instead of sitting doing nothing in the cold slit trench, she volunteered to help on the searchlights in the town, since many of the male youth brigades had now been deployed to the front. She and the others would trail their beam across the sky like a river snaking through a valley, spotters and listeners. There were other lights arranged around them, hundreds of metres away in all directions, so that when they found a plane and began to judge the elevation and azimuth, and opened the shutters, three other beams would appear, honing in until each line of light formed a pyramid, the plane at its crest perfectly triangulated even as it crossed the sky. Then the flak guns would begin firing. They would simply continue like that, the pilots knowing they had been seen, the lights leading directly back to where they were being observed. The planes would fly in formation, and so couldn't deviate from their course. Once the azimuth had been calculated, the lights would follow them perfectly. The guns would fire and fire, and sometimes a plane would be hit, but more often than not, the plane crossed the sky, lit up like an angel, the pyramid of light tilting and skewing and finally toppling altogether. It was dreamlike and futile, this ritual shared between two enemies. It seemed strange to think it had anything at all to do with corpses and ruins.

When the Allies were approaching Paris, rumours began to circulate that the city would be destroyed rather than turned over, but then no more was said of it. For a while after that, the city was no longer mentioned. Instead, they heard stories of a tank commander who had retaken a whole Allied village single-handed, or another major push on the eastern front. It seemed that Paris hadn't been destroyed in the fighting, but no one knew what had happened. Elsa slept fitfully, and ate little. The days began to blur so that she began to lose track of weeks, and knew only the seasons, the crickets in the clear summer nights, the cruelty of the searchlight during the new moon, the rains, the frost that made the grass brittle. She never felt she was among nature, for the nights were accompanied by the thumps of flak guns, flashing red from the barrels all around her in irregular intervals, like a jagged heartbeat.

For months at a time she was distracted, enervated. She had stopped paying attention to the others, except where it concerned the Allied advance. It was becoming clear that everything was lost. There had only ever been two options: victory or annihilation. The question now was who would find them first. If it was the Russians, they would all be killed, or hope to be. In East Prussia, the Red Army had gang-raped women and girls ten at a time before shooting them. When they were too drunk to go through with it, they used a broken bottle instead. The British and Americans were held to be safer, but rumours abounded about the French colonial troops, dark animals with inhuman strength, capable of terrible violence. Algerian soldiers were known to attack Aryan girls as young as twelve.

Knowing that a convent school would be the worst kind of target, Elsa had started to steal or hold back any scraps of imperishable food she could, aiming to stockpile enough to hide for a week or so in the copse, until the worst of it was over. She had originally thought about disfiguring herself in some way, but had decided that it was unlikely to be of any help. Whenever she could get away without being discovered, she would go to the copse and continue digging out a foxhole that she had started under the brambles. She collected newspapers as they were thrown away and began to think about how to allocate her few items of clothing, concluding that she must keep them indoors and wear as many layers as possible during her escape. Some of the other girls took a different approach, aiming to fight on after occupation, copying blueprints to pack tins of Heinz oxtail soup with plastic explosive, using pencil detonators, or practising techniques for garrotting. Others passed around suicide pills that had been obtained surreptitiously from a boyfriend in the Hitler Youth.

As winter turned to spring, there were fewer fanatics among them. Someone had tuned the radio to the BBC and no one reported it or tuned it back. When women and children began to arrive on trains, having evacuated Berlin, Elsa had to laugh. Did they expect it would be better here? And then came the far-off rumbling, like a thunderstorm, drawing nearer by the day. Elsa judged that there were no more than two days left until the fighting reached them.

Elsa went out that night to the flak battery to relieve the girls who had been there all day. Some of their ammunition had been diverted to the east, so the guns fired slowly, lazily.

Before the sun had gone down, they heard firing and shouting in Russian. The Hitler Youth working on the nearest flak gun reversed the motor, bringing the barrel sweeping down and across towards the gate. Elsa took her chance and fled. She heard gunshots and knew they were aiming for her back. She ran down the track and along a row of hedges, more afraid of being caught by Russians than of dying. There was heavy gunfire behind her, now, and she pelted across the field in plain sight, not slowing down until she was under the cover of the trees. There were no voices. With each loud, crackling step, she felt she might be leading the enemy to her hiding place. She found her foxhole in the brambles and climbed in, scratching her arms and neck. She rubbed soil on her skin. She listened to the cracks and occasional screams.

No one found her there. She listened for what must have been days, her legs cramping, the sky sometimes falling gloomy, sometimes bright white through the gaps in the leaves. She ran out of water and had no way of opening the tins. A rabbit grazed on the edge of the field. She couldn't imagine killing it now. There was a shower of rain, which fell unevenly through the trees and kept dripping for some time afterwards. Eventually, while she still had the energy, Elsa climbed out and went to see who was alive.

In order to get her ration card, Elsa was put on a bus and driven to the concentration camp situated ten miles away, staring out of the window at the twisted metal of a collapsed bridge. The stench at the camp was impossible to ignore or forget. There were piles of dead, stacked like rotting logs in great pits, their bones visible, their skin wrapped into the cavities of their ribs and pelvises, their eyes and cheeks hollowed. The soldiers made her walk to the very back of the camp, where, beside an empty watchtower, a desk was set up with a young man in uniform, writing down names.

'Why do I have to come here?' Elsa asked him when it was her turn. 'I didn't kill these people.'

'Yes you did,' said the young man.

'How could I have?'

'Do you think they poisoned themselves?' asked the young man, his face tight with hatred.

When Elsa finally arrived back at her parents' apartment, her few possessions tied up in her bleach-stained bedsheets, it didn't feel like a return. It felt like travelling to a city she had seen in an out-of-date photograph. Her brother wasn't there, and would never be again. The shop had been completely turned over, the windows smashed, despite the signs proclaiming that *Looters will be punished with death*. Her mother wouldn't leave the apartment. She muttered to herself, clutching her cardigan about her neck, as if afraid to show her skin. Her father tried to manage the shop, but with so little to sell they were left to rely on their ration books and the burgeoning black market trade at the Tiergarten. Every now and again, they would go to a restaurant and hand over three ten-gram fat coupons for a meat dish, receiving a bare spoonful of meat padded out with dumplings.

In the French Zone where they lived, school was closed and three-quarters of the teachers had been dismissed. She would walk around the neighbourhood, staring up at the sky through the blasted windows, the walls no longer keeping anything in or out, their purpose burned away like the dunes of bricks and dust. She liked to walk past one apartment missing its external wall, where a whole family still lived, their sitting room exposed to the street like a doll's house. The wife would hang up washing across a line to obscure the view, but one could nearly always see whoever was on the sofa. She watched women passing buckets of debris down a line and boys playing rag football barefoot to preserve their shoes. Elsa's own shoes fitted her, as did her dress. They had inherited them from a neighbour whose diminutive wife had died, and who had given her possessions away immediately, asking for nothing in his irrational grief. He could have asked for butter, eggs, ham; if he'd bundled them up he probably could have asked for a telephone or a radio, or a mirror, and he'd have got it. But he just gave them away. The country was filled with stupid people who didn't know how to survive. They were dust, walking dust.

Elsa would walk to the Gendarmenmarkt and sit on the dried-up fountain, looking out at the square filled with the riddled metal carcasses of cars and half-tracks. The French cathedral had been badly damaged, and the German cathedral opposite destroyed completely. The State Theatre was closed, as it had been since 1944, the rendering burned away in patches, but it stood. She watched the patrols walking and chatting, translating snatches of French or Russian when she could pick them out. The Russians were obsessed with watches – some wore five or six on a single wrist. Occasionally she pulled experimentally at a crease in her dress, hitching the material up over her knees, but the soldiers invariably passed by without looking. She knew she was as bony as a pigeon. Elsa would swing her legs back and forth, back and forth, watching others pick their way across the square. Summer, the sky through windows, her hot skin. Dust.

When the sun passed overhead, she might search for floorboards to sell for coffin wood. It seemed to Elsa that the soul had been invented out of a perfectly natural need to understand the lifelessness of corpses. It stood to reason that something must have left, if one couldn't imagine the same shape breathing or kissing one on the cheek. And if it didn't affect a corpse's weight, it must be light, lighter than air, and it must rise, like oil in water, to the sky.

In one pile of rubble she found a gun, in another a hand. It was presumably still attached to the body, the hand sprouting from the masonry like a seedling, visible up to the wrist, wearing a ring. Elsa crouched next to it and tugged at the ring with her thumb and index finger, careful not to touch the sallow skin. The hand was swollen around the ring. An old man rounded the corner with a shovel and she climbed down, walking past him and on towards the Brandenburg gate with her stray boards tucked under her arm.

She liked to walk past the bakery, where the soldiers unshouldered their guns, watching people as they queued quietly for their bread, the skin and nails of the German people growing dull as their conquerors' brightened. She imagined the soldiers' shining hair under their helmets, glanced furtively with hopes of seeing their teeth. She knew she too had changed, was changing still, but couldn't imagine how else to be.

When school reopened and the teachers that had been dismissed were hired back, Elsa didn't register. The world was as it was. Elsa could see a new Berlin emerging, like the hardy weeds growing up through cracks in the road. Terrible things had been done in the name of the final victory. But there was none. There was only knowledge. Elsa lived above a shop that belonged rightfully to Jews. She knew it was her father that had denounced them. Her brother had certainly shot crying children, may even have raped their mothers.

Every sentence and action began with the ghost of another. An official's face said, 'I set fire to a house full of civilians,' as they said, 'Here is your ration book.' A neighbour asked, 'May I borrow your iron?' and, as Elsa went into the apartment to fetch it, she considered what it would be like to use the iron as a weapon. Buildings were not bodies – they could be rebuilt – but they were embedded in the silt of knowledge, which one had to tread among. Elsa watched the blank faces of passengers on the trams that glided past. The people were not ashamed but exhausted. There was nothing left to be said, nothing done, except to get on here and off there, to watch one's hands peeling vegetables. They had all been prepared to suffer and be ruthless in service of a grand vision of the future, without seeing that all one is left with, in the end, is the past.

Elsa started going out to the clubs at night. Jazz was no longer banned and she, like many others, was fascinated by the black musicians that had arrived to reclaim the city – did they really have tails? She would go out in her only dress, sometimes standing on the balls of her feet in imitation of those who wore heels, and watch the bands, the cabaret singers, hoping someone would speak to her. The music was exactly as she had been warned – uninhibited, full of expression and disunity. It was the music of solos, improvisation, discord, a howl against order.

There were hardly any German men left in the city, but there were plenty of foreigners. The best clubs were to be found in the American Zone. She didn't dance at first, only watched. She learned how to lean against the walls, how to look at a man, how to cross her legs on a bar stool. The men were invariably in a good mood. Their money was worth everything here, and their duties were simple. Not one of them attempted to speak German. She would practise her English or French.

She liked to lay her hand on the muscle of their arms, or to stand close while they were speaking. She liked to arrive dizzy with hunger and feel her head swim when she was bought a drink. She liked to see how many cigarettes she could persuade away from their owners. It was a beautiful game, a game without victims. A new cigarette was worth fifteen marks, the American ones closer to twenty. The first time she was given two Chesterfields in one night, she took them straight home out of fear for her safety and sat looking at them for a long while, elated, imagining the reckless joy of lighting one.

Her father shouted at her, even hit her once or twice, but without enthusiasm. He knew as well as she that they couldn't live off stray lumps of coal or potatoes picked up from train sidings. Sometimes men would question her age, but more often than not they were interested in finding a room, since she expressly refused to have them set foot in her family's apartment. She did not like every man she slept with, but the act felt revolutionary. Her body was her own to use and take pleasure in. It was not for men, nor Germany, nor children. Her body became a way of taking. She smoked in bed, drank liquor from the bottle. Of the two or three men she saw regularly, it was possible to demand a new pair of nylons, or shoes. When another family was moved into their apartment, she managed to get hold of a mattress, which maintained goodwill between them for the whole summer, soured eventually by certain pointed remarks about the hours Elsa kept, which led her to cut the mattress up with a bread knife. If one didn't want to get along with her, one wasn't obliged.

It was Theo who taught her to dance. He was a captain

with the Free French. For all that people had talked about rank throughout her childhood, Elsa had never learned quite how senior a captain was, but it seemed elevated enough to operate with impunity, which, after all, was what mattered.

She met him while interviewing for a post in the translation service, transcribing documents from German to French or vice versa. If her Russian and English had been better, she might have found work as an interpreter, but as it was she was confined to a typing pool in an office, listening to the other girls gossiping all day.

Captain Lambert would have a sheaf of new papers delivered to her in a batch, and send someone to collect whatever had been done by the end of the day. Sometimes, he would walk into the office himself with a single sheet that he had written out in longhand in French, and ask for it to be translated into German. Generally these were instructions for civilians or official correspondence with one of the German civil bodies that operated in the French Zone, and with which the French army were having to cooperate. He had a remarkable way of seeming to smile while keeping a perfectly straight face. She sometimes felt the two of them were communicating a private pleasure solely by the timing of their glances, their faces straight, their tone unwavering.

One day, he delivered a single sheet in French and asked that Elsa type it out in German. It was important enough for him to wait. He stood in the doorway, smoking, while she read his letter: *Dear Theo, Thank you for your kind invitation to meet me after work to watch the Badewanne performance. I would be delighted. Please meet me at the Femina at 8pm. Yours affectionately, Elsa.* She typed it out in German, rolled the paper out, clipped the translation to the original and held it up for him to take.

That night, she borrowed a pair of earrings from one of the other girls in the typing pool, promising not to trade them away on pain of death, and went home to change into her dress. She had no lipstick, no perfume. She so wanted to mark the occasion. She decided to wear her high heels, despite the long walk.

YOU ARE LEAVING THE FRENCH SECTOR

She passed the Tiergarten, holding her earrings tightly in her hands so they could not be ripped from her ears.

YOU ARE ENTERING THE AMERICAN SECTOR CARRYING WEAPONS OFF DUTY FORBIDDEN OBEY TRAFFIC RULES

Theo stood outside the entrance in high, wide trousers, smoking pure money. As she approached, putting on her earrings, his smile grew wider, and he took her inside on his arm. They had a table in a corner by the stage, from which they could survey the fauna of the new jazz scene, the Tommies and Amis, the Negroes, the black marketeers. High up on a wall above where the acts sat in mime costumes and feather boas, a crocheted motto: 'Let the world do its thing; my house shall be my resting place'.

Theo sent out for a bottle of French wine that wasn't on the menu, and they drank it together, Theo savouring the taste, Elsa watching how slowly the level of liquid in his glass went down and trying to keep pace, when instinct told her to throw it back. He asked a few questions about her life, but they were dead ends; she didn't want to talk and couldn't believe he would want the answers. He was free to indulge his memories, however, and told her all about growing up in the south of France, where it was never this cold. He spoke of the wide fields, the Riviera. There was good bread there, soft and white, not like the kind you got here, and the cheese was soft too, and creamy. When the rain fell, it turned the grass a Technicolor green. It hardly seemed possible to Elsa that such a place existed in the middle of Europe.

The night's acts varied, though Elsa didn't like any of them. They were surrealists and nihilists, determined to persuade the audience of their own pointlessness, and Elsa was inclined to let them have their victory. One act was a staged suicide. In another, a young woman got in a large champagne bucket – presumably the bathtub after which the cabaret was named – and several men proceeded to pour champagne over her, soaking through her slight clothing, while the accordion played in the corner. When Theo offered her a cigarette, she smoked half before stubbing it and trying, discreetly, to put it in her purse.

'Finish it,' he said. 'I'll give you another.'

Then, when the performance finished and the music started, he pulled her up, and showed her how to dance the boogie. He made it look easy, but she soon found herself flushed keeping up, and nearly screamed when he grabbed her by the waist and flipped her over in a somersault. She found she couldn't stop laughing. It must be the wine, or the warmth in the room. She hadn't been in a warm room for what seemed like years. One could feel the bodies radiating heat. He took her to one side and stroked her hair and kissed her, on the cheek. She looked into his handsome face. He was half distracted by the music, but still she couldn't stop smiling. It seemed to her then that he was exactly how a man was meant to be. As natural as Elsa was studied. Not that he wasn't capable of reading people, but that it didn't much matter to him. The world would go his way without intervention. She could never feel that way herself – to her, the world was a bloody struggle – but she liked to see it in him.

'I've been wondering something,' Theo said as they walked back through the unlit streets together. 'Why do people write 88 on the walls, and on our trucks?'

'I don't know,' she replied. H was the eighth letter of the alphabet. It meant *Heil Hitler*. Elsa found the scrawlings profoundly irritating. Who wouldn't want to break with the past by now? As they stopped outside her father's shop – her real address – she found herself asking whether she would see him again.

'Of course,' he replied. 'I'll see you tomorrow.'

He planted his lips on her cheeks, close to her mouth. And he smiled at her as if he had already won her, and she had only to realise it.

His conduct in their courtship was impeccable. Elsa gradually stopped seeing other men, occasionally mentioning the captain to her parents when recounting her day at the office. Theo would turn up at her desk occasionally, but never often enough to arouse suspicion of fraternisation, standing in the doorway with a perfectly straight face and another urgent letter. Elsa would read through what she was about to write to him, pleased and frustrated by the act of ventriloquism.

'Thank you, Elsa,' he would say as he took the translation and original from her. 'With your help, my German is improving immeasurably.'

It was certainty he was offering her, and she knew it. She need only continue along the prescribed course. No one mentioned love. But then, the idea of love seemed faintly absurd to Elsa. What would one do with it?

One day, Theo stood in the doorway and asked quietly whether Elsa might come into his office. The other girls glanced over, smiling at their keys. He wasn't, after all, so very different from the other men, but had taken longer to feel at ease with what he wanted. He held the door open for her and she took a seat – the same seat she had taken during her interview. He closed the door and sat down in his own chair, keeping the desk between them.

'I'm sorry to interrupt your work,' he said.

'I don't care about that,' she said, nervous suddenly at having admitted it, since he was acting so much like her superior. All else being equal, she did need the job, and the money.

'No, I don't suppose you do.' He smiled to himself. 'There is so much going on outside.'

They sat for a moment listening to the sound of a plane overhead. At one point, not so long ago, the Soviets had cut off all access to West Berlin, and the whole population had been under siege. For almost a year, the city had been supplied by air, with planes taking off and landing at a rate of one a minute.

'You're leaving, aren't you?' asked Elsa. Theo caught her eyes and looked down at the desk. He nodded.

'My father is setting up a new business in France and wants me to help him run it. I've been here almost five years. I could be demobilised as early as June.'

'That's good news,' said Elsa. 'I imagine you'll be glad to leave.' Elsa thought she might be, too, in his position.

'I wanted to ask if you would think of coming with me,' he said.

That was the real shock – not that he was leaving, but that he would consider bringing a little piece of the wreckage home with him to lie in his bed and eat his soft bread.

'We'd have to be married, of course, or you wouldn't get a visa. There shouldn't be a problem. You were a child when it all happened. Anyway, Father has a lawyer to deal with export visas, so I expect we can get help if we should need it.'

'Is this a proposal?'

'Only if it's a yes.'

Elsa shook her head at the thought of it. Then, seeing his face, she reached across and took his hand.

'Will you come for dinner one night? I would love you to meet my parents.'

There followed a flurry of activity at home, including the difficult negotiations, conducted between mothers, for the other family to leave the apartment for the evening. All the while, Elsa's father followed her between rooms, lamenting that she had made the invitation, that he must entertain the enemy, that they would have to feed him with bread from their own mouths. It was only fair that the British and Americans should occupy their city – difficult as it was to swallow, they had after all been beaten – but the French had not fought at all, and it was wrong for them to claim a part in the victory. The French had even welcomed them into their country as allies, and now they claimed to stand with the enemy. Well, it was too much.

The evening that Theo came to dinner, Elsa's mother kept the conversation alive with a determination Elsa had rarely seen in her. Elsa found herself deeply grateful for her mother's agreeableness, which had always previously struck Elsa as vaguely contemptible. Her father, on the other hand, sat back with his arms folded in an attitude of belligerence. He discharged his duty not to jeopardise the prospect of a marriage, but without conceding anything as undignified as approval. Seated between them like a condemned prisoner was Theo. He thanked Elsa's mother for everything that was put in front of him, ate all of it and declined seconds, complimenting the family on their home without condescending, despite the obvious difficulty of finding anything positive to say. Throughout their meagre meal, he steered between icebergs of unpleasantness with such grace that Elsa found herself truly drawn to him; now that the decision was effectively taken, it was as if she had permission to be proud of his many good qualities, since they would be present in her children and were now in some way hers. They would have good children; the phrase that came to her was *biologically valuable*.

Thinking back on her wedding day, it occurred to Elsa that she had never explicitly agreed to marry him. As she sat in her dress at the vanity table, she had felt strangely disembodied. She could see herself in the mirror, beaming from three angles. This is real, she told herself. This is real. Theo had proposed a life to her, and it had seemed greatly preferable to the one she had, and it promised a shedding of moral debt, to be in France, with a French husband. The dresser pinned her hair up, and she thought, *Enjoy this, this is the most beautiful you will ever look, don't cry before the photographs. It is for the best your mother is to give you away; you love your mother. Best not to feel the tension in your father's arm, nor catch a glance between him and Theo.*

Her brother wasn't here to see her. She hoped he wasn't anywhere. If he were, it would be in a work camp, stamping a shovel into solid, icy ground, or picking away in the pitch darkness of a mine. He'd have loved it here, a beautiful old church in the south of France. If only he had found a way to stay.

They had agreed Theo would not wear his uniform today. She wished she could wait with him, watch him shave his face smooth and neatly part his hair. She wished they could go out together to face their relatives, arriving as a couple, instead of feeling their eyes on her alone, his family stood at both sides because so few of hers were present, as she approached him at the far end of the chapel, watching his back, thinking about tripping on her dress or on the slight furrows of the red runner.

She didn't expect him to be perfect. But that was a good thing – it would be hard to disappoint her. No – that made it sound tragic. Rather, she saw that he was human. And he was charming. He offered before she thought to ask. He seemed to perceive weaknesses in everyone, and forgive them. Young though he was during the war, he must have made a formidable enemy. And his wealth was not a cold consideration. How could anyone contemplate their future without an idea of its security? Did anyone ever wish for hardship? Elsa didn't accept that it was wrong to

love him in part for his money. The truly cruel choice would be
to bring a child into the world without knowing how to feed or
clothe it.

Her mother stood behind her.

'Dreaming already?'

'I didn't hear you come in.'

'You look so beautiful. Are you nervous?'

'Why should I be nervous?'

Her mother said nothing, only smiled.

Two months later, Elsa stood at the kitchen window, looking
out at the fields and the aqueduct on the other side of the village.
This was the quiet world Theo had promised her. Peace of mind.
The country air. The birds had been singing when they came to
see it, and she had thought how glorious it would be to live in a
house filled with birdsong. But when they moved in they found
that the birds flew off and didn't visit for days and, when they
did, they whistled in the night.

It had all looked quite splendid when they had first come to
visit. There was a neat little garden and the previous owners had
painted the front steps a deep ochre. Red steps! What would the
neighbours say? There was a beautiful hardwood door, and you
could see by the grain that it had all been one tree. She liked
to imagine it as a great oak, standing sentinel over the ancient
woods nearby, guarding the inhabitants. Inside, a carpeted
lounge and a large kitchen overlooking the village. Upstairs, a
bedroom, with a smaller, second room off to the right – a study,
perhaps, or a bedroom for a child.

Theo had already been to see the house with his agent; he had
only asked Elsa to look at it once he had made his decision, as
if her permission were part of the due diligence. She'd told him
that she was sure if he was sure. She told him she trusted him.

She told him he knew what she liked. But he wanted her to see it anyway. Perhaps he didn't want the responsibility of having chosen. Perhaps she didn't either. What if she chose this place, and they hung up paintings, and filled the cupboards, and what if it was perfect, and she wasn't happy? If she knew by process of elimination that the problem was hers, that it resided within her and that she had brought it here, just as she would bring it to any house? Perhaps she hadn't thought that at the time, and was only imagining it now. In the months after their marriage, neither of them had refused the other anything. They had agreed instantly, manically, every assent standing as proof of destiny.

Three weeks after they moved in, Elsa had tried to bake a cake for her new neighbours, whom they had invited around on the Sunday. She had discovered larvae and cocoon shells in the flour as she kneaded it. She had crushed some of them without noticing. A live one squirmed in agony on the ball of her thumb. She threw out everything in the house, cleaned out all the cupboards and bleached the floors.

From that day on, she had nightmares that they were in the food. Theo assured her there was no harm done – *it's maggots you have to watch for, moth larvae aren't poisonous* – but she kept imagining the little worms growing inside their stomachs and intestines. One night, standing on the cold flagstones of the kitchen in the moonlight, she drank a tall glass of whisky so that she might flush them out, if they were there. She was terribly ill, and spent most of the night in the toilet at the bottom of the garden, listening to the screams of foxes and the rustling of terrified hedgehogs. She was back in bed before dawn. Theo didn't notice. To him, sleep was something that dragged one off by the feet; when he read in bed, he would bookmark each new page, like a climber clipping himself onto a new peg. His mother said he had slept through his own christening.

In the mornings, she found herself spitting at the sink, hoping for some trace, some confirmation of an invasive body. She made herself sick once or twice more, as one might if they were poisoned, but there was nothing. Somehow, not finding the expected evidence was worse, as if confirmation would have soothed her that this was not a disease of the mind. And yet she knew there was something inside her, digging in, feeding. It made her so tired she would lean on the kitchen counter, aching from the cold, even though it was late spring, and stare at the aqueduct for minutes at a time, listening to her heart beat in her ears. One day the sweet peas on her windowsill died, and she cried as she picked up the dead buds and threw them out the back door onto the dry compost heap.

At dinner, Theo would try to coerce her into feeling better, or at least feeling bad about not feeling better. The sight of pork made her feel sick, and when she told him so, he dutifully speared it onto his own plate and asked whether he could make her something else.

'I don't want anything,' she said.

'It doesn't matter if you don't want pork,' he replied reasonably. 'You have to eat something.' He took her hand. 'Come on. What would you like?'

She felt tears welling up.

'I don't want anything,' she said.

Theo bowed his head, which was his restrained way of showing exasperation, and rolled all her peas onto his plate. He ate her pork chop in silence, while she felt the cold creeping up her shins and along her forearms. She folded her arms over her swollen, aching breasts. When he was done, he took up the plates and placed them in the sink for her to deal with in the morning, picked her up from the chair and carried her to bed. He went to sit by the fire with the newspaper for half an hour, utterly untouched. To him, none of this was war. When he was finished, he came through, undressed, and lay down next to her, his weight tipping her towards him. She put a hand on his chest as it rose and fell, and was about to speak when he started to snore softly. She lay listening to his breathing, wondering whether first to apologise, or to insist that he understand what was happening to her, or leave a note and run away from this place altogether, back to Berlin, as if this were an elaborate pretence, and she was not an adult, nor married, nor living in France, nor pregnant.

The moths kept on breeding. She bought mothballs. It was hardly a secret why moths didn't like them; anything with a nose didn't like them. If anything, it made her resent them all the more because they lived like her. They felt the chill. They seemed to subsist on flour. They couldn't stand the smell of mothballs. They sometimes struggled to embrace the light. Their wings were dusty, and unlike those of butterflies would fold away neatly, as if the ground was theirs.

Elsa wondered whether she might have a little girl. She opened the wardrobe and took out her wedding dress. It was the loveliest thing she had ever owned. She had always intended to keep it for her daughter, when she had one. It was not the pure, artificial white of so many dresses – it was the natural colour of silk, a lovely milky white, which had shone as she turned in the sun.

She laid it on the bed and pulled off the cover. It was shot through with holes. It was as if her fears had been confirmed and the little beasts were living within her, shedding and unfolding and flying from her mouth while she slept.

When the time came for Elsa to give birth, her heart wouldn't stop pounding. A woman from the village, whom she barely knew, began ordering her around, telling her to use the bathroom. She didn't remember ever having asked for her; perhaps it was decided by Theo. He waited in his armchair with a drink. She needed him as the terror seized her, needed his calm assurance, his love. For once she was desperate for his certainty, his presumption that all would be well, as she slid off the edge of her lived experience, not knowing when or where she might land. She lay on the bed, alternating between dread and pain. The dread was worse, for now. She had the urge to flee, but the object of her fear was internal, inescapable, like a grave illness. The pain came in slow waves. A deep, wounded howl, her own.

She cried out for Theo, over and over. Had he left, or was he listening from his armchair? Did her suffering not move him? *Fuck you*, she spat, *you coward. I hate you.* Other words came to her, words she hadn't heard or uttered since she was a child, and she forced them back. No one would ever hear enough to piece the whole of her together.

The stranger pushed her legs wider. Theo wanted to be with her, he must want to. He had left to preserve her dignity. Would he leave her side at her deathbed, too? She lost control and, at certain points, had to be restrained by the midwife, who chided as she pushed Elsa back into her pillows. *Stop this,* hissed the midwife. *You'll frighten the baby.*

She was told to push harder, and she pushed to be rid of it, to be left alone. Pushed because she was stuck, rooted to the pain, and the only way was to tear it out. She pushed again. Again. The midwife lifted it away. She panted. It was still attached. The cord was cut. The midwife pushed painfully on Elsa's stomach, and the placenta came. Elsa wanted to close her legs now, lie on her side, but the baby was placed on top of her, curled up and puckering. It made her think of the *alp* of bedtime stories, sitting heavily astride girls' ribs in the night and sucking the milk from their breasts. *Wad up the keyholes,* she thought, as she drifted into sleep.

It was a boy – Pascal after Theo's father. She spent the next six months on the brink of tears, vacillating between fear – that this little boy had been entrusted to her care, and that she didn't know how to care for him – and flashes of awareness that there was more beauty in the world than a person could conceive. She would wake up at five and listen to the birdsong, watch the sun rising over the viaduct and the fields, the birds twitching and flitting between the trees, the sky above her still steeped in night. The perfect cold of those mornings reached the joints of her toes and knuckles. On windy days, clouds of birds would puff up into the air, swirling around on unseen currents. Then the baby would start crying, and she would calculate the hours until his nap as she went to feed him.

Once, she watched past dawn as a great murmuration of starlings, tens of thousands strong, blotted the pink sky. They shifted and spread, now a gathering tornado, now a mushroom cloud, now a snake or river, and it felt true, more so than the sound of the boy upstairs, crying on and on, or his breath catching in his father's arms, or Theo in his dressing gown, shaking her, shouting. What did it have to do with her? She shrugged him off and walked down into the field to get a better view of the sky. Alight, roost, launch, climb, bank, glide away.

5

RALF, Paris, June 1958

Ralf arrived early and stood with his face to the sun, trying to see whether he could cheat time by not thinking or moving. Her note had arrived a few days earlier, simply telling him to meet her in the Tuileries today at one o'clock, making no allowances for the possibility that he wasn't free. He understood why, now – she had a husband. He rolled his shirtsleeves up, avoiding his watch face. This had to be the fountain she had described, and yet he imagined her standing by another just like it elsewhere. He could have used the time to explore the gardens and make sure, but by now he had left it too late to abandon his post. She was still not here. It was still early. Looking around, he saw that a goat had been tethered to one of the garden's slopes, and was eating the grass that the lawn-mowers couldn't reach.

He saw her approaching. She had dressed as she meant to be remembered. She wore a dress of polka dots, fanning out from the hips, her shoulders bare. Her lipstick was bright and red. And this was how Elsa would remember him: dishevelled, with rolled-up sleeves, like a bank clerk on a busy day. He was freshly shaven but his aftershave had run out, and he couldn't stand to wear another. As Elsa reached him he felt odourless, unable to cast an impression.

She raised her clutch bag as if to hit him and he raised his arms, smiling.

'I haven't done anything this time,' he said.

'You have.'

'I should be the one hitting you.'

'I'm glad you won't. I've seen how hard you hit.'

Ralf stared into the fountain. 'I'm really angry with you for not telling me,' he said quietly.

'I didn't think I needed to tell you.'

'Was I supposed to guess?'

'You refused to know.'

He turned towards her without looking directly at her. Her neck looked thin, weak like a bird's. A modestly sized pearl glowed in her ear. He turned back to the fountain.

'So – tell me. About your childhood, about Germany, about him.'

'What is the point? You don't want to hear the answers.'

'I do.'

'No, Ralf, you don't. You never asked me about myself because you wanted to sequester yourself in the present. We both did.'

'That's not true. I opened up to you. I wanted you to know me. I've told you about parts of my life that I've never—'

'When? You mean your father? Ralf, it's sad, it's terribly sad, what happened, but it was thirty years ago. Your life and his are different eras. So much has happened since, they were barely . . . I'm not saying this to be cruel.'

'Saying what, exactly?'

'You are not your father.'

'I didn't claim to be.'

'He doesn't explain you. This is your life.'

Ralf looked hard at her.

'No, this is not my life. We may struggle one way but we are all being dragged another by our heritage, by history.'

'But you can't let that history define you.'

'Do you think your life would be the same if you were ugly? Deformed, even? If you were born a hundred years ago?'

'That's it, Ralf, you are bound to a wheel.'

She swept her skirts behind her knees and sat in the middle of the gravel.

'What are you doing? Get up.'

'No.'

'What are you doing?'

'It's pointless to struggle. I shall sit here and life can find me.'

'Yes, very good.'

'I'm serious.'

'You're getting dirt on your lovely dress.'

She squinted up at him as if he were the sun.

'It's what history wants.'

'Oh, come on.'

Ralf bent down and put his shoulder to her stomach, lifting and tipping her in a fireman's lift. She shrieked as she turned upside down.

'This is not very dignified,' she said to his bottom as he walked.

'History is a bumpy ride,' he replied.

'Put me down.'

He set her down in the shade of a tree. He knelt to her, unsure whether he still had tacit permission to kiss her, or whether that was over. She pointed up above his head. A fat, green caterpillar was moving along a branch.

'You know what they do to silk moths?' said Elsa. 'They boil them alive and unravel the whole cocoon using tiny looms.'

'I didn't know that.'

'No. All sorts of things have happened here. I think it's untoward for a garden to have so much history.'

'Elsa.'

She looked up at him innocently.

'Yes?'

'What do you want from me?' he asked.

'Ralf.'

'Anything.'

'No.'

In his frustration, Ralf felt an urge to control her, to physically contain her. His fingers closed around her arm so hard that he could feel the bone.

'You'll find someone else,' she whispered.

'No. It has to be you.'

Elsa's eyes began to well.

'Will you please let me go?'

'Say that you love me.'

She shook her head.

'Or that you loved me once. Elsa.'

She put her arms up between his and tried to push him off.

'I have a boy, Ralf. I have a family. Even if I love you, I already had a chance at a life, and it may not be—'

'What? It may not be what?'

'But I took it. I already made my choice.'

'You came to me.'

'I'm not disowning my actions.'

'Why? Why did you need me, if nothing was missing?'

'I thought I needed something else – something more than I have.'

'But it turned out that you didn't? It was simply a useful exercise, to be reminded of your options?'

'Can I not have more than one reason? And what does it matter, if we can't be together?'

'Is it really all a game to you?'

'No, it's not. I wanted it to be. I had an idea that we might both derive some simple pleasure from it. I didn't know we would get far enough for this.'

'Were there others?'

'Ralf, please—'

'Answer me.'

'No.' She opened her bag and took out a clean handkerchief. 'Who do you think I am?'

Ralf couldn't be angry. She looked so human. He had never been angry at her, not really, but had tried to be for the sake of his pride.

'It was never fun, for me,' he said. 'It was always love.'

She nodded. 'Yes. I know.'

'This is it, then.'

'Yes.'

She took him by the hand and they walked east, on past the floral candelabra of the chestnuts and the Louvre. They walked the streets in quiet expectation, holding each other's hands tentatively, like children on a ledge. Her hair blew across her face and she didn't stop it, seeming to Ralf constantly on the brink of a declaration. Ralf felt a reckless joy at knowing their time was spent, so that every action had an impressive air of finality: the last time he stopped to let her through a narrow gap; the last time he touched her lower back; the last time he gave her a cigarette; the last time he lit it; the last time she looked up at him, willing him to beg. Stoking the burning full stop of the cigarette's tip. Sucking in poison, breathing out sea spray. She reached up and held his jaw in her palm, regarding him coolly as she took another drag.

'Ralf, my love, let's go before it gets too dark.'

'Yes, I suppose we ought to. Shall we take the river?'

They were alone on the path.

'You don't have to come back with me,' said Ralf.

'What do you mean? Don't you want—?'

'No, I do. But if you feel you'd rather get back, I won't be . . . I'll understand.'

'Ralf, I want to stay with you tonight. I know you will think ill of me, but I want to try to make you understand before I go.'

'I will never think ill of you.'

'You will. You'll resent me, in the end, thinking I have strung you along, denied you a life to protect my own. Perhaps you'll think me a coward for not wanting to take a leap into the dark, for standing at the edge and being too afraid to really jump. But I assure you the only choice I have now is between varieties of misery. I just want a last evening with you, so that I can memorise everything. I want to rebuild your room in my head – the warp of your staircase, the view of the rooftops, your stove, your bookcase, your armchair, your rumpled bedsheets – so that I can go there any time and be safe, and no one can find me.'

'Be safe?'

'Yes. And lie down out of reach.'

'Of Theo?'

'Of anyone. Out of time. You've never wanted anything from me, never demanded anything except that I exist. Don't you think that was perfect, that timeless haven in your room, even if it couldn't last?'

Ralf put his hand against the stone balustrade while they waited to cross the street. The booksellers along the river were putting up their boards for the day.

'I'd have made a number of demands if I ever thought you'd meet them, but I always felt you'd slip away at first light.'

'Ralf, there is nothing we could have done.'

'That's not true. We could run away right now. We are only ten minutes' walk from Saint-Lazare. We could get on the next train.'

'And do what? Run a guest house? Become seaside photographers?'

'It is a choice, Elsa. It is still a choice you are making.'

'Please, let's not argue again.'

They walked in silence along the rue de la Verrerie, past a family of Orthodox Jews dressed in black and white, walking patiently down the narrow paving in single file, led by a solemn young boy, his dark ringlets bouncing. Elsa trod carefully along the cobbles, past the cheese shop, past Speiser's.

'I've always wondered why you live here,' said Elsa, 'when you barely have a drop of Jewish blood in you.'

'Well, it's cheap enough.'

'Half of Paris is cheap enough. It doesn't seem much of a coincidence.'

Ralf thought for a few steps as they passed the synagogue.

'I don't know. Maybe it comforts me to see others belong.'

'Because you feel that you don't.'

'I have never felt that I belong anywhere.'

'You're on first-name terms with almost everyone in the street.'

'Dague is a racist. I don't even know Jacques' surname. They aren't my people.'

'But that's just it – belonging means indulging people you don't like, yawning through church and putting party hats on other people's ghastly children once a year. In return, someone will notice if you fall ill. You don't have to like them all.'

'Are you hungry?' Ralf asked.

'I'm fucking starving.'

'Let's stop here.'

They found a window table at Jo Goldenberg's, where they had beef brisket with a bottle of wine, commenting on the people walking past to draw themselves back together, to see the world through a single eye again. Jacques passed the window, blinking in a daylight unfiltered by dirty windows, to deliver a boy to his mother by the scruff of the neck. Two old women compared their groceries, one apparently disappointed with the leaves of her cabbage.

Ralf and Elsa fell into a cordial silence after their meal, in the afterglow of shared food, sipping violet liqueur, watching Paris go about its business, her hand on his, and they smoked, smiling to themselves at the quiet rebellion of this public gesture, as if they were teenagers eloping. Then round the back, through the courtyard, as the light thinned. Up the narrow wooden stairs. On each landing, they could see the windows of neighbouring buildings until they were level with the rooftops, the skyline glimpsed through the gaps. They stood on the landing, their faces almost touching, he looking at her just to see, just to exist in sight of her. Her gaze flitted between his eyes, as if to check his attention was really on her, and not something behind her, and a smile broke across her face, balanced on the moment, tipping over into sorrow. As she fell into him, grabbing his waist, her cheek against his shoulder and her small breasts pressed against his lower ribs, he felt absurdly as if it were he leaving her, as if a kind word were the only thing necessary for her to take up grateful residence in his apartment.

'I love you,' he murmured into her hair. She sobbed and clung to him. He stroked her back, trying to soothe her. He murmured to her, calm as the sea, until she pulled away to find a dry corner of her handkerchief. Ralf let them in and they settled themselves, taking off their shoes and taking it in turns to cross the landing. Ralf went over to his record player and slid his Satie from its dust cover, matching the disc to the platter and dropping it over the pin. He started the belt and placed the stylus onto the first ring of the dense spiral. It crackled over invisible dust. Then it started up, the tentative waltz settling into languor. The tempo *slow and forlorn*. Elsa joined him. He took her hand and her hip, his cheek to her temple, and they swayed. The last time they would dance together. He drew her closer and combed his fingers through the hair at the back of her head, feeling the tightness where it was pinned up. It would have been almost impossible to see them dancing; their movements were slight. Ralf closed his eyes as the mood of the song clouded over, offered a counter-argument. It turned hopeful, unresolved, then repeated on itself, reliving the first bars. They stood still. The piece was only a couple of minutes long, but over its course they had crossed the threshold into their private world, and now only the two of them existed.

Ralf went to the cupboard for wine, taking down two glasses. He worked a knife into the cork, twisting and levering. Elsa sat forward in the armchair, hands on knees, as he carved it out of the bottle. Ralf had expected sarcasm or laughter, but she sat patiently until the wine was poured.

'Sorry about that,' Ralf said.

'About what?'

'The corkscrew is broken.'

'Oh, don't be silly. It looked rather fun.'

She loosened his tie, slipping one end through the knot and throwing it on the floor. He undid his top button.

'To your health,' he said.

'No! That's too dull.'

'To Paris.'

'Paris doesn't care about us.'

'Well – to us, then.'

'Yes. To us.'

Their glasses tolled together like distant bells. He put his down and reached back up through her hair, pulling out pins, trying not to snag them.

'I'm not made of porcelain,' she whispered.

He smiled, but continued as before, stopping once so she might sip her wine. She looked younger with her hair down, truer, somehow, her impulse showing through her poise. The last time he took off his tie; the last time she let down her hair.

'Earlier,' he began.

'Yes?'

'When we were walking down to the river. You said "my love".' Her lips tensed. He prompted: 'I don't like the idea we can't see each other, but to believe that it meant nothing . . .'

'Please don't do this, Ralf.'

'I only want you to tell me you love me.'

'I can't. I can't. Don't you understand? You're making it harder.'

'Then why are you here? If it's so important that you leave, why don't you leave?'

Ralf stood. Elsa remained sitting. She held her hands, folded her elbows into her stomach, curling around them like paper in a fire, sooty tears falling between the polka dots of her dress.

He studied the scene, watching to see what he would do. What did he want himself to do? He reached out his hand to her. She made no move towards him. He wished they could return to their earlier intimacy, but perhaps it would always spiral in on this moment.

'I'm sorry,' he said.

She was crying steadily now, and he went over to a drawer for a clean handkerchief. The act of passing it to her seemed to quell her tears, and she dabbed the inside corners of her eyes, which were ringed by make-up, the corona of an eclipse in negative.

'You're a bit smudged,' he said. She went to wash her face, moving tentatively as if sadness had stiffened her joints.

He thought about turning on the radio but baulked at the idea of channelling the outside world, so he turned over the Satie and put the needle down on the *Gnossiennes*.

She returned with her face scrubbed and pink, her lips swollen from the effort of crying, a thin strand of hair stuck to her forehead.

'I look horrid,' she said.

'No,' he said. 'You are the most beautiful woman I have ever met. When I look at you I could forget to eat or sleep.' She shook her head. 'I have tried to hold something back, but I may as well have tried to throw a stone into orbit. I can't do it any more. I give up. I love you.'

'You don't.'

'I do. You think I'm only in love because I can't see every-thing, and that if I could, I wouldn't love you. But I do see you, and I know who you are, and I love you.'

Elsa kissed him, pushing him back until he could feel the edge of the bed against the backs of his legs. She pushed him down on the bed, knees on the edge, holding his collar so tight in her fist that he could hear the thread of a button snap.

'I love you,' she said, her face so close that he couldn't hold her in focus. He felt a surge of loyalty – he wanted her, he had her, she was his – and he gazed at her as she undid his shirt, pulled her dress over her head, so caught up watching the moment fulfil itself that he fell still within it.

'What's wrong?' she asked.

'Nothing is wrong,' he said tenderly. 'I am happy. This is perfect. You are perfect.'

And he lifted her and placed her gently on her back, her head on his hand on the pillow, and she closed her eyes as he kissed them one by one, and he took off her bra so that he might run his hands over her skin without breaking contact, her hands on his shoulders and arms, exactly as if she were memorising his contours.

They lay side by side, perfectly tessellated: right arm over left shoulder, left arm around waist, left legs interlocked. It was perfect, or would have been, if that had been Ralf's last day, but our lives go on and on, if we let them.

In the darkness, his hand reached out for her warmth, and found the familiar indentation, shaped in a soft negative of her presence. The cold pillow cupped around her absence. The cold mattress and the flat blanket. He listened for a sound from the pipes or the stove, but there was nothing. Around him was the darkness of the Marais, a timeless, oceanic darkness that approached black without ever reaching it.

She could be anywhere. She could have caught a train. She could have returned home. She could be across the landing right now, hands balled against the cold. And yet somehow he knew she was not. She would have clambered over him, left the blankets pulled back.

He moved over to her side of the bed, looking for some physical reassurance, a make-up mark on the pillow cover or a blonde hair. He moved across and lay where she had been, in the cold. He tried to lie like her, curled up, facing the window.

By degrees, the light began to work its way through the gaps in the shutters. It was quiet enough for him to hear the bell of Saint-Paul-Saint-Louis striking seven. He stayed like that, lying there, as the bell chimed its way through quarter-hours, not wanting a day without her to start. He heard the baby in the next apartment crying. His own apartment barely had room for one, and he wondered where the young family could all fit.

Her underwear was on the floor under his shirt. She might still be here. She might have been taken in the night. He would have woken. And no criminal would walk the ninety-six steps to his room when all the valuables were in ground-floor shops.

An hour passed. Two. He got up to relieve himself. She was not there. He put his hands on the cold porcelain of the sink and looked at himself as if his own impassive face might hold some clue. It was light enough to shave now. He unscrewed the bulb above the sink and carefully placed it on the floor in the corner, picking up the thieving plug and screwing it into the light fitting, before plugging in the razor. He shaved his sideburns, his neck, his chin, his moustache. He looked back at the disappointing familiarity of his face and wondered about growing his facial hair, obscuring his features in some way.

There was a letter on his doormat. And of course it wasn't from her, because why then would it be addressed and stamped, but even knowing it wasn't from her he felt a thrill on picking it up, thinking that it might contain some cryptic note. *Today I opened the cage of the macaw and in the confusion I fled,* or *I have killed him, I can't move him on my own.* As the flap of the envelope sheared open, it occurred to him that she might have posted it on the way to the Tuileries, knowing that she would be gone before it arrived. It might contain words of comfort or even of hope. *Pack your bags and meet me at Saint-Lazare.* But this was idle nonsense, because the address specified France, and the stamp was English, and the letter, when he unfolded it, was written in his mother's cramped, parsimonious hand, on tissue-thin paper, the pen pressed so lightly as to fail to draw ink on certain letters, so that the paper might not tear.

Ralf went back inside and sat in the armchair. The letter said *My darling Ralf.* The letter said she had marked the anniversary of his father's death alone last week. The letter said that she had gone to the local cemetery and laid fresh flowers on a headstone that had weathered to blankness. The letter said she knew very well it was not his grave, but it cheered her to think that it might be, and laying fresh-cut flowers down was a way of thanking whoever was really buried there, and unforgetting them. Fresh-cut flowers. I found this beautiful: I killed it for you.

The letter said she thought of Emil every day, without exaggeration, and that despite the pain it still made her happier to mourn him, and to talk to him as if he were there beside her, than if he had never lived and died. The letter said she knew he would have hated the idea that she talked to him, and he would have tried to remain patient as he explained that he was nothing but a group of cells that had found a way to band together and replicate and protect one another, and that what she called Emil was only the continuity of those cells, living and dying every second, but carrying each other through space and time, and when that continuity ended, Emil no longer existed. And she knew what her response would be: he had shown her how his brain worked over fourteen beautiful years, and she had moulded her thoughts to his, until she had a faithful copy of him that nothing could destroy, not even Emil, and so even if she had lost her faith, and knew that she could not reach out to him, nor even picture him, she could still talk to him just as she could still love him.

The letter said she hoped that Ralf would find such a love, one day, and that he would know when he had found it, and when he did, he must do everything to keep hold of it, because it might not come again, as it had not for her.

Ralf read back over the letter with his coffee. It was a bright day. It would be the perfect day to receive Elsa. He imagined that she had gone home to change – she might be downstairs now, sat in a chair with her gloves on, talking politely with M. Dague, waiting for Ralf to appear. He wished there were a way to know whether there was anything he could have done to keep her. She had said she loved him, but even if she did, he had nothing to offer her; he had no career, no possessions. She hadn't been crass enough to say as much, but he wasn't a complete fool. He wanted to tell her that whatever happened, it would be good – if she entrusted herself to him, he would make sure of it. They could live wherever she wanted, do whatever she wanted. He would make whatever sacrifice was necessary. He only wanted her by his side.

He walked down through M. Dague's shop.

'Good morning, my brave,' said Dague, who was sat at the bottom of the stairs by the telephone. 'A late start?'

'Yes,' Ralf said abstractedly. 'You didn't see a . . . you didn't see anyone this morning, did you?'

'Not a soul. And I should know – I haven't moved all morning. These newspapers seem to get longer and longer. Anyone would think more is happening in the world than it was ten years ago, but the reality is that people only want to talk. When I was young, being talkative was a kind of laziness. We admired men of action.'

'Yes.'

Ralf sat down in a waiting chair.

'I would send you out for apricots, but it's no use – you never remember. Besides, Nicolle is . . . ah, here we are, my beloved, ham and Emmental, and it comes with my wife in tow.'

M. Dague beamed up at his wife, who put the little bundle down on the coffee table next to Ralf's knee.

'Good morning, Ralf,' she said.

'Good morning, Mme Dague.'

'Is everything all right? You look as if someone has walked over your grave.'

'He's fine, stop bothering the boy.'

Nicolle sat down in the other waiting chair, next to him. She was about his mother's age, and had arrived at the time of life when all one's hardest edges are buried beneath soft tissue, her expression achingly sympathetic.

'I won't pry,' she said. 'I know the last thing you want is someone telling you they have felt the same, because it doesn't seem like it could be true. But the only way to think of it is that, if it were going to happen, it would have. If you know that you tried. Yves and I were never blessed with children, but we didn't want children with anyone else. This is the love we were meant to have.'

M. Dague was still smiling, but more as if encouraging himself than exuding happiness.

'Life is not a picture postcard,' he said. 'One cannot practise, nor make decisions twice. But it is better that way. What would life be like if one could plan it out in advance?'

Ralf bowed his head and felt the warmth of Nicolle's hand on his shoulder.

'There is always tomorrow,' said Ralf.

'There is always tomorrow, until there isn't,' M. Dague chuckled, wagging a finger. Nicolle shot him a look.

'Thank you both. I'll be fine. I just thought – this time . . . but it's already so late in the day, I had better . . . Thank you.'

Ralf got up in a daze and walked out the door. It always sounded so simple when it happened to someone else. You find someone you like. You promise to be kind to one another. One of you makes the sandwiches, the other dotes. It was all well and good to say, *this was the love we were meant to have*, but perhaps none of it was meant. Perhaps it was just happening to people.

This felt so much like the end, but it was a beginning, it had to be, because time was not lived along a line: it was a series of cycles, some describing their circle in a minute, some taking hours, or days, or years. One saw the true shape of time in the tides or seasons, some in their whole course achieving only a step in another, larger cycle, seconds in minutes in hours, phases of a moon, spinning round the Earth, spinning round the sun. Each of these cycles had its idiosyncrasies: the moon spun in perfect alignment with Earth, so that one only ever saw the same half of its globe; perhaps stranger still, the moon was four hundred times smaller than the sun, and four hundred times closer to Earth, making the two bodies appear almost exactly the same size, so that ours was one of very few planets to experience a perfect lunar eclipse. That was how life sometimes appeared, to Ralf: the personal seemed to eclipse by its very proximity the grand events of history, of which he only ever felt he could observe the corona. But we all share suns, never moons.

Ralf went out and bought a *croque*. It had really been the last time, even though he had allowed himself to believe there must be some loophole, some last-minute overturning. The city was beginning to empty out for the summer already, the traffic intermittent and lazy, no one on the pavements. Everything in its season.

A wasp weaved back and forth across Ralf's vision, interested in the ultraviolets of his white shirt. Summer had arrived late this year, and they were frantic. Convinced it had found a god among flowers, the wasp looked for the hidden entrance to the nectar around Ralf's collar. Ralf batted the wasp forcefully to the floor and trod it into the stone. He bought a packet of filtered cigarettes, to see whether there was any difference. He found a new café on the rue des Barres, wedged next to Saint-Gervais-et-Saint-Protais, with its thin Gothic spires, and sat looking up at the gargoyles, jutting out ready to spit rainwater on passers-by. The sharp light drew new intricacies in the crenellations, flying buttresses sticking out of the roof tiling as if the building were still half finished all these centuries later. He did not look at the couples gathered here, nor at the children chasing and hitting one another as they tripped along the cobbles. Ivy had over-taken the building next door, a little porthole cut out for the window. He transferred the cigarettes to his case, crumpling the carton. He had two matches left. This was a beginning. It was a beginning.

Ralf had been drinking before he arrived at Jacques', hanging his new hat on the rack. It struck him that not a single fixture had changed since he had moved into the area. It had not been renovated, nor visibly degraded. Its very lack of regard for the arrow of time was profoundly comforting and yet somehow disconcerting.

'Are you well, Jacques?' Ralf asked.

'I persist.'

'A red wine at my table please.'

'It will be waiting for you at the bar.'

Ralf drank in great gulps, looking over at the bar where he had found her. He hated her, hated loving her. What had she been doing here in the Marais? She had warned him, feebly, but she had gone along with him anyway.

Ralf finished his wine and examined the grease on the glass. Around him, the same old faces were talking, their voices low and pleasant.

Ralf knocked the side of his empty glass against the table. He knocked it harder and it made a loud noise without cracking. He raised his forearm and brought the glass down hard enough to break it, watching a couple of pieces skitter across the table and off the far side.

There was a brief lull as Jacques came round from the bar, before the murmuring resumed. Jacques leaned over him, brandishing his index finger.

'Don't make me sick of you. Ralf? You are a loyal customer. You can even be likeable if you put your mind to it. But if you make me choose between you and all of my other customers . . . Look around you.' He raised his voice a little. 'These are the most handsome and charming men in Paris.' There were a couple of laughs and invitations to fuck himself from the surrounding tables.

'Another wine, please,' Ralf said, righting his broken glass.

'Ralf—' Jacques began in a low voice.

'I am an adult. I've never owed you a centime. Just get the wine.'

Jacques went back to the bar and Ralf sat back, dismayed to have been rude to someone he liked. Fouad was smoothing down his moustache, awoken by the commotion. He looked exhausted, adrenally fatigued, the blood drained from his face.

The skin under his eyes was puffed up, thin as tissue.

'Please, brother – join me.'

Ralf got up, collected his wine from the bar, and sat opposite Fouad, drinking.

'You shouldn't have woken me up if you didn't want to talk,' Fouad said.

'What is there to talk about?' Ralf asked.

'A bar is not the place for solitude.'

'There is no wine left in the apartment.'

'Is this about the woman from the Ninth?'

'Yes. There isn't any other.'

Fouad's brow darkened.

'You must put it behind you.'

'I can't.'

'Compulsion is not love.'

'She is the only thing that has ever felt . . . the only time I have felt utterly convinced.'

Fouad sat back in his chair, reluctant to follow Ralf down an indisputable line of argument.

'Has your ability to love grown over time, or diminished? Has it brought you outside yourself?'

'Of course it hasn't.'

'Then it is not love; it is hunger.'

They had talked a lot that night. Fouad was perhaps the only person Ralf trusted to talk about it all. Ralf had come back to Jacques' every night after that for a week, hoping to see Fouad again, but just when Ralf had begun to seek him out, he disappeared. No one seemed to know where he had gone – there was a rumour that he was hanging around the Three Cats with some of the other Algerians, but no one there seemed to know him. The other possibility was that he had finally found a place in

Nanterre. Ralf had never been there before, but it was on the Métro. How far could it be?

Forty minutes, as he discovered the next day. Reaching the barriers at the other end, Ralf realised he had lost his Métro ticket, and was reduced to waiting at the exit until a kind old woman let him shuffle through with her.

Fouad had to be here somewhere – Ralf couldn't think where else he would be. He walked past a building site, red and white cranes leaning over as if to tamper with the clouds, a new wall full of braces. Some of the buildings were close to completion, and their bright, square concrete stood as a counter-argument to the teetering, sylvan growth of the Marais.

Ralf followed the road, hoping to ask someone for directions. Next to the cleared land of the building site was an improvised town, laid out in rows to give the impression of planning, of order – a place where great pride and care presided over mud and scrap metal. Ralf felt conspicuous, leaving the safety of the road, entering the huddle of low buildings. He could hear a chant, high and metallic, as if through a cone. People were coming out of their homes, holding mats, rushing down the path. Ralf followed, seeing others converge on a crossroads with a standpipe, sprouting up out of wet mud.

Some washed quickly while others rushed off down the street, organising themselves in parallel lines in front of their mats. Ralf stood eastward, out of respect, watching those in his sightline ready themselves. The imam chanted, each of the men standing still and ready – they were all men – then, as one, they lifted their hands, palm out, either side of their head, suggesting listening, then up, supplication to power. They grasped their forearms. A fireman's grip with nothing to anchor it, an arm gripping an arm in mutual support, with no world to pull against – an internal grip. Ralf was the only one who was not praying, but for now he was completely ignored by the others. He stood under a sheet-iron porch in the vain hope that he might blend with the contours of the street. *Alla'hu Akbar. Alla'hu Akbar. Alla'hu Akbar.* They were on their knees, their heads on their mats, prostrate, like all other Muslims in their time zone. Ralf imagined the many groups of Muslims across the world, praying as noon broke across newly minted countries – Bangladesh, India, Pakistan – facing towards Mecca, a continental wave of kneeling supplicants breaking westwards as the sun rose directly overhead. The supplicants facing west, south-west, south, south-east, like flowers tilting in the sun, until the prayer was taken up in Paris and Algiers, the next wave already broken and approaching from the east.

Why were so many men here during working hours? Ralf had expected the place to be largely empty, and to have to knock on doors, but with prayers over, men stood unhurriedly by the water tap, filling jerrycans, laughing and talking. Ralf stepped forward and approached the nearest group, one of whom spotted him and seemed to want Ralf to leave a safe distance between them, as if these were the first uncertain days of a plague.

'Hello – I'm looking for my friend Fouad.'

One of them, shrugging, responded in Arabic or Berber, which would have been convincing if Ralf hadn't seen their glances. They didn't want to be understood. Lucky for them; they could have been making it up for all Ralf knew.

'Does anyone here speak French?' Ralf prompted.

The man continued talking in Arabic or Berber, shooing him back towards the road and the train station.

'Is this the rue de la Fontaine?' Ralf asked. 'Where is the tree?'

'Ralf? What are you doing here?'

Fouad was approaching, apparently angry.

'Finding you,' said Ralf. 'No one has seen you for weeks.'

One of the men began to argue aggressively with Fouad in Arabic and Ralf followed the progress of the argument by visual cues. Both pointed repeatedly at Ralf. Fouad seemed to be pressing an advantage by pinching his thumb and fingertips together and flicking them at the other man as if throwing a grain of salt. The man threw a hand up in the air and said something involving Allah, and one of the others, who continued to ignore Ralf, muttered something while clutching his friend's forearm.

'Let's go,' Fouad announced abruptly, dragging Ralf down an alleyway.

'What was all that about?'

'You can't just walk in here and strike up a conversation with the first person you meet. You're going to get us both killed.'

'Who were they?'

'Algerian nationalists. Sometimes they are good people. But they are also murderers. It depends on their mood.'

'Where have you been?'

'I'll explain later.'

Fouad led Ralf through the streets, where their gaze was met with a mixture of curiosity and open hostility. After a few minutes, Fouad knocked and showed him into a low room, where a mattress had been pushed up against the wall, and a woman was balled up next to a portable stove, cooking. She stood as she heard them enter and tucked a stray wisp of hair under her head covering.

'This is my wife, Fatima,' Fouad said.

'It's nice to meet you,' Ralf said, nodding politely and self-consciously, feeling that it would be a mistake to try to acknowledge her more intimately with a kiss or a handshake.

'You must stay and have lunch with us,' Fouad said.

'I don't want to impose.'

'Nonsense. You've only just arrived.'

Fouad smiled thinly. He was a terrible liar, but Ralf didn't press him, since it suited him to stay. The rich smell of cumin and cayenne pepper filled the room, and Ralf hadn't had nearly enough human contact this past fortnight. The naked flame, the smells of cooking and Fouad's obvious pride in his home gave Ralf a nostalgic feeling that made his apartment in the Marais seem quite desolate by comparison. When they had first met, Ralf had made the lazy assumption that Fouad was a man to be pitied, who had no access to the privileges conferred on Ralf as an educated European, but he was wrong; Fouad had everything, and he had come by it without vanity. Fatima had joined him, and he was complete, and did not need Ralf as he had thought, but indulged him. Ralf suddenly felt incredibly stupid for having come here, embarrassed to have assumed that no one else would notice Fouad's absence, when it was he who had left the Marais without a word uttered and travelled alone, and might be gone for days without arousing suspicion. Whose only lasting mark on the world had been a deep scratch, nothing more, which would heal in time and perhaps had already, in a person who had loved him little enough to leave him. When he thought about it, as he did constantly, Ralf wished he could have inflicted a deep and lasting wound, because the very capability would have proved something. His consolation prize was that he couldn't be accused of spite.

'Ralf?' Fouad had indicated two crates in the corner.

'Sorry. It's so lovely to meet your wife, at last.'

'Are you all right?'

'Yes, yes.'

Fouad took out a backgammon board, and they whiled away half an hour while the lunch was prepared. Ralf tried a couple of times to include Fatima, but she didn't seem to understand what he was saying, and after Fouad had translated, and she had responded briefly, each attempt ended in an inconclusive silence.

'So why haven't you been coming to the Marais? Has the work moved elsewhere?'

Fouad shook his head.

'It's the FLN. They have a lot of control over who gets the shifts. We are going to start a family – I'm not going to defy them – but I don't want to be involved in their schemes, so I get passed up some days for work. A number of men have been killed recently in fighting back home so their families are getting more work in compensation, and there are only so many jobs available.'

'I did notice a lot of people around earlier.'

'No one is working today.'

'Are you on strike?'

Fouad picked up the last of his chips.

'My game. You know, even a monkey should win sometimes.'

Fouad packed up the board and Fatima served lunch, Fouad insisting that his wife take a crate. There was just enough food for two on the three plates, and Ralf felt terribly guilty, but did not want to offend his hosts by drawing attention to the fact. He took his time over small mouthfuls, remaining hungry as he scraped up the last grains of couscous with the side of his fork. Afterwards, Ralf and Fouad stood outside while Fatima cleared up, Fouad standing protectively in front of the entrance. The hill they were on afforded a good view of Paris, and Fouad scanned the horizon as they chatted.

Far off came the deep, unmistakable plosive of a bomb. A column of grey smoke rose somewhere on the Left Bank, a little south of the Tour Eiffel, Ralf guessed.

'What was that?' he asked rhetorically.

'A minister's apartment,' said Fouad. They stood alone on the deserted street.

'You knew about this?'

Fouad called to Fatima and, hearing her response, beckoned Ralf inside.

'The FLN aren't being heard in Algeria, so they're bringing the fight to France. There will be another before evening prayers.'

'Where?'

'I don't know, but it will be at an official address. You'll be safe in the Marais. You should leave now, before it happens. Don't go anywhere else today – just go home.'

Ralf had never heard Fouad use the imperative before. It jarred with his normally faultless courtesy, but the brittleness of his manner assured Ralf that it was no mistake.

'I'm sorry not to have seen you for a while. It was kind of you to come and visit me here – you are a good friend – and I'm glad to have had the opportunity to introduce you to my wife. The police will doubtless be arriving in La Folie soon, so it's best if you go.'

'Yes, of course. Thank you so much for lunch.'

Fatima was looking nervously at the two of them, and Ralf nodded to her again, half bowed, really, excusing himself and striding back up the dirt track towards the station.

On the Métro, Ralf became conscious of the number of Algerians travelling back into the centre of the city with him. The atmosphere in the carriage was sullen. Now didn't seem like a good time to be travelling, despite Fouad's assurances. It was an odd time to be travelling into the city at all – the bars were on their afternoon break, the shops would be shutting soon. Two of the passengers seemed unnecessarily nervous. They wore baggy suits like Chicago gangsters did in the pictures, and despite talking low, their voiceless, velar fricatives made him think for a moment that they were speaking German. But these sounds were more fundamentally guttural, more aggressive, it seemed to Ralf, as if they were working up to spit on the floor of the carriage.

One of them was carrying a briefcase. It was absurd to think that it might be a bomb, even knowing that a bomb was due to be set this afternoon. The chance of it being this man, on this train, was low. Not impossible. But even if it was a bomb, he would want to get it to its destination. Very little might be achieved by blowing up other Algerians and Ralf, who was not even French. The thought made him homesick, but for where? Germany was not his home, and the little patch he knew had been firebombed so comprehensively that he wasn't sure the roads even followed the same schema. England was not his home; that had been made abundantly clear to him throughout his schooling. If France was his home, how then did he feel homesick in the midst of it? German had other words, farsickness or longing-addiction, but what use was it to name the feeling when he would still sit, unbelonging, on this seat?

The only consolation for Ralf was that he no longer felt belligerent for any patch of soil – let these Algerians carve out some little black globe of it, as long as they didn't kill anyone, which home-made bombs so rarely did. At the heart of territory, even of property, was the assumption of inequality and exclusion. Ralf possessed nothing, and his soul was light.

The two men stood and one of them glanced in Ralf's direction. Ralf raised a bland smile and looked down at the floor as they got off. Yes, he could almost believe it, except that he did want to possess: he wanted to have a wife, he wanted the two of them to have a child, to hold it, and if he had these precious things, he would want to give them a safe place that was theirs, that he could protect, ringed concentrically by a safe neighbourhood, in a safe city, in a safe country, and so the whole godforsaken race was doomed to kill itself, out of love. Ralf thought he heard the low rumble of a detonation overhead, but perhaps it was just the tracks.

6

ELSA, Nîmes and Paris, 1957–1958

●

'Would you like to go to Paris?' Theo asked one day as they sat down to supper. Elsa didn't reply immediately, sensing there must be more to the question. Pascal began to torture his salad the moment Elsa served him, and she occupied herself with settling him down on his chair.

'It might be nice to get away for a few days,' she said eventually. 'See a show.'

'There's so much going on there. We could do anything.'

Theo took her hand and she found herself smiling shyly.

'Yes,' she said, not daring to get excited without knowing what Theo was planning.

'I know you must find it dull sometimes, out here in the country.'

Elsa tilted her head as she chewed. She had never been bored – only painfully aware of the world around her – but it was true that here there was nothing to distract her, and that made her hate it.

'We could take an apartment there,' he said.

'What do you mean?'

'Well—' here was the real news '—I've been offered a job.'

'That's wonderful. In Paris?'

'Yes.'

'That's just . . . wonderful.'

Paris. Drizzling boulevards. The chopping block. Freedom.

'I know you've grown attached to the cottage, but we can keep it. We'll come down on weekends in the summer and go on long walks.'

Elsa almost shouted, *I never want to see this place again!*

'But it's an exciting time,' he continued, quite animated now, 'we are on the verge of a new era. It's happening already in the big cities. People don't care about politics any more. Politics is embarrassing, it's what happens to people when something goes wrong. We could enter another war tomorrow and do you know what people would talk about? Rationing.

'People want to live well, and for the first time in their lives, they can. There is a new movement in the world, where nothing needs to be repaired, nothing cleaned, perhaps not even reused. We have this incredible industrial power, truly incredible, and plastics that are cheap and easy to mould and durable. There are supermarkets with miles of shelves, filled with every imaginable product in the same building. We'll have machines to take care of our homes. And it's already started happening. We can be a part of it.'

'So you're going to be opening supermarkets in France?' Elsa asked. 'I can just imagine—'

'Pens. We're going to be selling disposable pens to the big foreign markets. Hopefully even America, eventually.'

'Why would anyone want a disposable pen?' Elsa asked, bending down to pick bits of salad from around Pascal's chair and putting them on the side of her plate.

'First you make it possible, then people want it. Look at slavery. First we build the factories, the Industrial Revolution and so on, then when we no longer need the manpower, we discover a moral objection. Britain only objects to our slave trade because they have already built factories and we haven't. Travel becomes simpler, so we become tourists. Women fight for equality for over a hundred years, but it only comes when the men have gone to war and the women are needed to keep everything running. The economics comes before the ideals – one needn't ask whether people want disposable pens. They exist and they are cheap, so people buy them, and when they throw one away, they buy another.'

Elsa picked up their plates.

'So they make them good enough that people want one, and bad enough that they don't mind throwing them away.'

'No,' he said. 'That's the old way of thinking. You can make each pen a work of art, but if it is cheap, people will throw it away regardless. That's the beauty of it.'

Elsa didn't object to this world of abundance; it was simply that she couldn't imagine it. To her, each item of clothing, each meal, was precious. She loved her possessions dearly and felt wounded when they were lost or broken. She tracked them in her head, knowing where each of them was in her orbit. She remembered every unreturned book she had ever lent out. A beautiful set of pearls that Theo had bought for their first anniversary, formed over years, dug up from a seabed and wrested from their shells, in their satin box on her dresser. Their oak bed with its firm mattress and feather pillows. Their kitchenware, their mirrors, their record player. Each had its function, but more than that, it seemed to insulate her from her final meal, to confirm her security. When Elsa thought of Paris, she thought of boutiques, of restaurants stocked with food and drink, of endless cigarettes. To her the city promised an unhurried plenty, one which was to be enjoyed, rather than discarded. She thought of the pictures of German soldiers in their smart uniforms, enjoying real coffee on the terraces. Paris, and the end of wanting.

Theo found them a beautiful apartment in the 9th arrondissement, with a spare room for a live-in housekeeper. Elsa decided that they might as well ask her to nanny, so her main stipulation was experience with children (the unspoken stipulation being that she mustn't be needlessly attractive). They put out an advert, and after several interviews, found a Mme Lefebvre, a heavy-breasted, matronly woman in her late forties who skirted around her husband's death, and who creased around the eyes at the appearance of Pascal. She took the first salary offered her and moved in two days later with a single battered trunk, a stranger in the midst of their strange home, an apparent immigrant in her own country.

The apartment was larger than their cottage, and they had left a number of necessities behind, so Elsa busied herself in the first weeks with getting the place in order. Once the apartment was furnished, Elsa went out to the shops simply to look at what was on offer, having got into the habit. She memorised the city's quarters and their connections. She walked along the row of pet shops on the Right Bank with their canaries and parakeets flitting about, the stands selling used books, the grand floors of the Bon Marché. She loved the flea markets and the antique shops of the 7th, the Louis XI chairs, armoires with carved panels, ornate candlesticks. These things would have been impossible in the austerity of her youth.

The first time Theo went away for more than two days, Elsa trailed around these shops in abject misery. Out of a kind of desperation, she bought a pair of Chinese lion statues from the Qing dynasty, one with its right paw on a ball and the other with its left on a cub, and had them delivered to the apartment. Mme Lefebvre made no comment on them, only rocking them away to clean around the fireplace before rocking them back. Theo, when he returned, said he liked the look of them, but didn't mention the cost, which he couldn't have failed to notice. No one suggested they be returned. Elsa talked about starting classes in dressmaking or dance, and Theo didn't react to the idea of her meeting people in the city; indeed, he seemed to think it was a good idea.

When Theo went away again, this time for a week, she decided it would be best to avoid the antique shops, and instead spent her time tapping at the glass of aquaria and kissing at puppies. She basked in the shopkeepers' pleasure at their own expertise.

On the second day, Elsa decided to take Pascal with her – she had hardly spent more than an hour with him since they had moved to Paris. She spent all day with him naming the animals and showing him how to put his hand out to be sniffed, or how his finger might be bitten if he prodded. He seemed so pleased to be by her side, holding her hand, and when he saw something he liked he would look up at her to check she had seen it as well. They were both quite taken with a large blue parrot at the back, its eyes ringed by yellow, which the owner claimed was very rare and almost never seen in the wild. Elsa hoped he was telling the truth, because it cost a fortune.

They caught a taxi back with the cage. The parrot was not used to French drivers, weaving as they did to make gaps and avoid running over mopeds. It shrieked and clung to the side of the cage with its talons like a prisoner rattling the bars. Pascal was caught between terror and glee at the sight of its dinosaur eyes and its curved, smiling beak.

They set the cage up in the sitting room, Theo's quiet space, where it could shriek to its heart's content. Pascal went off to tell Mme Lefebvre about his day, leaving Elsa sitting on the two-seater, thinking that she didn't really know her son. Was it simply that he was too young to know himself? Or was this the sign of a failure in her? She tried to call to mind what she had most wanted from her parents, but found her memories scrambled by the effort of self-censorship. She had wanted to be a good German girl. She had liked having her hair braided, and singing in class, and gymnastics, endless rows and columns of her peers moving in perfect synchrony, the feeling that one was lifting a thousand arms, bowing a thousand heads.

Mme Lefebvre prepared a salad and cold ham for supper. Elsa sat wondering whether she appeared as cold to her son as her mother had appeared to her. Perhaps; but this was why the nanny was so important. It was possible to own one's faults, and to mitigate against them. Her son need not be as unhappy as she had been.

Pascal fidgeted in his seat. He was enervated by the excitement of the day and wouldn't eat.

'When I was a little girl we didn't have any ham,' Elsa told him. 'All we had was potatoes. It's very rude not to eat your food when Mme Lefebvre has gone to . . . such lengths . . .' She forced herself to a stop, got up from the table and went to lie down on her bed, leaving the door open so that she could hear the nanny making excuses for her.

When Pascal had gone to sleep and Mme Lefebvre had gone to her room to look at her photographs, as she did most nights, Elsa retrieved the stack of letters from under the bed. She ran her fingers over Theo's looping cursive, clipped to Elsa's translation. He had kept them all, and brought them with him to Paris, as if they were letters from her. The idea had seemed so romantic at the time, but she had been absented, abstracted.

She got up, put on her shoes and went downstairs. She needed to feel the cold. She would take the first turning she found and be back at her door in no time, approaching it from a new direction. Mme Lefebvre was there if anything was needed.

As Elsa strayed farther from the apartment, she began to feel the danger of being alone at night. Anything could happen to her. It was a wide, empty street, and she was alone. When she kept going without taking the first turning, or the next, no one stopped her. No one knew where she was. There was no one to call her back. She was, in a certain manner, free.

There were no sirens, nor planes. Lamps but no fires. Few people. Being out at night seemed to break some internal curfew. There were too few people around to call it a society any longer; there were only animals, wandering through an expanse, weighing the shadows. That first night, the feeling made her lose her nerve, and she turned back to safety, staying up to watch the dawn, the white sunlight streaming in through the windows, casting curlicued shadows against the wall.

On the next nights, she strayed farther, but didn't speak to anyone. She was content to walk among the revellers, the tramps and the lovers, a silent witness to their joys and troubles. Paris was wide open and uncontained. Pedestrians on the other side of the road were too far away to seem threatening, and the bridges afforded unexpected views. One might tumble down alleyways and wash out into a wide, straight boulevard that ran to the horizon.

She began to fall into a routine. From her apartment, she would walk to the river, sometimes down to Concorde and across to the Tour Eiffel, but more often turning east, past the Tuileries and the square, silent Louvre, to the river. Her senses came alive at night, so that she perceived the true distance between objects, their motion, their texture. She would place her hand against the trunks of trees, trail her fingers along the smooth walls. Down by the river, she would stare through the water at the seaweed, looking out for the darting shadows of small fry where the stone banks sloped into the depths.

She would cross at the Pont des Arts or the Pont Neuf. She liked to walk to the very tip of the Île de la Cité, through the gardens there, stepping quietly in the shadow of the willows, watching couples sit with their knees up, leaning into one another, murmuring. If their backs were turned, she could stand very close and watch them for many minutes, glancing occasionally behind to make sure she herself was not being watched. How beautiful it would be to sit there with Theo like that, watching the tips of the branches trail in the dark water. To bring a bottle of wine or Calvados, to pass it between one another while one listened to the water, to feel simultaneously at the tip of Paris and at its very heart. Filled with longing, she would retreat silently on the balls of her feet, and walk back up the stone steps, surveying those along the banks from the top, where the statue of Henri IV looked down on his city.

The islands were not busy at night. If she wanted to feel close to people, she would continue on towards Saint-Michel, where the terrace cafés were full, the heaters lit. There, one would find tourists, buskers, shouting and laughter. Sometimes she walked past the entrance to a jazz club, knowing that she was building the courage to go in one night, but that to do so would change the nature of these walks, or rather confirm their nature undeniably.

It was not freedom from Theo. When he returned, she was happier than ever to see him. He got in early one morning, waking Elsa as she lay in bed, he looking fresh as the dawn. He jolted at the sound of the parrot and she was laughing before she could explain, drawing him down onto the bed, holding him there, though she could tell he was restless and wanted to get up. She told him about the parrot and, when Pascal had woken up, he got into bed with them, and Theo asked what the parrot was called.

'The Blue Parrot,' said Elsa.

'What does he eat?' asked Theo.

Pascal looked up at Elsa.

'I don't know,' she said, 'we'll have to ask Mme Lefebvre,' hoping the bird hadn't been starving all this time. She left the bed, ostensibly to use the bathroom, went over to the cage and was relieved to find a feeder half full with seeds, clipped to the side of the cage. So really there was no cause for concern.

Theo stayed in Paris through the autumn and into winter. He worked hard, but he came home, and they went for walks together, and when it rained they stopped at a café for a pichet of wine until the rain abated, and when it was sunny they went out in the car, with the roof down, driving along straight, tree-lined roads, out to nowhere and back on the weekends, and when people had to come round for dinner, which they sometimes did, Elsa would listen to recipes and cleaning tips in the kitchen while cigar smoke wafted in from the sitting room, thinking how small a concession this was, really, when one considered it.

When the New Year came, Theo was excited to be reassigned – he was going to be wooing American clients. It was a huge market, perhaps the greatest opportunity of his career. Ideally, they would move to America for the year, but Pascal would be starting school soon, so they agreed to stay in Paris. It meant a lot of travelling for Theo, but he didn't seem too put out; indeed, it was his suggestion. Elsa had to wonder why, if he truly loved his family, he was intent on putting thousands of kilometres between them, but he dismissed her.

'It's a good opportunity. That's all.'

And so he left, again. Elsa wept at the airport, knowing what it would mean, and he called her a silly thing – it was only a week – and she begged him not to go, though of course it was too late. The problem was not in him. He kissed her and promised to bring back candy for Pascal, real tooth-rotting stuff, and to write her a postcard on the flight.

She went home and kissed Pascal goodnight and held him, and then went and lay in bed, hoping for sleep to exonerate her. But the darkness of the room wore off, and every way of lying seemed to make her neck uncomfortable. Keeping her eyes shut felt like an effort. She could feel the cold air seeping under the door.

Elsa wouldn't let herself up until dawn, when she went to

stand at the window and watch as the neighbourhood opened up and the first flowers unfurled. Her bones ached and her eyes itched. It would be another day before she would receive Theo's postcard.

She tried to think of French foods that Mme Lefebvre could teach her to cook. She considered and rejected a number of ideas that sounded more like architecture than pastry. Millefeuille? Perhaps not. The morning crept. Noon. Lunchtime. Three. One had, at some point, to get fresh air. She put on her lipstick, threw some essentials in a handbag, and went out for a walk.

She dawdled for a long time in the Tuileries. Eventually she kept on east, crossed the river, walked along the Left Bank, and then back over another bridge, past the Tour Saint-Jacques, towards a part of the city that she didn't know. The houses around her crumbled progressively. She turned off, into a high, thin road, almost an alleyway. She saw signs in Hebrew. She felt her openness to the city and its people retreat. She had been a different person once. She knew unutterable words, could see the faces of these men shaved and bound up in the square with signs around their necks, had lived above a stolen shop, praised for not being them. But they lived on as evidence that a complete crime was impossible, that you cannot create a new world, only set new conditions. What would the world have been like without this? These bakeries, these men with hats and ringlets, brothers, husbands, sons, who stepped onto the road to let her pass in safety.

Say they had been a corrupt people, and it was possible to extinguish them. The act of killing tainted the purity of the vision. One could not separate what one was from what one did; one did not accept the truth from a liar. She herself had helped to shoot down planes, the pilots burning in their shells. Some might call her a murderer. What would be done with her and people like her in the coming decades, the damned, silent mass?

She approached the synagogue, where men were asking passers-by if they were Jewish. They fell silent and smiled at her as she passed. She was not like them; they knew it as well as she did. The winter night was drawing down over the rooftops, a cat blinking lazily as it stretched for the hunt. Some shops had already shut. A barber was hooking wooden boards over his windows, barring and bolting them. A waiter laid cutlery, straightened it, wiped a butter knife on his apron, sniffed it, put it back. It was one of those pleasant streets, so rare in Paris, where people didn't care if you were looking at them.

It had just gone five, but she didn't feel like walking back yet. As long as she was out of the apartment, her problems seemed suspended, pending, unconfirmed. Negotiating the cobbles, she found a quiet neighbourhood café, a little greasy but above all anonymous, with round wooden tables and plastic ashtrays, the room small enough that one could smell the waiter's dishcloth from the other side of the bar.

She put her bag down on a stool and ordered a glass of wine. She would have one glass and go home. The barman made a crude joke to one of the regulars, who didn't respond. Perhaps a third of the way through her drink, an Arab came and sat in the corner. A few sips later, he was joined by another man.

When she saw him, she recognised him. She did not mistake him for someone she had met before, but she recognised him, in the way that one recognises a gift one had asked for long ago and forgotten. She knew that if she spoke to him there would be trouble, and she knew that it was the sort of trouble she'd half had in mind when she had left the trodden path of her usual walk.

He was dressed smartly for a bar like this, the only one in here who was clean shaven. Ex-army, she guessed. She didn't catch his eye. He was talking animatedly to the Arab, and she thought at first that they were arguing, but then one of them slapped the other on the back and laughed. What was a soldier doing with an Arab at a time like this?

He looked over towards the bar, towards her. That decided it: she stood to leave. She fumbled for a note that she had in her coat pocket and put it on the counter, leaving without waiting for change. She walked away quickly, free and light, too light – she'd forgotten her bag. She stopped and looked back at the bar. She didn't want to go back. And yet she couldn't leave the bag behind as evidence that she had been drinking alone in a strange bar at a strange hour. She would have to be quick.

He was there, the man, rifling through her life. Terrified and furious, she swung at him. She had to get rid of him, get away. She hit him over the ear and he cried out plaintively, like a beggar.

'Thief! Give me my bag!'

She hit him again and he barely put a hand up to defend himself, only looking at her with tenderness and confusion, as if he would rather suffer than retaliate. He passed her the bag, apologising profusely. He had a beautiful voice, his accent neither French nor quite her own. He stood stock still with his arm half raised, looking into her eyes almost with pity. She laughed in spite of herself. Standing there cowering like that, he hardly seemed a threat. She would have one drink, then she would go.

It had been snowing all the way back from Deauville, falling in thick flakes, resting on every roof and road in clumps of down. Elsa and Ralf returned to a white Paris, silent as a memory, and the snow kept falling as they parted, separating them like a curtain. But even as Elsa walked the short distance to her apartment, the footfall and traffic began to turn the whole city into a grey mush. Soon, it would be sluicing off roofs and overflowing from the medieval drains. She felt cold, and dreadfully empty.

The apartment was dark except for the inconstant light of the fire in the sitting room. There were wet footprints in the hallway. Theo's coat was hanging on the stand. She touched it. It was damp.

Elsa took off her boots and coat and went in. Mme Lefebvre was on her knees by the fire. She pushed a log in towards the centre and a part of the fire collapsed with a shiver of embers.

'Your husband is home early,' she said.

'What did you tell him?'

Mme Lefebvre began to sweep the coal dust around the grate. Elsa knelt beside her, the fire steaming her cheek. She picked up the poker and put it to one side, then took the brush from Mme Lefebvre's hand.

'Please,' she whispered hoarsely. 'What did you tell him?'

Mme Lefebvre looked up, over Elsa's head.

'Hello, darling,' said Theo.

'You're home!' said Elsa. She got up and threw her arms around his neck. He didn't lift his. 'Did you just arrive?'

'Yes. Mme Lefebvre kindly lit the fire for me.'

The nanny excused herself and retreated to the kitchen.

'Can I get you something?' she asked.

'I'd better not. I had a number of drinks on the flight.' Theo loosened his tie and stood in front of the fire. 'It's horrid weather out there,' he said.

'Yes, I know – I just got back myself. Didn't Mme Lefebvre tell you?'

'No, she didn't.'

'How funny. I thought she'd have—'

Theo turned and cuffed her over the head. One moment she was standing, the next lying on her back. The parrot shrieked fearfully.

'No,' she said faintly, a blanket denial wrought out of confusion.

'Again. That's what Pascal said. Again. Mummy is gone again. Is Mummy going away again?'

'We must fire the nanny,' she mumbled from the floor.

'What are you talking about?' Doubt was creeping into his voice as he saw what he had done. He lifted her and set her in the armchair. 'Come on now, explain. I want you to explain.' He shook the armchair once, emphatically. 'Explain.'

'I went away.'

'You went away.'

Elsa felt her eyelid swelling shut.

'Yes. I went to see my father.'

'To Germany?'

'Yes. I know you and he don't get on, but he is my family.' The two of them would never be in the same room again. Her father might not have approved of such a lie, but he had always believed in self-preservation.

'How long did you go for?'

'Two days.'

'To Germany?'

'It was better than nothing. I haven't seen him in eight years.'

Theo looked at her face, down at her body, and chewed his tongue. He went over to the sideboard for a cigar.

'Why didn't you tell me?'

'I didn't lie to you.'

'You didn't tell me.'

'What would have been the point?'

Theo returned with his cigar and leaned down to put his hand on her belly. She flinched.

'Do you think it's okay?' he asked her.

She looked up at him and concentrated on keeping the hurt out of her voice.

'I don't know,' she said.

Theo went to the bedroom while she stood at the kitchen tap

soaking a cloth, and held it against her eye, ignoring the sting of contact. The night she had met Ralf, she had run from the restaurant almost out of an instinct for survival, hoping that he would not follow her back to her life. If he had, it would have changed everything. What was she doing, pursuing an affair, when she already had what anyone might hope for? She had not always had a good life, but she had one now, and she had to protect it. All she had to do was walk away.

Part Three

7

RALF, Paris, 1961–1968

'Ralf!' shouted M. Dague up the stairs.

'Yes?'

'There's an Arab down here for you. He says he's your friend.'

'He can come up.'

'He's waiting in the courtyard.'

Ralf went out to see him.

'Your landlord still pretends he doesn't know who I am,' said Fouad, as they set off towards the rue Vieille-du-Temple.

'He's a bourgeois soul, trapped in a slum. I feel sorry for the poor fucker.'

Jacques was ill and hadn't opened up this week, so they whiled away a few hours on a terrace in the Latin Quarter, enjoying the ribaldry of the expats and the self-conscious flirting of the students.

'You see this?' Fouad asked.

'What is it?'

Ralf took hold of the card, the picture of Fouad looking him dead in the eyes.

'My residence permit. I'm not a citizen, but I'm allowed to stay.'

Ralf looked up at Fouad, then back down at the card.

'That's terrific. I'm really happy for you.' He flagged down the waiter. 'This calls for champagne.'

'Only if you're paying,' said Fouad.

A bucket was brought, the cork popped, the napkin draped to catch the condensation.

'They actually asked me to join the police as a *harki*, but I refused. What is the point of bringing my family here if I'm going to spend all my time catching and torturing other Algerians? I might as well have stayed at home. I think my military service must have counted for something, though.'

After their drinks, they walked up as far as Maspero's bookshop.

'Do you mind if we stop in?' Fouad asked. 'I want to get that Jules Roy book and see if he has any copies of the Frantz Fanon under the counter.'

'I thought you didn't believe in violent struggle?'

'I certainly don't believe in being there when it happens. But no, for my part, I believe "those who show no mercy will receive none".'

They browsed for a while, chatting with the other customers and looking through assorted radical titles, a few that were officially censored, and even a few that had been published by the shop itself.

'Aren't we going to miss your curfew?' Ralf asked.

'Probably,' said Fouad. 'But most of the Algerians I know are protesting the curfew tonight. When the FLN says it's counting on you for support, you'd be surprised how many people decide to show up. They want it to be peaceful this time. Everything is changing. First the French generals go crazy and start their own secret army. Then they throw grenades around in Algerian cafés – but so what, that's Algeria and no one here cares—'

'Not no one.'

'It's true, no one here cares. But then they try to assassinate de Gaulle and bomb a newspaper office in the middle of Paris. The stupid bastards are starting to make the FLN look like the party of common sense. We already know from the referendum that seventy-five per cent are in favour of Algeria's self-determination. So now all we have to do is demonstrate peacefully.'

'I hope so. Quite aside from the matter of independence, it's absurd to place a curfew on "French Algerians" or "French Muslims", it violates the principle of equality,' said Ralf. 'We've had this before, separating people out into races. It gets my back up.'

'Well,' said Fouad, without elaborating.

They walked past the rue de la Huchette, and Ralf tilted his hat down.

'Let's cut through,' Fouad said.

'No, we have to go around.'

'Why?'

'I can't walk past the Caveau de la Huchette any more. Had a bit of trouble there once.'

Fouad looked amused. They waited at a crossing next to two city police in their blue cloaks.

'On the signal,' said one of them.

The second muttered something Ralf didn't catch.

'The velodrome, I expect.'

Ralf and Fouad turned as one and kept on down their side of the pavement. Fouad checked his watch while Ralf glanced back to check that the police had crossed.

'Do the police know about the protest?' Ralf asked.

'Of course, it's not a secret. But that's why they have to keep it peaceful. They can't give any reason to attack. We have women coming, and children. No weapons. No bombs. It's about asserting our right to be on the street. That's the headline we want in *Le Monde* tomorrow.'

In a little shop next to the cabaret El Djezaïr, at least one Algerian had defied FLN orders and was doing a roaring trade in grilled lamb.

It was 8.30pm as they reached the fountain, with its statue and its spitting dragons.

'Remember the rue de la Fontaine?' asked Fouad. 'The little standpipe?' He looked up at the Fontaine Saint-Michel. 'Well, you see this, and you can't help but laugh.' He didn't look like he wanted to laugh. 'How can anyone feel we are a threat, when we are happy with so little? We are not asking to overturn the glory of France – we would be happy enough to be left in peace, to have a tin roof and a water tap, to be allowed to walk around at night.'

'Don't look straight away, but isn't that the FLN over there?'

They were sat at a table on the quiet side of the square, blending with the crowd in their suits. They seemed quite innocuous sitting on a terrace drinking coffee.

'They meet there often,' said Fouad. 'Lots of escape routes. Under the arch, there's Gît-le-Coeur – the one with the Beat hotel – as well as Saint-André-des-Arts, an entrance to the Métro, and then the boulevard itself. The second they set foot in an Algerian hotel, the police have them under surveillance. Here, out in the open . . .'

It would be hard to chase anyone through the bustle. However, there was surprisingly little traffic coming over the bridge, and they could hear far-off chanting and ululating over the idling of motors and impatient horns. A *darbuka* started beating out a rhythm and Fouad smiled reflexively.

Ralf felt a few droplets of water on his face, which he thought might be coming from the fountain. They had both spotted the two policemen approaching the bridge but there were only two of them, and the happy crowd was swelling to fill the width of the road. Ralf felt an instinctive aversion to violence, but perhaps this peaceful way was only possible now they were winning: de Gaulle would support their self-determination, and only a tiny number really believed Algeria was somehow part of the French mainland.

'Do you want to join in?' asked Ralf.

'Me? No. I am happy for them, but I have my card; I am a French resident.'

A police van pulled up at the far end of the bridge, and another on their side, at the entrance to Saint-Michel Métro. One of the officers went up to the window to talk, and as the crowd approached he opened the door and pulled out two white sticks, over a metre long. Others were setting up metal barriers and beginning to push back the French crowds. Ralf nudged Fouad. It wasn't just spotting, now, but raining. The police were waving the march back across to the Right Bank, but those at the front couldn't resist the insistent press of the crowd behind.

They heard a disturbance farther back, and the crowd on the bridge stood still, their chants dissolving in confusion. The men looked around for information as the women spoke to their children and shifted the weight of those they were carrying. The doors of the van slammed, the police lining up to cut off the wide mouth of the bridge as another van pulled in behind them.

Fouad crossed the road towards the crowd, shouting in Arabic to an older man on the bridge, who strained over the noise, holding his hands up in supplication. Fouad turned back to Ralf.

'He says they are trapped. The police are on both sides telling them to get back.'

Ralf caught up with Fouad and walked with him to the police line.

'Excuse me,' Ralf said to one of them. He didn't turn around. Ralf didn't want to tap his shoulder. 'These people can't go anywhere. They aren't being allowed off the bridge on the other side.'

The officer turned around.

'Step back,' he said.

'But how can they—'

'It's past the curfew.'

'I'd like to speak to your commanding officer.'

The policeman stepped forward and shoved Ralf hard as two others grabbed Fouad by the arm and hair and dragged him through the police line onto the bridge, Fouad protesting. There were screams from the far side of the bridge.

Ralf took his chance to burst through the temporary gap in the line. The two officers had Fouad doubled up against the low wall of the bridge but Ralf could barely see them through the seething crowd, much less get to him, before they had lifted him and rolled him over the top, into the air, into the Seine. A baton struck Ralf on the side of the knee and he was dragged over to the verge. People were openly attempting to escape past the lines now, as reinforcements arrived. It was the police's turn to chant: *dirty rats, into the Seine.* The only aim of anyone now was to flee.

Ralf staggered down the stone steps, more bodies falling from the bridge: unconscious divers, frogs in a hurricane, the silhouettes falling slower than gravity, nauseatingly slow, all the size of adults, thank God. Only one or two, resurfacing downstream, came up swimming.

At the bottom of the steps Ralf turned left with the current, passing under the bridge, where the screams were surreally dampened. Two homeless men sat on the stone ledge staring dumbly. The clouds had drifted apart to reveal an almost full moon, and he stepped out from under the bridge into its eerie blue light.

He saw a clump of dark hair bob to the surface, and a shoulder, still travelling slower than the current so that the water parted around it. It looked like a clod of earth. He moved closer. A siren wailed far above. It was a head, unmistakably. He ran downstream of it and took off his shoes and jacket. The ledge was high on this side, designed for mooring boats. He would have to get them both over to the far side by the trees, where the bank sloped up onto the Île de la Cité. The head and shoulder and upper arm were drifting closer. He took his moment and jumped. As he hit the water the shock filled his lungs and he wondered, absurdly, why he hadn't taken his trousers off. The current was stronger below the surface, and Ralf fought the drag of it, and the drag of his clothes, trying to stay afloat, to reach Fouad. He nearly lost him but grabbed at the hair, took the dead weight of the thick shoulder, going under, suddenly concerned they might both drown, unable to see but thrashing with his legs, across the width of the river. He hit the concrete with the top of his head, grabbed its rough edge, hiked the shoulders, the torso, the legs, up the steep bank, and climbed, panting, onto the cold promenade. He sat catching his breath, picking floating weeds off his body, the branches of a willow blowing about his head. On the other side, no people, only boats. There was only moonlight. Ralf realised that the police had turned off the street lights.

He heard the cry and splash of another body, and came to his senses. The puddle around him was cold and clear like the rainfall. The puddle forming around his companion was opaque. He was heavy, Ralf could now see; heavy even on land. Ralf rolled him onto his back. Thick lips. A bulbous, crushed nose. A thick beard. It wasn't Fouad.

Ralf looked down the river in despair. There was nothing to be done. Crying, he sat up the body, its spine rolled, its legs bent, babylike, and began to slap it on the back. In his frustration, Ralf slapped harder and harder, and the body dribbled at the mouth, but Ralf didn't stop, his powerlessness confined now to the blameless task of raising a stranger from the dead. He switched hands, landed bruising blows. The neck abruptly regained tension and the stranger coughed, pitched forward nearly into the river, and vomited. For a little while, the body was still bound to its reflexes and convulsions, but by degrees, the man began to take in his moonlit surroundings, seeking to understand. And he saw Ralf, and he couldn't tell, it was clear, whether Ralf had thrown him in or saved him, and Ralf pointed dumbly up at the Pont Saint-Michel, and the man started to kiss Ralf's bare feet, weeping.

'Stop it. Get up,' Ralf said. 'There are others in the river. We have to get them out.'

The man nodded, chastened, wiped the blood off Ralf's foot and drew a sleeve across his beard. They were both shivering. The clouds had closed over the moon, but even from the uncertain way he stood, Ralf could see he was in a bad way. He would have to stay on the bank while Ralf went back in.

It was a long night. They pulled two more bodies out of the river before the police came down to the bank and they had to run. One of the bodies was alive, the other had its hands cuffed behind its back. Neither was Fouad. The next day, the newspapers carried brief, terse reports of a disturbance, suggesting a few had been injured during FLN rioting. In his grief, he walked back down to the Pont Saint-Michel. The scene looked the same as it ever had, almost as if nothing had happened here last night, except where, on the bridge wall, someone had painted, in foot-high black letters, *Here they drown Algerians*.

After Fouad's death, Ralf began to drink in a more dedicated way. There was no one he saw regularly. He no longer wanted to be himself. He dreamed of being abandoned while he slept, one of those horrid dreams when one knows one is asleep and is desperate to wake up, and he would often wake up three or four times that way in the night. In other dreams, he was watching bodies fall through the sky, out of reach. He would have a drink when he woke up to settle his nerves, and sometimes continue on through the day, too full of shame to go to Jacques'. Once he lost his tutees, he worked occasionally as casual labour, often not bothering to take off his overalls or boots between shifts. When he didn't get work, he'd sign on at the Assédic, and there he fell in with a shifting crowd of itinerants, expatriates and self-professed intellectuals. They hung around bars, hoping someone would join them with enough money to pay the bill; if no one did, they ran away and found somewhere else.

A few of them experimented with drugs. Ralf tried marijuana, psychedelics. They displaced him, put him to one side for a time. Frankly, it was a relief, not to be himself. He liked to journey out to the far shores of consciousness, where his biography couldn't find him, sometimes laughing with the others, sometimes content to travel alone, briefly excused from his loneliness. He made a little money by buying too much of everything and selling it on.

There was a girl called Muriel who sometimes bought marijuana to sell on to her fellow students in Nanterre or the Sorbonne. This wasn't really her world: she would have a good life one day, a good job or children, or both. He tried to watch after her, when he could. He and his associates had coalesced because they were all, in some way, deficient, and he knew better than to leave her alone with certain of them. She was too trusting.

He started to visit her in Nanterre every couple of weeks, to save her the trip, but more often than not he would drink through the day and retreat in the evenings, taking long walks or lying on his bed, the world spinning on its axis, everything travelling at 1600kph.

The night that he overdid it was not all that different to his routine. He had been drinking solidly in the day, not to get drunk but to maintain stasis, and he had eaten a light lunch, which he sometimes didn't manage. When he got home, he had a glass of wine and ate some pieces of mushroom, forcing himself to ignore the brackish taste, which lingered long after he had swallowed them. He measured his reaction by the smell of his sweat, which had all the rancid sweetness of fermentation. Ralf went and sat in his chair. The longer he watched any one spot, the farther it receded into its self-collapsing world, a mirror inside a mirror inside a mirror. He tried to make himself sick but couldn't.

He looked at his reflection, standing at the sink. When one looked – really looked – it was quite ridiculous to have one's face sprouting hair. Above the eyes, all over the top, down the sides, on the neck and cheeks and mouth. He was a ball of hair, nothing more. Skin was really just the soil.

He pulled away and lumbered down the stairs, crushing populations of bacteria underfoot. He only got as far as the Place des Vosges, where he sat watching the sky darken on a bench near a large statue of a man riding an ecstatic horse. The cloisters around the square were already cloaked in shadow, the sparrows rearranging themselves in the hedges. The fountains had been switched off for the night, leaving still, flat pools at their base. Next to Ralf, the gnarled roots of a tree curled in on themselves, writhing like fat brown snakes in a fire.

Ralf took an unknown pill out of his pocket, crunching it between his teeth. Why did these things always taste so foul? His tongue and gums started to go numb. Ralf hoped he hadn't just swallowed a heavy anaesthetic, or anything else that might close his throat.

He watched two pigeons wandering around the square while he waited for the pill to do its worst. You had to take your mind off these things, especially in the first few minutes, when the urge to call for an ambulance was at its height. The ground was warping and tipping under him so he focused on the pigeons. The cock was chasing the hen, who seemed torn between a desire to run and a desire not to expose her rear to her pursuer. Whenever she stopped to face him, or, forgetting herself, paused to peck at an unseen grain, the cock set up his stall in the hen's eyeline and, when he was sure he had her attention, spun full circle on the spot, first clockwise then anti-clockwise. He was showing off the iridescent green and purple plumage of his superior neck, Ralf realised, making it flash and ripple in the light. She, for her part, was succeeding in not being impressed. The females were always the gatekeepers of affection. The males were always running round in circles.

He thought about Fisher's runaway hypothesis that strong males develop useless skills. Peacock feathers. Elaborate songs. They take up far too many resources to be worthwhile. But that's why we do them. To prove we can. Lesser males don't have the resources to spare on making themselves different colours or having useless tails. That's how you know who the real man is. He's wasting everything he's got.

Wasting everything he's got, sang the birds.

You know who the real man is. Wasting everything he's got.

Wasting everything.

Useless tails.

To prove—

Ralf vomited over himself.

To prove—

His blood ran cold, his body banking sharply left though he could see he wasn't moving.

His body was being washed to the left, as if by a strong current. He watched his right hand rise from his lap and drift over, past his left arm, felt his body follow it. In normal tempo – the only moment in normal tempo – he fell and hit the back of his head on the gravel, a sharp stone sticking into the back of his head. His ear burned, but it wasn't important. He saw the clouds and he was with them. Such colour, greater than life, pure colour. Waves of a different length would heat you until you burst, but these were beatific, life-giving, benign. Up there, everything was as you would wish it. Elsa would have liked it there. The cool spray of condensed vapour. A human being would provide a surface for the water to coalesce, he was covered in a sheen of little droplets, carrying him left and up into the sky where he could look around him at the vast indifferent universe and be free. His body was completely numb now. He wiped his chin off. Yes, there. Up there where all that existed was perspective. Into the outer atmosphere, where probably there was a straight line between him and Elsa, and if she looked hard enough she might see him, and he could signal to her, *It's okay, I forgive you everything. Just come back to me.*

Ralf lifted his head, lifted his eyelids. Someone was replacing the music.

'Play the Steppenwolf,' Ralf said.

'Fuck you.'

'Play it.'

'No way. We've listened to it five times already.'

He looked over to where the student called Roger crouched over the LP player, watched him place the needle ritually on the disc, the warm crackle starting up like a long draw on a dry joint. Ralf observed his blood turning icy as the words crept in. *She seemed so cold to me, and I remember when I loved her.* He sat up, the new perspective allowing his attention to latch onto his surroundings. They were in a large storage cupboard on the third floor of a concrete cube in Nanterre, which had been gradually accruing furniture and decoration over the two months since the campus had been officially closed by the administration, until it had come to resemble a pad in Chelsea. From the thick fur rug on which he lay, he could see the player and the lava lamp in the corner, numerous large cushions, a broken guitar, a small piece of broken mirror, and an uneven detritus of tobacco, rolling papers, jumpers, unclaimed knickers and empty bottles. Next to him lay his construction hat.

Roger was rifling around for wine, and Ralf passed him a bottle. Ralf hadn't really wanted to drink last night but he had fostered certain expectations, profited from them. It was no longer for him to decide who he wanted to be; his presence was required as master of ceremonies. And so as he had turned the light off, lying in intimate darkness in the colour-changing glow of the lava, drawing in the perimeter of his consciousness until it was just the room, just his bedding, his body, just a pin-point between his eyes, he had heard a knocking, and some of the students had arrived with wine and cigarettes, and Ralf had propped himself up against the wall, cold with lack of sleep.

She seemed so cold to me, but I remember when I loved her. Now we are strange . . .

'Will you put something else on?' asked Ralf irritably.

'Like what?' asked Roger.

'I don't know. You choose.'

'I did choose, and you don't like it.'

'The Doors, then.'

The mood had been relaxed but alert at first, the students exchanging ideas about the ongoing protests and telling stories of their daring exploits. There had been three that Ralf didn't recognise, sitting cross-legged on the far side from Ralf, one plaiting another's hair, but Roger had been there as he usually was, cutting lines on the mirror with his knife to impress the newcomers, Muriel soon curled up with her head in Ralf's lap. Others passed in and out. The news filtered through that the de facto leader of the protests, Dany the Red, was 'in the building'. Roger had been down to the École des Beaux Arts, where the art students were making posters, dozens, he said, 'The Struggle Continues', 'Be Young and Shut Up', 'Beauty is in the Street', 'A Youth Too Often Worried about the Future', 'CRS: SS', 'We

Are All Undesirable'. One of the slogans was plastered across a sinister shadow of de Gaulle, still holding the reins of power a quarter of a century after the liberation. Roger himself had come out with a couple of gems, which Ralf had suggested he graffiti on public walls. They had made a shortlist of favourites on the back of a poster. The girl with the plaited hair had suggested, 'The thought of tomorrow's enjoyment will never console me for today's boredom', and Roger had countered with, 'The more I make love, the more I want to rise up; the more I rise up, the more I want to make love', staring balefully into the girl's eyes. Ralf had suggested, 'beneath the cobblestones, the beach', and Muriel had purred on his lap, putting a hand up to stroke behind his ear, her eyes closed, her smooth, unblemished legs bent into a question mark.

Roger had been going on about freedom again, and Ralf had got into an idiotic argument with him about it. Ralf had pointed out that one person's fantasy was another's nightmare. Roger had argued back. Ralf had asked what would happen if Roger wanted to sleep with the girl with plaited hair, but the girl with plaited hair did not want to sleep with him. Whose freedom did he respect? Roger had started shouting and waving the knife, Ralf in fits of laughter, Roger threatening to cut his face up with Muriel hanging off Roger's arm. Ralf had tried to ask what should happen if Roger wanted to stab him but he didn't want to be stabbed, but he had fallen onto his side coughing, Roger holding the tip of the knife an inch from Ralf's face as he shouted and the three in the corner edging on their bottoms towards the door, too terrified to do the sensible thing and stand up.

Muriel took the whole thing very seriously and tried to ask Roger to leave, even after new people arrived and poured a little cold water on proceedings by suggesting they all smoke. Ralf calmed Muriel down and Roger sulked for about half an hour until someone began to talk about the march planned for the next day and he couldn't help but participate. They talked over the plans for a little while with Alain, who was among the newcomers, and Muriel had quietly slipped off to find her Jacques Dutronc 45, which she loved to play at 5am. She returned with drunken, shining eyes and put the record on, dancing in front of Ralf and trying to get him up and dancing, without success. A couple of the other men in the room watched her and she turned towards them. Ralf watched silently as she flirted with Alain after the song had ended, feeling that she would be better off with someone like Alain. He watched and thought of ice cubes, of their utter cold brittleness and the low crunch through the molar and through the jaw and through the skull. Roger didn't know that true violence came not from disdain for the victim but disdain for oneself. Ralf nodded along to 'Green Onions', determined to listen properly to Roger so as not to alienate himself from the room, but thinking more about listening than he was listening.

God, well, the dawn had been sickly. It was one of those dawns that creeps in through clouds and turns everyone's skin grey, and one suddenly discovers one's chewing gum has lost its elasticity and turned to pulp in one's mouth, like a wad of soggy tissue. They were all young and looked a little depleted, but Ralf felt exhausted, sick to the skin, his kidneys aching dully as if he had been holding his bladder too long. And suddenly the room was empty but for him and Muriel and Roger. The LP crackled over invisible dust, having reached its end.

'What time does the march start?' asked Ralf, playing two moves ahead.

'I guess around midday,' said Roger. 'We'll start over the river, cross the bridge and head down towards the Sorbonne, the Boul' Mich', I guess.'

'In for the long haul, then.'

'Yeah.' Roger patted each of his pockets for his possessions, probably his worst tic while high, which he conducted surreptitiously but almost constantly, feeling the contours of his wallet, tobacco, flick knife, keys. He looked around at Muriel, who was busying herself tidying up. 'Well, I guess I should get some sleep.'

Roger shook Ralf's hand and stood for a couple of seconds waiting to say goodbye to Muriel, who didn't acknowledge him, before leaving. Muriel rolled her eyes at the door as it closed.

Ralf turned off the LP player.

'You know, Alain says I shouldn't hang around with you. He says the revolution is about moulding society to our minds, not moulding our minds to society.'

'Perhaps he's right, but he's very prescriptive for a free thinker.'

Muriel sat down on the rug, and he sat beside her.

'Did you want to sleep here?' he asked.

She smiled and nodded. He started to move away but she pulled him back and kissed him. It was unexpected, insofar as anything was to Ralf by now, and he hesitated. She crossed her arms and removed her orange jumper, unzipped her pleated skirt and folded them in a neat pile next to the rug, utterly unselfconscious. Her thighs were soft and smooth, her stomach the barest curve, stopping short of her breasts. Ralf undid his shirt, which was only partially buttoned in any case. The room was warm enough, but Ralf felt conscious of his slack body, its irregularity and bulk. Muriel was still at the age when there is no distinction between how one feels and how one appears, but for Ralf, sex now required a kind of wilful delusion or diversion.

He lay down beside her. Nothing made him feel so old as this young woman, the health of her skin, her utter certainty and impatience. He would be happy just to stroke her skin, to feel its softness and, if not love, at least be reminded of love. She kissed him. It seemed as if she were granting him permission, coaxing him back from a voluntary exile. The truth was that he didn't want to touch her. For him this physical closeness implied intimacy without conferring it. To be blunt, to admit to his own cruelty: he was not present, but he was weak enough to rely on her for solace.

She kissed his collarbone, his rib, his hip. He turned his head away and sighed. It was somehow worse that Muriel was good and kind. He sat up and she paused, unsure. Separating her hair into three thick ropes with his fingers, he kissed her on the cheek, and pushed her gently onto her back. She lay back, lifting her chin towards the window so that her face caught the weak morning light, and closing her eyes. He ran his hands over her, wondering whether they were so calloused as to scratch her skin, and stroked her inner thighs and her soft, warm belly. He kissed her, deeply, wondering whether it was better to treat someone properly for the wrong reasons than be true to a destructive passion. Without feeling, he might make their morning coffee, go to work and come home some days with fresh tulips. He might have a routine. He kissed her, and stroked her, willing himself to be what she saw in him, determined to be present. She held his face in both hands.

'I want you,' she whispered.

'I . . .' His voice cracked. 'I can't.'

Her eyes filled with tears as she nodded, holding his face, and smiling, swallowing back sobs. She started to cry and drew her knees up to her chin, looking all of a sudden more like a child than a woman, and Ralf held her, all of her, her shoulders and her shins, bundling her in the blanket.

'I'm sorry. I'm sorry.' He didn't know what else to say. He knew neither how to explain nor how to assure her. 'I'm so sorry.'

She tried to brush her long fringe out of her eyes. Her hair was hanging down over her face like half-drawn curtains.

He closed his eyes. This was not home. When had he last been in the apartment? He didn't even know whether he had paid the rent. He thought of Dague picking through his clothes, his wife folding up the bedsheets. On his table, letters from his mother asking him to come back to her, to telephone, to write, just one line to assure her he was alive. She would not be angry that it had been so long, she just wanted to know that he was okay. *Just a word, Ralf.* Just a word. But what could he have said? I have no job, no wife. The woman that I loved left Paris ten years ago and I doubt I shall see her again. I cannot think of another future; it was not meant to go like this. Ralf rocked gently, calming Muriel, singing a lullaby in a language he had half forgotten, buried deep under the sloping ceiling of his first bedroom: *Do you see a half-moon, even though it's a sphere? That's the best we humans can manage, down here.*

Later that morning, he stood looking down on the campus and the jerrycan towns below. He thought about Fouad and his family. Algeria was independent, now, but what good had it done? The country was free, but the people were still poor. All that bloodshed.

He went out and bought bread and milk, heating the coffee on a little Primus stove in the corridor before going in to wake Muriel. She sat up, holding the blanket to her chest with one hand and taking the bowl of coffee with the other. She drank quietly. He gathered up his things and had a wash in the sink across the hall before putting on his hard hat and helping Muriel put her things in her bag.

Others must have seen Ralf's hat on previous days, because a number were now wearing moped helmets or hard hats stolen from construction yards. Students and citizens marched together, linking arms to pace out the procession, some waving red flags or banners.

When they reached the turning for the rue Gay-Lussac, they

spilled off, there being a thick crowd as far as the eye could see down Boulevard Saint-Michel. The crowd began to pack in tighter, eddying around the dense middle, where some of the leaders were. One could spot Dany easily, his nervous, boisterous energy, sometimes switching his megaphone on briefly to save a chant that was fraying around the edges. He climbed up onto a plinth where others were waving to friends, and switched on his megaphone with an audible pop.

'They don't want us to stand up for ourselves,' he shouted, 'so we'll sit!'

The crowd milled around for several minutes more, until it became clear there was no further plan, and group by group, the students started to sit down in the road, propping up their placards and flags wherever there were gaps between cobbles. An expectant hush fell, as if they were a theatre audience. Nothing happened, and the noise of lively conversation grew again.

The sky was cornflower blue, the clouds so thin as to be scorched by the sunlight. An anarchist had broken onto one of the rooftops nearby, and was waving a black flag as some down below rolled cameras or took snaps.

Roger's companion, an anaemic-looking boy with wild hair called Jean-Luc, handed round a baguette, which they ate with *sauçisson sec* and little truckles of cheese, with various complaints as to its taste, shape and consistency, before Jean-Luc, much aggrieved, pointed out the difficulty of finding cheese that didn't stick to the fingers or require cutting. Roger took the opportunity to point out that he had a knife, if they had needed anything cutting, at which even Muriel had to laugh. Someone produced a bottle of wine and they passed it around. Roger explained how they might siphon petrol from a parked car, later, in order to turn the bottle into a Molotov cocktail, adding a little motor oil to thicken it. He had brought lighter fluid to soak the cloth wick. Ralf mentioned another method, which would be safer to carry as it didn't need a lit wick, but would require white phosphorus.

'Do you have any?' asked Roger.

'No,' said Ralf.

'A typical intellectual. You have a hypothetical weapon, no means to create it, and no will to use it.'

'Have you ever actually killed a man, Roger?'

'I object to violence,' Muriel said. She took off her crown of flowers and began to pick off the petals. Deprived of sleep and pulled in different directions by the residual effects of various drugs, Ralf's mind associated wildly as he watched her plucking the petals one by one. A striptease. A dismembered spider. Winter.

Jean-Luc put his hand out for the wine, reaching forward to take it from Ralf.

'Malcolm X said, "We are nonviolent with people who are nonviolent with us,"' Jean-Luc quoted.

'Humans have an evolved impulse to violence and tribalism,' said Ralf, 'and they justify it after the fact.'

'No,' Roger said. 'Look at Black Power, the Viet Cong. They are standing against oppression, for freedom.'

Ralf shook his head.

'Do you really believe you are oppressed and powerless, Roger? That your struggle is comparable to theirs?'

'I am in solidarity. With them just as much as the workers at the Renault factory. This is about fighting fascism in all its forms.'

'But what is it you want? There are the three demands, yes, but how did this all begin? Boys weren't allowed in girls' rooms.'

'It's more than that. It is about taking power back for the people, all around the world. Che Guevara. Chairman Mao.'

'Yes, I noticed the Mao flags. Which part of his beliefs do you subscribe to?'

'All of them,' Roger said, Jean-Luc nodding along.

'You are against ultra-democracy?'

'Yes.'

'The bourgeois aversion to discipline. Becoming complacent as your country achieves relative prosperity. Preferring comfort to work.' Roger looked at Jean-Luc, who stared back at Ralf. 'You want the university reopened, the police withdrawn and the prisoners released. You want it to go back to how it was.'

'It is more than that. People are striking all over the country.'

'For what? Do you think the communists want the same things as you? They want better pay, better conditions. You want to be free to fuck and to consume. You want most of all not to be reminded of responsibility. You want to relieve yourself of the duties of community, of the collective. That is why the workers can agree on why they are striking, but why you simply are striking, without goals, without direction. Are we all equal, or are we all individuals? You can't stand up for both.'

Muriel threw her flowers at Ralf's head.

'So now you are standing against the cult of the individual?' she asked him. Ralf shrugged. 'No, Ralf. You're not an independent observer. We make the world around us every day we are alive. I won't apologise for being optimistic about the future. Look around you, right now. There are millions of us, Ralf, and we are going to change the world. With or without you.'

'All right, all right. I'm here, aren't I?'

As the initial excitement waned, the crowd settled in and began to conserve its energy, chatting in groups of two or three. On previous days this period had been soundtracked by Roger's guitar, but that had been broken in a skirmish and he had been so upset over its loss that Ralf hadn't even teased him. Muriel leaned on Ralf, and he put his arm up to support her.

'I'm sorry about earlier,' he said.

'Earlier?' she asked.

'Before we slept.' She said nothing as she caught up. 'I don't mean to make excuses. I just wanted to reassure you that it's not about you.'

'Ralf,' she said sadly. 'Don't you see that's what I'm afraid of?'

Ralf opened his mouth to speak but realised that he had no response. He had not thought she would say that, and it was so different from how they usually talked – circumspect and wary of offence. She was not scolding him for it, but rather pointing out that he did not understand himself, which came as no surprise to her, clearly, but which he found disturbing.

'You are living faithful to a past that didn't care for you then, and certainly doesn't now,' she said. Bewildered, Ralf decided she couldn't know how her general referred to the particular. Had he talked to her about Elsa? Perhaps while drunk or high? The vertigo of unremembered nights and days gripped him with the possibility of so many lapses of thought or action that he wanted to cry out and disown himself, haunt a new body.

He pulled her closer, so that their sides were touching.

'Muriel, I dearly wish I could have woken up this morning, freshly minted. I wish that today could be my first day, this my first memory.'

'But look around you. We are living and dying by the present and the future. Which way do you look when you walk?'

Ralf nodded. He took his arm back and found his rolling papers. He picked off clumps of marijuana, laid down a paper and pinched off some tobacco, sprinkling the marijuana over it and rolling the paper back and forth to distribute it evenly, before using his thumbnail to tuck the near side in.

'Can you put a filter in?' asked Muriel, tearing a strip of cardboard off the packet. The face of the packet's Zig Zag Man was torn in half, one implacable eye peeking over a shamanic beard. Ralf took the strip and rolled it into a cylinder, slotted it in and licked the paper shut. Muriel lit for him and he unfastened the shoulders of his overalls, stretching out on the ground. She lay back next to him and took the joint. They looked ahead at the sky. Off to the left, just above the buildings, was a waning moon. Ralf took back the joint.

'Imagine,' he said. 'One day soon, humans are going to go there. They will get into a little pod and plug it closed, sealing in a little of the Earth's air with them. And they will travel up, vertically up, past our tallest buildings within a few seconds, past the clouds in minutes. They will watch continents reveal themselves and they will start to see the curvature of the Earth, tightening in circumference until they can see the whole planet through one window. And when they land on the moon, they'll quickly see it's just a rock, just a lump of inorganic debris, and they'll look back at the Earth, at us lying down here, and think . . .'

Muriel took the joint from him.

'Who do you think will make it first?'

'*Soyuz*,' he said. 'The Russians are perfectly prepared to lose a few men if it means beating the Americans.'

'The Americans have killed a few too.'

'True. So far the space race is a sort of kamikaze war. Poor astronauts.'

'And stray dogs.' She took a drag. 'But it's really about the possibility, isn't it? People are beginning to see that they can do anything imaginable. We can hit the moon in the eye.'

They watched her trace the joint's embers across the sky, trailing smoke, imitating the sound of a German whistling bomb without, presumably, knowing what it was.

Soon, the shadows washed in from the fronts of the buildings. The marijuana was taking over now. Ralf imagined Elsa getting out of a car, cutting through the protest, following her own path, undeterred. Her lipstick was immaculate. She would glide between groups without touching anyone, step over him and carry on over the bridge. He had no proof that she had ever known him, ever lived. No one knew her. She had not given him anything. She had closed his door quietly and walked down the stairs without disturbing the neighbours, and out and away, and he had stayed in Paris for her, he realised now, scanning faces in crowds, revisiting places he had seen her, keeping hold of an apartment he didn't live in so as not to fray the last threads of continuity between them.

He listened to the modulation of the crowd, now pushing forward, now dying off, rolling over him like waves and dragging Ralf back out to sea, spinning along the seabed, shoulder over knee. There was a turbulence here, underneath the friendliness, and it spun him off course until there was no up, no surface; only liquid in his ears and eyes and mouth and nostrils, and a thud, a dull thud, a knocking at the door.

Ralf felt a gentle tapping on his hard hat. He was a crustacean, his thermoplastic shell the first and only line of defence. He opened his eyes. It was dark. Muriel was looking at him.

'What are you doing in there?'

'I was asleep.'

'You weren't moving. I got worried.'

Ralf rolled off to the side to push himself up, feeling dizzy.

'I'm fine.'

'The crowd is getting tetchy. The CRS have been gathering at either end of the street for the past two hours.'

Ralf stood. Someone had broken the window of a parked car and released the handbrake. His friends were manoeuvring the car into position as the young man steered, legs hanging out of the window. There wasn't much of a barricade yet, but it was beginning to take shape. Roger and Jean-Luc were shaking a tree from side to side, pulling its roots from the sandy earth. Ralf wished they could have spared the tree its life, but they were nearly done now. Ralf went over and pulled up the iron grilles from around its base, passing one to a nearby stranger and showing him how to break and lever up cobblestones. Muriel began passing the stones along a line towards the front of the crowd. Behind them, a group of teenagers had lit a fire, and residents were looking out of windows. Someone threw down a blanket. Others waved. Some looked on at the gathering chaos as they might a news report of something that had happened hours ago.

Ralf lifted Muriel.

'What do you see?'

'They're lining up.'

'Linked arms?'

'No, they have their batons drawn.'

She got down. Ralf passed the grille to someone else, and they pushed forwards towards the car, which had been turned on its side. People were shouting at the police. This did not feel like a protest, as it had earlier in the week. It felt like revolution.

Someone lit the wick of a bottle and flung it, straight armed, at the police. It landed with a harsh pop of glass just over halfway to the front line, a puddle of fire spreading out between them.

The CRS stood in a row, their faces impassive.

'You fucking Nazis!' shouted Jean-Luc behind him.

The policemen faced forward. Their black steel helmets glowed darkly in the light of the fire, the trim of their coats gleaming like silverfish. They watched the barricade grow almost to head height in places as the puddle of fire died down and separated into two smaller pools. Ralf had his eye on their commanding officer, who was briefing them. They listened with their eyes on the protesters. One of them stared directly at Ralf. You picked your man, or your man picked you.

Ralf was pulled back by Roger, who handed him a dustbin lid. Jean-Luc was smashing a café chair against the floor and handing out the legs.

'We throw, you shield,' said Roger.

Ralf nodded. The crowd behind him seemed to have swelled to four times its number in the day, and he felt a kind of pride, arrogance, even, at their having outnumbered the police so decisively. He grinned at Roger, who held up a cobblestone with glee. Ralf raised his makeshift shield, blood pumping fiercely through his hands and head. Roger took a couple of quick steps and twisted sideways, coiling his torso and shoulder and catapulting the thick stone over the front line of the CRS. A cheer went up behind them, a renewed call for de Gaulle to step down, a chant of liberty. The line ahead didn't move except for the commanding officer, who was striking the edge of his hand against his palm as he spoke, his words inaudible over the chanting. Other students behind them held stones, but they were waiting to see how the CRS would react.

Ralf felt a tugging at his arm again.

'Roger, I'm—'

But it was Muriel.

'Stay behind me,' he said.

'I have to talk to you.'

'Now?'

'Yes.'

Ralf felt the glare of the CRS on one cheek, like the afterglow of a fire.

'Whatever happens tonight, I want you to know that I care about you enough to want you to find the person who makes you truly happy.'

Ralf shook his head.

'She's gone. She left years ago. I have no way of finding her.'

Muriel pulled back in confusion.

'Who's gone?'

'What? You just said—'

'Who? Who is she?'

A woman in the crowd screamed, and Ralf turned to see that the front line had parted. Two officers stood braced to fire what looked like thick-barrelled shotguns. They were wearing gas masks.

Ralf pushed Muriel behind him, turning side on and lifting the lid. The police both fired at once, the canisters shooting past and knocking students to the ground. They hissed, smoke streaming out as the crowd tripped over itself to get away. Ralf ran over to the nearest canister and picked it up, his eyelids melting shut, his nose and sinuses on fire. He turned back to the barricade and threw the canister with all his might back at the police, he hoped, coughing and involuntarily breathing more of the smoke, which burned and curdled down his throat and in the top of his lungs. The air was raw as onion, doubled and doubled again, growing exponentially hotter with each breath until he lost his surroundings and there was nothing but the burning. He had no voice, no time. The ground fell into him like a wall. Momentarily, his face was in the cold snow, he felt the blast of an 88, his friend's body was draped over a turret, aflame. And then a great shock of cold water, and he was drenched, and his eyelids unstuck. He was lying on the ground with another protester, looking up at a resident in a first-floor window, an old woman watching him with an empty bucket.

'Run,' she called. 'They're coming.'

Another canister knocked the old woman backwards into the darkness. He didn't know where the screams were coming from. Ralf stood shakily, casting around for Roger or Muriel. The police line crested the barricade, batons drawn. His man had found him. Ralf turned, began to limp off, but too late. He had lost his shield. Something had hit him on the side of the head. His last thought, as he fell down, was to wish that he had something left to give up, something to apologise for.

Ralf lay on his back, trying to breathe. He could hear others near him, coughing. One man was gasping with pain. The medic came to tell Ralf he probably had a broken rib, and he confirmed it was probably that. He was given some water, and he lay back, listening to the crackling of a nearby fire and the wail of a siren a few roads off.

It felt both strange and natural to lie on one's back in a garden at night. There was no moon, and the dark sky ahead appeared to have extinguished the stars, as if they were alone in the universe.

The siren was approaching. Ralf wondered who would be taken to hospital first. His injuries were relatively minor. He could probably even walk home.

The siren shut off and a door opened on the street. The young medic went out to meet them. As he began to speak, heavy boots sounded on the pavement, and Ralf heard the familiar strangled cry, the sound as of a dropped sack of flour, and he knew that the police had found them. He lay as still as possible. He heard them spreading out around the courtyard as the gasping man pleaded and was silenced.

One of them grabbed Ralf's ankles roughly and pulled him from the cot, and he landed hard on the floor, coccyx first. He curled up instinctively and covered his head, and the blows began to rain down again. Heavy boots bruised his kidneys. The smart wap of clubs sent shocks through his muscle tissue and into his bones. They kept on at the same spots, making them tender, bursting his capillaries and fibres until they turned to mush under his skin, every nerve screaming *you are breaking, you are breaking*.

The blizzard continued until the last man was called away, and Ralf lay there foetally, his rib barely registering now but his arm, kidney, hip, knee unbearably painful along his exposed right side. His body tensed and he heaved, his breath stuttering like that of a newborn.

No one came for him and the cold numbed him well, so he rolled over and knelt and stood. It was dawn. Limping slowly, he picked his solitary way down the Boulevard Saint-Michel, past an old construction colleague who didn't recognise him, dismantling a barricade with an earthmover. A municipal worker replaced cobblestones one by one. On past the Caveau de la Huchette, on to the river, to his apartment, wondering whether his key still worked.

8

RALF, London, 1972–1978

(

It was only when she was found by her neighbours that Ralf realised how long it had been since he had spoken to his mother. The police had called him as next of kin, and Ralf had spoken in faltering English, unable at first to articulate himself.

'Oh. That is. That is . . .' he had said.

'I'm very sorry,' repeated the officer.

His reaction had been stunted by the language barrier, so that he could not even grieve except vaguely. It was as if he had never learned to cry in English.

Now, he was in the neighbour's kitchen. For the past five years or more, his mother had rented out the house and moved to a small flat in this block, living off the rent. She seemed not to have known her neighbours, but when he had walked up the stairs past this man's door and on towards his mother's flat, the man had rushed out and asked whether he was Therese's son, and invited him in, introducing himself as Martin.

'You live in Paris, then?'

'Yes – well, no. I just moved. Am moving.'

'Tea?'

'Yes, thank you.'

Sobering, was probably the best way to describe the past four years. Not long after the riots, Muriel had found someone who was able to love her, and up to the moment she told him, he had been willing it, sometimes even engineering it, thinking it was best for both of them. But that moment, the moment she told him, he had begun to doubt every choice he had made for years, wondering at what he had done, and why. He would wake shaking and sweating – would hallucinate Elsa and ask her questions, and she would know the answer, but she wasn't allowed to talk to him. Muriel had been ready to love someone, but Ralf had ceded the probability of love for the possibility of pain, a shut bud in a fickle spring. He had pushed her away and she had gone only reluctantly, and he had abandoned his squalid little room – hadn't even gone back for his things, sick of the sight of the lava lamp and the square buildings, sick of the belligerence of youths, lovesick, withdrawing.

Oh, how he had itched. Staring at his clock, obeying the letter and not the spirit of his self-imposed rules: first cigarette at 11am; first drink at 2pm – no, 1pm, because one was allowed one drink with lunch; no spirits before 5pm; nothing to speed up the day; clear vision. Try not to rub your forearm. Try not to scratch your stubble. Try not to jog your leg. Sit up when you are supposed to sit up. Lie down when you are supposed to lie down. Lie on your back, do not curl up. There is no one in the room with you. Lie on your front if the coccyx starts up again.

There had been a couple of false starts. The way his hatstand had been glowering at him, shrugging its curved arms, looming in the dark, he had to break it up. The ceiling had crawled.

Martin the neighbour handed Ralf a cup of tea.

'What's that?' Ralf asked, pointing up at the ceiling.

'It's just damp,' said the neighbour, sipping his own.

'From my mother's flat?' Ralf asked.

The neighbour looked anxious.

'Did the police not say?' The neighbour's accent was either Irish or Northern Irish – Ralf didn't want to hazard a guess. 'They should have said.'

'Is there water damage? I am happy to pay for the repairs.' Ralf wondered whether 'water damage' was really a phrase in English, or whether it was a clumsy approximation.

'No, don't worry.' The neighbour started to roll down his shirtsleeves and button them. His wife had just come home with their children, and the wife pulled the kitchen door to. 'Is your wife . . .?' Martin asked.

'No,' Ralf said. The neighbour looked at him uncomprehendingly. 'I don't have a wife.'

The neighbour nodded.

'I didn't know her very well,' he said, after a pause.

Ralf motioned for him to go on.

'I knew she lived alone, but she kept herself to herself. I used to see her sometimes taking down the bins and I'd help her on the stairs – the bloody lift, it's always broken. But you don't see what's not there, do you? There was no routine to it, we just put them in the skips. I suppose I should have thought to check on her, but.'

Ralf tried to gauge whether the neighbour was implying negligence on Ralf's part, but it didn't seem to have occurred to him. 'Life gets in the way,' Ralf finished for him, after too long a pause.

The neighbour leaned in.

'One day. One evening, we're sitting down to supper, and I notice the ceiling.'

'She left a tap on, I suppose? The washer was worn out?'

The neighbour glanced over at the door.

'It wasn't water.'

What, then? A plumbing issue?

'She'd been up there for some time. She wasn't . . . When I found her. She wasn't all . . . together.'

'Oh dear. I'm sorry,' said Ralf. The neighbour looked confused. 'It was you who broke down the door?'

'Yes.'

'How long had she been there?'

'Two weeks, they think.'

Two weeks in summer. The green discharge of decomposing tissue. Autolysis and bloat. Hydrogen sulphide. Maggots, lique-faction, matter. Pupation.

'I just thought you should know before you went up. The police have cleared it up but it's—'

'Yes. I understand.'

Ralf pushed his chair back.

'I'll pay for the damage, of course.'

The man waved the offer away.

They walked together up the stained concrete stairs, a faint stale smell of urine being replaced by something more like the sweet smell of a butcher's apron. As Ralf found his key, he began to realise that there was no intermediary between him and what was left: behind the door would be everything but the body itself.

As Ralf entered the narrow hall, he was hit by the ripe tang of shit and bad meat. He covered his nose as the neighbour turned away behind him. A green bottle fly zigzagged out the door and Ralf could hear more in the lounge. He held a breath, strode through and began opening the windows, sucking in clean air as he did so, the numberless flies setting one another off in a great cloud, pacing themselves equidistant from their neighbours before spiralling in pairs and settling back on the floor, a carpet of metallic green dotted with deep red eyes. They twitched clockwise and anticlockwise, reacting to some unseen stimulus. Many were still.

The armchair was there, the one she had been found in. Beneath the animal smells was the unmistakable smell of the dead, diamines, putrescene, cadaverine. They had removed the body but the seat was stained, and the floor around it.

The neighbour came in hesitantly, and they agreed to take the armchair down to the ground-floor bins, as it was no good trying to clean it. Ralf didn't want to share this experience, either with a stranger or with someone he knew, so he thanked the man at the bottom and went off to the shop to buy bin bags and cleaning products. He took a second trip down the stairs with the contents of the fridge, some of which were in date, other items putrefying in the vegetable tray. Shrivelled apples, cheese, four pats of butter, some indistinguishable leftovers in a bowl. He thought about throwing the bowl away but ended up cleaning it, since he hated to throw anything away unnecessarily. He left the door open and switched it off to defrost.

In the cupboard were a great many tins: tinned peas; corned beef; some kind of reconstituted ham or ham substitute; tinned beans; tinned soups. At least six of each, stratified so that those at the back were covered with a speckling of dust. Pickled onions, pickled eggs. Years of food, stockpiled for the next war.

To have lived through both must have made her fear that it could happen again at any time, and who could tell her she was wrong? Ralf remembered when the great victory of the war had seemed to be of the left over the right in Europe. The US had held off from aligning itself one way or the other, since it had a great many sympathies with the right wing, and abhorred the Soviet experiment, but it was drawn in by its Pacific interests. In joining the Allies, it claimed a part of the victory for the soft right, the individualists, the consumers, the materialists. The US had really won freedom through collective action; they had tested the limits of their productive capacity. Following the unprecedented prosperity of the war, peacetime fell like a pall, and a new strategy had to be devised to stave off another, greater Depression. The liberal ideals of freedom, tolerance and personal expression were elided with the necessity of consumption. Communism was incompatible with these goals; so, too, restraint, self-sufficiency, community. It had happened around him and Ralf had believed he was plotting his own course, helping to forge a counterculture, but now he saw that he had fallen into the very heart of the trap: his life had consisted only of buying and selling, the primacy of pleasure over reward, self-definition over social meaning. And his mother had kept calling, and writing to him, because she understood what it finally cost to leave one's life unshared.

Ralf reached the top of the stairs for a third time. His mother still had that fucking chair in the hallway by the telephone, ushered through the past decade by new nails and careful perching. In the living room, he looked out of the window at the tops of nearby houses and the tall, brutal blocks of the surrounding flats, which had not been there when Ralf had known London. They had sprung up like bomb weed, determined to be the first to colonise the light.

He and his mother had stayed at the house of his father's cousin, when they had first arrived, in Stoke Newington, before their own accommodation was arranged by 'The Four Percent Industrial Dwellings Co., Ltd'. Ralf had been put in a room with a boy of roughly his age. They had shared no language but the boy had talked at him anyway, and Ralf had watched the boy's mouth moving, apprehending nothing. The boy hadn't seemed to mind but Ralf had felt his intelligence dwindle. They were left alone for hours, and the boy was reduced to showing Ralf a wooden toy duck, which he had thrust towards Ralf until he had understood that he was supposed to take it, it was his. The boy was being kind to him, an idiot who couldn't even open his mouth to thank him. Ralf had cried and cried, overcome with sobbing at the boy's unwarranted kindness, and the mother had walked in and started hitting the boy and shouting at him in that thin, frictionless language, and Ralf had run to find his mother, to explain what was happening, but it was too late, and the boy had hated him after that.

The man of the house had been a furrier, and Ralf had been scared of the implements in his workshop. He had a wooden fox head, which he used to shape the furs from the inside. He would shove it inside a fox's empty face, shape its nose. Dead animals would stare at Ralf when he looked in on the workshop, deflated as if they had been parasitised from the inside. He had hated his woollen coat, long socks, his shiny black shoes. He was not allowed to speak German. He was not allowed to talk about Germany. He could only speak about London, and he didn't know anything about London. He used to sit and listen to others, longing to participate, to feel the warm glow of their attention. He had learned not to ask anything of anyone, not to impose. He had such gratitude for everyday kindnesses. He could live off a smile for weeks. That was how it was now, too.

Ralf emptied his pockets of everything but the key to the flat, so that he could not be mugged, and walked down to the night. Ever since the end of the war, he had walked alone at night. He found it odd that no one else seemed to do it. It was a way of reclaiming the city while the throng slept, of occupying a patch of land a little bigger than he could afford to fence off around himself. In Paris, electric light was used as a mood enhancer, pooling around sites of interest. Smaller streets were unlit, and the Seine ran like crude oil. In London, lights were a defence against the night, meted out obsessively every few metres like breadcrumbs in a forest, as if one could not travel through shadow. No place was as empty as it seemed, but the company at a late hour was different, warier of space. He saw a woman like Elsa hurrying to put distance between them. Even now, everyone looked like her. He didn't follow any longer.

A fox was trotting along the pavement ahead of him, and as he trod over the metal of a basement stair cover, it stopped to assess him. Ralf continued at a steady pace so as to make his intentions clear, and the fox resumed its trot. Once you slowed down to look for life, it started to move: the lumped silhouettes of roosting pigeons; the near-static whorls of garden snails; a lone cricket; worms, some flattened at one end and flailing at the other, doomed by their genes to fight on past all hope; mice clearing open spaces, their heartbeats faster than human panic. No ants at night, no birdsong yet, but they were there. It must have rained earlier, because the air had the clean, earthy smell of ozone and plant oils and moist actinomycete spores.

The market Ralf was walking through was deserted, a damp cardboard box lying next to discarded peel and a blue plastic bag. His empty pockets felt soft – he had cleaned himself up and bought new clothes before coming over – and their slight sug gestion of comfort made his heart ache. Ralf did not feel better for the walk. He did not particularly want to stay out or to go back. There was no one for him here, nor anywhere else; no one with whom he shared a language. To speak to another human and to truly communicate, one had to share so many ways of looking, and Ralf had individuated himself at every stage of life by branching off, defined himself against the group. Ralf was not a German, not a Jew. He was not a soldier nor an academic. He did not believe.

How could one live through the war and entrust oneself to a group? But if one became a true individual, never subscribing to others' ideals, always standing outside, looking in, as Ralf had done, what was one left with? He had no career, no true friends, no wife, no child; his father was dead, and now his mother, too.

Since he was six, Ralf had associated death with his father, so much so that it hadn't even occurred to him that his mother would die, except in a remote, abstract way. So much remained unspoken between them, and he had always assumed that there would come one day a natural caesura in the mid-sentence of life, during which they would speak to one another not as mother and son but as creatures of five senses, creatures of feeling, forced to make structure out of the frankly incomprehensible experience of being alive. Instead, she had settled for trading itineraries by telephone on those occasions when he was not insensible, and perhaps the kindest thing one might say was that they had both known they had someone to talk to if they must.

She was always desperate for him to come home, but Ralf didn't feel that this place was his. He had believed, once, that Paris was his home, but now he saw that he had only borrowed it for a time. He had refused to be nearer to his mother, and she had accepted it, both of them knowing that she lived only to see Ralf find a family of his own, to take up the second half of life's bargain. His mother had asked nothing of him except that he would one day have a child and keep the flame of her beloved husband flickering, if halved and halved again, for another generation. She had witnessed bad people, stupid people, the money-minded, egotistical and boring, multiplying all around her. Ralf felt certain that his mother had died out of a failure of purpose, knowing that Ralf, the only remnant of her husband, was wayward, apostate, and that his selfishness and lack of resolution would kill Emil for all time.

Ralf moved into the flat, stripped the carpets, had his books shipped over. Soon he found work teaching a single module in academic translation at the university and took on a couple of private tutees, his meagre income more than covering his few outgoings. Once he had got used to speaking English again, he fell comfortably into a routine, each week characterised more by variation than by novelty. He would arrive at work early to beat the rush of commuters, sitting at the front on the top floor of the bus, gliding over the streets like a ghost, bearing down on the damp morning souls. He would watch shadows with umbrellas bobbing along. At the faculty, nobody troubled him with the past. His colleagues would talk cheerfully about trade unions or the weather, as nervous graduates tried to interrupt with half-plausible excuses for some piece of work or other. Ralf found it comforting to be sought out in this way. It made him feel necessary. And their gratitude when he let them off the hook filled him with warmth.

With no friction and no obstacles, time began to build pace. More often than Ralf thought necessary, there were fireworks. By the time he noticed the summer shadows had been getting shorter, they were already lengthening. It came to seem almost farcical to wind the clocks forward so soon after winding them back, as if one had borrowed an hour from an impatient neighbour. He found dust in his bowls. He had been teaching his module for four years. The local hardware shop had shut down in the time between visits, and now sold colour televisions.

Ralf still thought idly about Elsa, of course. He would invent unlikelihoods. She had moved to London. She passed him every day underground as he travelled in the opposite direction on its surface, their paths meeting and straying. What did she look like now? Each time he tried to remember her face, it was as if he were tracing over his previous effort, the act of recollection warping the original, a copy of a copy. Yet some nights, in a dream, her face would come to him perfectly, and the shock would wake him, and he would lose it.

Her surname! He had forgotten it. He knew it wasn't Laval, but for some reason the name stuck in his head. Elsa Laval. No, it wasn't that, but it was close to that. Not Leventhal – that was too long – but he felt sure that it began and ended with an L. It disappointed him not to know it; he might have checked the phone directory. She had never been listed in France, but there was always a chance, however slight.

And yet at the same time, a benign sort of fatalism began to settle over him – not even concerning Elsa specifically, but life, everything. As a young boy, he had been happy enough, because unaware of injustice, then angry, when he discovered the extent of it. As a young man, he had been idealistic, believing he might change the world, then depressed, because he hadn't. Now, he could see that the wheels of the world simply turned, and one hopped between them, there to rise or fall in a greater or lesser arc. Ralf had lived through certain decades with a certain status and certain natural qualities or inclinations to struggle. If one saw clearly how little the individual mattered, how determined a life was by its context, one would have to conclude that no one was responsible for their lot. If the rich were not literally gifted with wealth, they were determined to succeed by dint of their genetic inheritance, by sex, by height, attractiveness, impulse control, aggression, conscientiousness, charm. So, too, murderers. The Nuremberg trials had twisted everything, because the Nazis had argued the opposite of what they believed, claiming that their individual actions were subordinate, and the Allies had argued, by way of punishment, the case for individual responsibility. But Ralf had never believed – couldn't believe – that he lived out of history's reach, when his life had so neatly followed its course. Simply by being Ralf, he had lost his father, lost Germany, loved Elsa, lost his best friend, fought for a world that never came. In this light, there could be no thought of his own happiness. What remained was free to nudge others towards their own fulfilment.

For the first time in his life, he stopped thinking of the future, preferring instead to watch the world as it was. He started to perform small acts of kindness when he knew no one was watching. It felt like a kind of subversion, an irrational assertion of free will. He sorted through his books and, writing notes of recommendation for five of his old favourites, posted them through the letterboxes of unknown homes. He laid his overcoat on a homeless man while he was sleeping. It didn't make sense, and no one could stop him. His days began to swell with potential.

There was an old restaurant he liked in the West End, where the steak was good and red and the waiters were convinced they knew better than the patrons. Ralf went there whenever he could afford it and the maître d' would never ask whether he wanted a table for one. One Saturday in late spring, he found himself smiling down at his plate, almost unable to look at the young couple seated in the window. They looked younger than half of Ralf's students, but they were the smartest dressed in the room, he in an oversized suit, she in a long dress. They both looked sick with nerves, each stealing glances at the other. She laid her hand on the table, half open, and he noticed it. He kept offering her bread and topping up her wine, determined to provide, or to put off the end of the meal, and she nodded, and touched her earring, her hand reaching out for him across the table, an open invitation.

Ralf called the waiter over and asked for their bill as well as his own. The waiter's face lit up and he turned towards the young couple but Ralf grabbed his arm. He wasn't to interrupt them while they were eating. Not a word, until after Ralf had gone.

9

RALF, Paris, 1992

ELSA, Paris, 1958

(

Ralf was back in Paris, after all.

As he left Saint-Paul Métro, the light blinded him. The weather didn't know what it was. Everything shone, the city made reflective by the recent rain. It was still spotting, the drops hitting his face and hands so lightly he could have mistaken them for pins and needles. He didn't care. He wanted to sit outside today, under the sky.

As he had grown older – not grown, though, but rather fallen away into old age – his memories of Elsa tended to seem less like evidence of some emotional crime, and more like a fixed image passing across his eyes like the landscape through a train window.

Ralf had come to feel that he proceeded in life by dead reckoning, triangulating where he was by where he most recently had been and where he believed he was headed, though he could not see it, a ship with a compass and map but no way of measuring the current or the winds, or the drift that took place while he slept, scanning the horizon for landfall. It was no one's fault; it was the only method available.

A girl had appeared on the bench next to him. She was

unpacking a large travelling rucksack, which seemed to contain the necessities for living on the road for some time. Her thick blonde hair was trussed up in dreadlocks, a stencil of white shoulder straps against the bronze of her shoulders. She had a number of piercings in one ear and what looked to be a life's collection of bracelets on her wrist. She was unpacking a small medical kit, from which she removed a plaster. She peeled off the protective backing and carefully stuck the plaster over a blistered heel. Then she set about packing everything once again, meticulously, as if the topography of the bag was inviolable. She still hadn't looked at him. These days, people appraised him the way they might look at a shrub or a wire fence: he simply happened to be there.

He hadn't spoken to anyone at all since he had arrived, other than a beggar at the Gare du Nord, where he'd been too slow and aimless to escape her cue card.

'English?' she'd asked, holding up a begging note in English and French.

'German,' he'd said to get rid of her.

She'd immediately flipped the card over to reveal the other side, which was in German and Italian. She deserved his loose change for the timing alone.

He closed his eyes and sucked in the cool, moist air. His throat was scratchy, and the phantom twinge at the base of his spine had started up again. But this was a pleasant enough place, and time. One had to admire the present. He opened his eyes. The setting moon was a faint sliver, a C, but one could see the shadow of the whole if one really looked. There was still now. He looked across at the girl. Her manner was of one who would change the world. Yes, there was now. Better not to think of love or war. Better to live by the small moments, to hop between rock pools of contentment, than to try to carve out a reservoir with your bare hands. Rock pools held their own little worlds, their animals and warm water, and that was enough to sustain a person until the next tide came in.

The girl had nearly finished packing her bag. She would go soon. He should have said hello. One might talk to anyone, if one did it straight away, but once the silence set in, that was it.

He ate lunch at Jo Goldenberg's, his pleasure at being back on the rue des Rosiers dampened by the bullet holes preserved in the restaurant's window. The attacks had been all over the news, even in England. Two men had thrown in a grenade and machine-gunned any diners they could see. It was said that the attackers were Arabs, and that it was an anti-Semitic attack – after all, this was a Jewish restaurant in a Jewish neighbourhood. There was a commemorative plaque outside for the six people who were killed. The first name on the list was Benemmon, an Arab.

Ralf decided to walk over to where Jacques' bar used to be. He wondered what was there now. He went down the few short steps one at a time, placing his left foot next to his right so as not to overextend. He felt like an old man. Which is to say, he was old, but not so old he should be reduced to this. Still, it could be worse – he could walk, which was more than some could say, after the police were done with them.

The façade of Jacques' was unchanged, which Ralf thought a nice touch. Whoever had moved in had taken care to preserve their share of the area's history. He waited to cross. The bell of Saint-Paul-Saint-Louis struck decisively twice. He approached the filthy chequered floor, the old suited men in the back, drinking sullenly. It looked uninviting, even hostile. In short, it looked the same as ever.

The barman finished pouring out a beer for a customer. They had a beer engine, instead of old-fashioned taps, but otherwise the place was just as Ralf had left it twenty years before. The barman turned to him. They both smiled.

'Hello, Jacques.'

'Oh – hello, Ralf. Enjoy your holiday?'

'I can't believe you're still here.'

'Someone's got to serve these miscreants.'

He had come around from the bar and gave Ralf a hug, and Ralf closed his arms around the barman's big shoulders, breathing in his yeasty smell. Strange to think he was here again, at this very spot.

'Beer or wine? I warn you, my prices have gone up.'

'I'll just have a coffee at the counter.'

'There was a rumour going round that you'd drunk yourself to death. You can imagine how I felt when I heard it.'

Jacques went back behind the emotional rampart of the bar.

'I would have, if I'd carried on, but I've changed a lot since then,' Ralf said. 'Everything has changed around the Marais, too.'

'It has. We're fashionable,' said Jacques.

'I barely recognise it. No Yiddish signs. I saw a shop which only sold bonsai trees.'

'Dague's old shop has become a gay tea room,' Jacques confided.

'I'd love to know what he'd think of that.'

Jacques chuckled. 'But why haven't you visited?' he asked. 'You could have stopped in. I'm not going to force beer down your throat.'

'I don't know. I didn't think anyone would still be here. Or if you were, I suppose I thought everyone would have forgotten me.'

'What made you change your mind?'

Ralf stirred his coffee.

'I received a letter.'

Ralf looked down at the neat square of paper he was holding, and back up at the house. This looked to be it. He pressed the button marked 'Lambert', and listened carefully to the disembodied voice that came to him. Male, a little higher than his own, which was

rough as gravel since his throat operation. Assured. Had he noticed a slight American accent, or was that simply his expectation?

Sophie was waiting for him at the top of the stairs, beaming.

'You must be Monsieur Wolfensohn?'

'Please – Ralf.'

She kissed him on each cheek and led him into the apartment,
offering him coffee. Ralf could not quite concentrate on her.

Paul was there, waiting by the phone buzzer, looking almost
as nervous as Ralf felt and tucking a loose shirt tail into his
jeans. He broke into a smile, but he didn't say anything. His wife
excused herself. The two men each studied their mirror, respec-
tively a memory and a prophecy. Paul had a straight nose, dark,
defined eyebrows, brown hair and Ralf's heavy lashes. A certain
raptorial intensity. He might almost look effeminate, were it not
for the density of his stubble and his build, thicker round the
neck than Ralf had been even as a young man.

There were too many questions.

They shook hands firmly.

'Please, come through to my study.' They walked through to
a room lined on one side with books – novels, mostly – with
a hi-fi wedged amongst them. Paul moved a pile of papers so
Ralf might sit down before falling back into his office chair. A
personal computer took pride of place on and under the desk,
which was pushed up against the room's only window. Paul
noticed him looking at the family photo propped up next to the
monitor, where two small children giggled hysterically, clutching
their mother's legs as she fought to keep her skirt up. It was a
picture of joy. When had people started smiling in photos? Ralf
wished he had photographs like these of his parents. In the few
he had, his parents looked overwhelmed by the significance of
the act, stiff-backed like sitters in a portrait, steeled for the flash.
Here, the children hadn't even caught sight of the camera.

'I wanted you to meet them,' Paul said. 'They're at school at the moment, but they should be home in an hour or so.'

'They're beautiful. What are their names?'

'Aurélie and Julien.'

'So I'm a grandfather.'

Paul smiled warmly.

'They're a little older now. Nine and seven.'

'You've been married a long time?'

'Almost fifteen years. We were "high school sweethearts",' he said in English. Then, remembering something, he swung round in his chair and picked up an envelope, which he handed to Ralf.

Inside was a photograph. A young couple standing alone on a beach, the wet sand behind them reflecting the sky. Ralf was younger at thirty-one than Paul was now. He was smiling and squinting like a man possessed of an untold happiness. Next to him stood Elsa. He did not have his arm around her, but she was leaning into his side. She had the expression of a wildcat that had fallen into a trapping pit and would fight the first person who looked in. It shocked him how clearly he could see it. She was so beautiful, glaring at the lens. No one in the world looked like this any longer, nor ever would again.

Ralf leaned over to put the photograph on the desk.

'That's for you,' said Paul. 'I have a copy. She wanted you to keep the original.'

'Oh. Thank you.'

Ralf remembered the way Elsa had clung to him on the train, the billowing of her skirt in the wind as the sand piled up against the houses. He remembered her talking about Paris as if she were a runaway, denying her home but longing for its comfort.

'My mother told me that was the day she had her miscarriage.'

Elsa finished her make-up and put on her shoes. Her shoulders felt exposed in her polka-dot dress, although it was hot enough outside. It had rained all spring – at one point, the Seine had reached the shins of the Algerian *zouave* statues on the Pont de l'Alma – and now it felt almost indecent not to be wearing a raincoat and a scarf.

The Tuileries was always beautiful on days like this. She often saw couples flirting together by the fountain, or strolling down the long main path. Ralf might be there already, dividing his attention between the entrances like a sentry. Perhaps he wouldn't come at all. She wouldn't blame him.

Elsa still hadn't told Theo about the bleeding. He had been overjoyed when she had mentioned that she was late . . . Theo was immediately convinced he had another son on the way and had actually grimaced when she'd reminded him the odds were even, and that it was too early to know whether she was even pregnant. Privately, however, she had known instinctively that she was, hadn't needed to wait for an omen. She had spent two weeks thinking only of soft little heads, warm moist skin, the unmistakable scent. Then spotting, and then the trouble in Deauville, when she had locked herself in the bathroom, crying, not knowing whom to confide in or what she might say.

She had always been sure she didn't want another child, feeling inadequate enough about Pascal, not knowing how to hold him, or keep him from crying, laying him down in his cot like a hasty confession. But something was changing. The ground had begun to move. She now felt something she would never dare articulate to anyone – a feeling that brought her shame, when she had for so long dismissed the very idea of shame. She had begun to feel, now, ready to have a baby, she who already had one, and who felt keenly what she lacked as a mother. She wanted a new child; she felt she might now care for a life.

Ralf had been rough with her in the hotel room. If it weren't for that, she really might have told him everything. She believed that he would understand. It was the way that he spoke to her – not even what he said – and the way that, when he laid his hand on her skin, the warmth spread, so that she didn't want to be away from him, physically. As if he was the cure for her unknown illness.

She had been shaking when she had got back to the apartment on the night she met him. She had been desperate to see him again, had even arranged a time and a place, but one of Theo's trips had been cancelled at the last minute and she had sat inside all day, imagining Ralf driving past her window. She had looked out at the traffic as if it were possible to see through a roof, wondering what car he drove, or whether he was wearing a moped helmet. She had spent days wandering around his area, hoping to bump into him, somehow afraid to go back into the bar a second time, or even to send Pascal in with a note – he was well into the age, now, when everything had to have a reason. And then, when she had found Ralf, he had agreed to go on a trip with her, just like that.

She had wanted to ask him about everything, all the little details that would have bored her terribly coming from anyone else: the barber below his apartment; the Algerian he drank with in the evenings. How did one befriend an Algerian in the first place? She had wanted to ask, but didn't dare risk revealing the poverty of her knowledge.

The problem was that she couldn't stay away. Elsa had only got a few hundred paces down the road but already she felt nervous. Perhaps it was a bad idea to see him again. She stopped for a second, balanced between desire and futility.

She had built a life with Theo; Pascal needed her. But she loved Ralf. Every time she saw him, it was as if she was climbing into another life she might have had, playing make-believe. All the while, she felt a desperate sense of loss, because she knew it wasn't real, one couldn't live life twice.

Week by week, however, it had been easy to pretend. After Deauville, she couldn't disappear for days at a time, but she could slip out for a day or a night and she could be near him and talk to him and look at him. She had tried so hard not to scratch him to see whether he bled, but she couldn't help it – it somehow mattered more with him, who she dearly wanted to believe was a good man, could not be blackened, would not rise to bait. But of course he was human, and of course it couldn't last, and he was a brute like other men. Worst of all, worse even than his violence, he had followed her, as she had feared, all the way back to her other life, and declared himself, like a verdict.

Theo was many things, but he was not gullible. He had known what she was the moment she had sat down in his office to be interviewed, and he had shown her the role she must play, and she had gone along with it willingly. He had seen her staring out at the empty sky long after the swallows had gone south. He saw her now, and had given her a way out of the lie. The only reason he didn't beat the life from her was his belief that she was carrying his child. He treated her as if she were in quarantine, finding excuses not even to touch her.

What did it matter if Theo believed she was pregnant? If no child materialised, she would blame the night he had hit her. And if there was a child, she would love it more dearly than anyone could imagine.

She walked through the entrance to the gardens. She would give Ralf up. She saw that she had to. But first, she would give herself to Ralf, or rather, let him give himself to her. She knew it seemed like a deception, but to her it was the truth, a kind of truth she had never before had the chance to express.

The photograph of Deauville quivered in Ralf's hand. In the hotel room she had been angry or upset – she had locked herself in the bathroom, he remembered now – but he hadn't understood.

'I thought you knew,' Paul said.

'She never told me.'

Paul lowered his head and they sat in silence. Paul toyed with a lighter and Ralf could see that he was holding back from smoking out of politeness, but smoke now smelled to him like exhaust and he couldn't be cheerful about it.

'When I was born, my father didn't think anything was amiss,' Paul continued eventually. 'Her pregnancy had not been confirmed when she lost it, and when she found she was pregnant again, she lied about the timing. There was no ultrasound in those days. They induced me because they thought I was weeks late, but I was still premature.'

'She must have been terrified, to have done a thing like that.'

'I turned out fine,' Paul said quietly, flicking the wheel against the flint with lazy little sparks. 'You and my father don't look worlds apart.'

'I met him once,' Ralf said.

'You did?'

'Yes. We had a stiff little conversation in the apartment in Paris. I kept hoping his parrot would interrupt us, but of course it was very well behaved.'

'What did you talk about?'

'I don't know. I remember thinking it was vital that I confront your mother, but I have no idea what I hoped to achieve, other than to refute the impossibility of my dropping in for tea. I think I was trying to pursue the consequences of honesty, thinking it would work in my favour.'

'What did my father do?'

'Nothing. He refused to change course, to make any outright acknowledgement. He entertained me rather cheerfully – kept offering me his box of cigars. He was utterly impervious. I realised then that there was no chance of my whisking her away.'

And yet he felt irrationally optimistic, all of a sudden, at the thought that she was still abroad in the world. It sometimes seemed everything between them had happened in a closed world with its own rules and limits, but it was this world, this city.

'Is she still – I mean to say, does she live here? In Paris?'

Paul's eyes flashed with a suppressed violence, perhaps Elsa's, perhaps his own.

'She doesn't want to see you.'

Ralf drew breath.

'No, of course. I'm terribly sorry.' Ralf began to stand, one hand on the back of the chair, another on the seat, tipping slowly to avoid bending his wretched spine. 'I can see I have intruded on your family, but it has been so wonderful to meet you—'

'No, no,' said Paul, putting out a hand as if to catch Ralf. 'Please, stay. Stay. Here, let me . . .' He stood quickly and left the room, returning with a cushion for Ralf's seat. Paul sat back in the desk chair, agitated, picked up the packet on his desk and absently lit a cigarette, dragging a clean ashtray over with his middle finger. Ralf's throat began to tickle and the only way not to cough was to hold his breath.

'The knowledge is still a little volatile,' said Paul. 'I only found out a few weeks before I sent you the letter. She knows I'm meeting you today and asked me to pass on her best wishes. Look.'

Paul reached across and turned over the photograph. There was a short note written on the back.

They say that of all forms of caution, caution in love is the most fatal to true happiness. I suppose it's the sort of truth one can only recognise when it's too late. I hope you have forgiven me, Ralf.

Ralf nodded to himself for some time.

'Thank you,' he said hoarsely. 'Thank you.'

'My mother has told me about your early life in Paris,' Paul said. 'But none of us know what has happened to you since. It wasn't easy to find you – we thought you were still in France.'

Ralf coughed into his fist. 'Excuse me. My throat is . . . What did you want to know?'

'Everything. I have begun to record our family history, and I don't know anything since—' he looked down at a page '— 1958.'

'Well, there's a short version and a long version.' Paul stubbed his cigarette, spun in the chair and picked up a handheld Dictaphone.

'We have an hour before dinner.'

Ralf started to talk about his building work, how he'd got it through an Algerian friend, and he was glad, he realised, to be telling someone about Fouad after so many years; Fouad, who wanted only to belong. He saw Paul frowning at Ralf's account of the massacre in '61 and resolved to find some official document that might support him. He started to gloss over the loss of his job and his slide into more unorthodox business, but Paul kept probing, and he found himself having fun recounting his hippie phase. Each of these memories was defined sharply by how alive he had felt, how physically solid, how present. He could forget a thousand days of coffee, of laundry, of quietly chopping onions, of waiting at the post office to send a letter to his mother. Not that he'd written all that often – standing there, in his mother's apartment, without her, he'd seen for the first time how easily one might neglect those one loved by chasing the big story, the big lie that history was a matter of ideals and not compassion. Paul seemed to be looking at him with pity and Ralf wanted to shout, *But I survived, I outlived all of this, here I am!*, like a punchline.

'I suppose it comes down to something my mother once told

me about my grandfather. How happy he was to see my parents together. He bent everything in his life to accommodate them, fell out with other family members, gave them money he didn't have. It was as if, in my parents, he had finally found proof of the existence of love, and he spent the rest of his life out gathering wood for the fire, happy to see it warming his family through the misted window.

'Well, that's how I felt when I met your mother. One might settle easily into a job and a routine if one had never felt the force of a love like that, supposing that there was no more to be done with life – but I lived in a different world once I had proof. After she left, I found nothing that matched it, no one that could be her. I was single, or my relationships failed. I could stand the loneliness, but it made me very unhappy to think that I would have no son or daughter, that my own fire would ebb and glow, and grey, and die before dawn. It's only now I have reached this age that I can detach myself. I can see now that the only purpose of life is the continuance of life, and all conflicts arise from the inference that it is our life, ours particularly, that must go on.'

'Can you really believe that?'

'Oh, I know it. Rationally, I know it. But I am an animal. I can't deny how much it means to me to see you here. One of my kin. It makes me want to shake my mother back to life and show her.'

Ralf smiled through his wet eyes, and Paul rested a hand on his shoulder, moved, but not to tears.

'When did your mother die?'

'1972.'

'And your father? My mother mentioned a few details, but it would be good to hear you tell it.'

Ralf became aware that he was being recorded, the Dictaphone on the desk spooling in a thin, black, unbroken line of time. He cleared his throat again and attempted to explain, but he found it hard to know what to tell and what to leave out – how does one render a whole life in words?

'If we have time after lunch, I'll give you the long version – my mother's story, really, since my life overlapped only briefly with his. I suppose you already know the ending.'

There was a knock on the door, and Sophie pushed two little children in. They ran from their mother to their father, staring at Ralf openly once they were in contact with Paul.

'This is your uncle from England. Say hello.'

They recited their hellos. His grandchildren. Ralf felt his eyes sting with tears.

'It is good to see you, little ones.'

'I don't know you,' said the oldest with the unshakeable certainty of youth.

'Ah, but I know you already. I knew a little bit of you before you were born.'

She looked to Paul for confirmation that they were humouring a deranged old man.

'Come on,' Paul said, chuckling, 'let's go eat.'

At the table, Ralf watched the children chomping obliviously through their food. Theirs was the gnash of uncracked teeth. If these children lost one, they would grow another, regenerate. Nowadays Ralf chewed tentatively, as if every mouthful were toffee that might unroot a tooth or popcorn hiding a pebble in a soft husk. Ralf didn't dare bite down, but ruminated, chewed cud.

In his first days in London, as a boy, he had had dreams that his teeth were bleeding, and he had worked each of them back and forth, pulling them up. He knew how it felt, by then; he had lost a couple of milk teeth. The detaching of nerves from the bed of his gums, the dead, inanimate alienness of the tooth in his mouth, newly an object. And in the dream, or nightmare, he had levered them out and swallowed them, feeling them stick in his throat, until he was all gums, an old young boy, a gummy zoo creature. Often he would wake to find he really had worried one of his teeth in the night by clenching his jaw or pressing with his tongue, confirming his worst fears by enacting them.

When he had first arrived back in London, he'd had the dream again. Never in Paris. The dreams seemed inseparable from London, the locus of his exile. The only difference the second time had been that the levering of teeth had felt like a revolutionary act, a toppling, like students rocking municipal trees in the Boulevard Saint-Michel. He had spent so many years trying to distract himself from the life he might have had. And now that he had finally arrived at a happiness of his own, a complete happiness, he found himself here, sat at a table, sharing a meal with his child, with his grandchildren. Tragedy and comedy, separated only by time.

'Why don't you tell your uncle about *Mémé*?' Paul prompted.

'She bought me a Game Boy,' said Julien, shovelling beans.

'That's wonderful,' said Ralf. 'What does it do?'

'There's a game with blocks and you have to get them before they fall or it fills up and you die and there's a game with Mario and he jumps on the things' heads and you go in the pipes.'

Aurélie raised her eyebrows at Ralf (*kids, eh?*). He smiled at her.

'How old are you?' she asked.

'I'm just old enough,' he said. 'Sixty-five.'

Julien giggled.

'What are you going to do with the rest of your day?' he asked them.

'Swimming!' Aurélie said.

'Do you enjoy it?'

'Yes. I can swim two hundred metres.'

'Gosh. I don't think I've ever swum two hundred metres. You must be very good.'

She nodded.

The children got up and helped to load their plates into the dishwasher, while Ralf marvelled that a dishwasher could exist in a Paris apartment. But that was one of the strangest things about getting older: one could only keep pace with change a certain while, after which one was more inclined to retreat into the relative stasis of memories.

Out in the hallway, Julien was already wearing his goggles. Ralf gave them each a hug, their fragile bodies clamped to his chest like the orphans his mother had taken in before the war.

'You are quite wonderful,' Ralf said to them. 'I can see why your parents are so proud of you.'

Sophie beamed at him as he put a hand against the wall and straightened up. Paul was standing a little farther back. He could see that Paul had inherited Ralf's incurable habit of appearing aloof when it mattered most to be demonstrative. A taste of his own medicine.

'If I've missed anything, please let me know, and I'll do my best.'

Paul nodded.

'And if you're ever in London,' Ralf went on, 'please let me know. I can show you where my mother lived.'

'I will. You never know, though, perhaps you'll be in Paris again soon.'

'I don't know. Perhaps.'

Maybe he would, maybe he wouldn't, he thought as he stepped out into the spotting rain. It didn't matter any more, not in the slightest. Life went on, was going on all around him, carried on the air, walking the boulevards, pirouetting through space on a ball of lava, trying everything, inventing every possibility, a tactic which had never lost. Not all life need strive. To be one of the living was a miracle; to feel alive, to really feel it in one's bones, stranger still. How rare and lucky it was to have felt joy and pain, fear and love, to have eyes that could know the shape of everything along an unbroken line, ears that could read the ripples of particles miles away, and to be able to express it to one another, and to create new life together. Only life could have made itself like this. It was as precious as it was momentary. Eventually he would leave it behind, or rather, it would leave him, and he would lie down and nourish the earth, and he would be many things after that.

Paris was perfect this afternoon, enough people busy on their way, enough sitting with coffee and cigarettes. The river bled by, parting around the islands of Saint-Louis and the Cité, its stippled surface reflecting the bright, scrubbed façade of the police building opposite. A bank of cloud drifted overhead so slowly as to appear static, but down here on the ground the shadow leapt back, sunlight washing towards him like a wave. The city smelled of smoke and laundry, and any moment he would step over the shadow, and be drowned in light.

Acknowledgements

In my research for this novel, I owe a special debt to *Berlin* by Antony Beevor, *The Past is Myself* by Christabel Bielenberg, *I'll Always Have Paris* by Art Buchwald, *Exiled in Paris* by James Campbell, *Algerian Chronicles* by Albert Camus, the Paris diaries of Janet Flanner, *The King's Most Loyal Enemy Aliens* by Helen Fry, *The Jews and Germans of Hamburg* by John Grenville, *A Savage War of Peace* by Alistair Horne, *Postwar* by Tony Judt, *A Corner in the Marais* by Alex Karmel, *Paris in the Fifties* by Stanley Karnow, *1968* by Mark Kurlansky, *Muslims and Jews in France* by Maud S. Mandel, *A Hitler Youth* by Henry Metelmann, *Paris in the Sixties* by George Perry, *Parisians* by Graham Robb, *The Tender Hour of Twilight* by Richard Seaver, *Historic Maps and Views of Paris* by George Sinclair, *The German War* by Nicholas Stargardt, *Remembering Paris* by Denis Tillinac, *The Heroic City* by Rosemary Wakeman; *A Foreign Affair* (1948), *Germania Anno Zero* (1948), *The Third Man* (1949), *Le Silence de la Mer* (1949), *Le Beau Serge* (1953), *Les Diaboliques* (1955), *Ascenseur pour l'Échafaud* (1958), *Les Amants* (1958), *Les Tricheurs* (1958), *Pickpocket* (1959), *Les Liaisons Dangereuses* (1959), *Paris Nous Appartient* (1961), *Lola* (1961), *Bande à Part* (1964), *Paris Brûle-t-il?* (1966), *La Battaglia di Algeri* (1966); also to the Jewish Museum in London.

Thanks to Shakespeare & Co. for letting me sleep among the bookshelves in Ralf's old stomping grounds. Thanks particularly to Yoyo Chan, Melody David, Richard Fegelman, Baxter Jephcott, Laura Keeling, Clayton Knipe, Peter Kowalczyk, Rafaela Piovesan, Ryann Summers and Milly Unwin for the conversation, reading recommendations and wine. Thanks also to Tim Ashton and everyone at Soulton Hall for their generosity in lending me such a peaceful, not to say beautiful, place to edit.

Thanks to early readers Jon Bentley-Smith, Tom Campion, Chris Christofi, Janet Christofi, Alyson Coombes, Jess Hammett, Rebecca Layoo and Cathy Thomas for all the support and suggestions. Thanks to my agent, Jonathan Pegg, and his counterpart Doug Stewart, for their help and advice over the course of the drafting. Thanks to my editor Hannah Westland, who saw this novel hiding in the one I had written, and to Nick Sheerin. Thanks to all at Serpent's Tail, but especially Penny Daniel, Drew Jerrison, Ruthie Petrie and Flora Willis.